To Joshua, Zachary and MacKenzie

Every man, for his individual good and for the good of society, is responsible for his own development. The choices that govern his life are choices he must make; they cannot be made by any other human being, or by a collectivity of human beings.
—Barry Goldwater, *The Conscience of a Conservative*

I have no intention of placing my fate in the hands of men whose only qualification is that they managed to con a block of people to vote for them.
—Michael Corleone, *The Godfather* by Mario Puzo

Sniper Bid

By

Rick Robinson

Headline Books, Inc.
Terra Alta, WV

Sniper Bid

By Rick Robinson

First Paperback Edition
copyright ©2010Rick Robinson

Publisher Page
P.O. Box 52
Terra Alta, WV 26764
www.publisherpage.com

Tel/Fax: 800-570-5951
Email: mybook@headlinebooks.com
www.headlinebooks.com

Publisher Page is an imprint of Headline Books, Inc.

ISBN 0-929915-61-5
ISBN-13: 978-0-929915-61-6

Library of Congress Cataloging-in-Publication Data

Robinson, Rick, 1958-
  Sniper bid / by Rick Robinson. -- 1st pbk. ed.
     p. cm.
  ISBN-13: 978-0-929915-61-6 (pbk.)
  ISBN-10: 0-929915-61-5 (pbk.)
  1. Legislators--United States--Fiction. 2. Washington (D.C.)--Fiction. 3. Political fiction. I. Title.
  PS3618.O33367S65 2010
  813'.6--dc22
                    2010015990

Cover Design by Kevin T. Kelly, www.kevintkelly.com
Baseballs And Flag©T.W. Woodruff Photography, Thomas Woodruff, United States

PRINTED IN THE UNITED STATES OF AMERICA

Prologue

"So I think I like this new position you're in," said The Fat Man to Congressman Richard Thompson. The newly elected Representative from Kentucky and his former law partner, Joseph Bradley, known for his portly figure to friends and foes alike simply as "The Fat Man," sat in the dugout of Ed Smith Stadium in Sarasota, Florida, waiting for the ceremonial first pitch of the Spring Training game between the Cincinnati Reds and the Pittsburgh Pirates. Fidgeting like little kids, the two looked from side to side at the sights and sounds of a major league baseball game from the friendly confines of the home team bench.

"Yes, my friend, I think I'm going to like this job," said Thompson as he tried to look cool while ogling the players mingling around them. "The only thing that could make this day better would be if Meat Loaf was singing the national anthem."

For true baseball fans like Thompson and The Fat Man (and probably Meat Loaf for that matter), Florida in the spring means baseball. The cool breeze off the Gulf of Mexico hitting your face is matched by the hot sun roasting your arms and legs as you watch young players fighting for one of those last spots on the big league roster. You can see the tension on their faces as they realize that one booted ground ball may well be the difference between a plane ride to the "Show" or a bus ticket to some half-filled, Triple A stadium in the Midwest.

Prior to Thompson's election to the United States House of Representatives, he and The Fat Man made their annual pilgrimage to Florida's spring training sites to spend a week doing nothing more than totally immersion into pre-season baseball. The Fat Man likened the yearly trip—spending days sitting silently watching major league prospects—to the Zen experience of monks silently meditating while watching a bonsai tree grow.

The pair rarely spoke while sitting at the ball park watching a game. Their silence broken only by an occasional reference to some obscure baseball statistic or to some even more obscure player. In fact, to Thompson and The Fat Man, no game (spring training or otherwise) was ever complete without a reference to the Big Red Machine era, reserve outfielder named Angel Bravo, who had a grand total of three RBIs over two seasons in the big leagues. Any other hapless baseball player who made it to the field with such weak statistics would forever be referred to as "Angel *Whoever...*"

They became most animated when the pitch count was a Canaveral (3 balls, 2 strikes, 1 out) or a Milhous (2 balls, 2 strikes, 2 out), the former inducing each of them to make a rocket takeoff motion with his right hand and the latter requiring them to raise their arms in the air in mock imitation of the victory salute of Richard Milhous Nixon. It was not 'mound ball,' but it kept the two amused as they watched even the dullest of games.

This year's trip was cancelled due to Thompson's recent special election to the United States Congress. Cancelled, that is, until one of Thompson's subcommittee chairmen decided to hold a hearing in his home district to explore steroid abuse in professional sports, with a focus on baseball. The Democratic Chairman of the Judiciary Subcommittee on Oversight, Congressman Kevin O'Toole (D-Sarasota), needed a Republican to accompany him on the fact-finding mission. When Thompson heard that the subcommittee hearing would be held at the Cincinnati Reds' training camp, he was quick to volunteer his services.

As soon as Thompson called to tell him about the hearing, The Fat Man responded with similar lightning reflexes, offering to serve as an on-site advance man to assist the two Congressmen in their "fact-finding." In order to complete the illusion that he was doing something constructive, The Fat Man had flown down from Northern Kentucky two days earlier, rented a full-size, American-made car and already had a mild sun burn when he met the flight from DC that brought both of the Congressmen to Sarasota the next afternoon.

Thompson's Congressional colleague had not checked any luggage on the flight, so when they deplaned, he immediately made his way to some late afternoon function in his home district. As Thompson approached the baggage claim, he spotted The Fat Man grabbing his suit bag off the luggage carousel.

"Baseball in spring was made to be played in the shade of palm trees," The Fat Man said as he greeted Thompson. "I've spent all morning watching the bubble boys. If the pitching coach asks me, I have a pretty good idea who should be the sixth man in the five man rotation."

The pair of old law partners and friends dined at one of the best beachfront seafood restaurants before retiring to their respective hotel rooms (and their respective laptops).

Ed Smith Stadium in Sarasota is evidence that the allure of spring training in Florida's Grapefruit League is in the joy of watching baseball, not going to the stadium itself. The game field is housed in a nondescript concrete structure in the middle of an older neighborhood with overpriced beer and hot dogs. The daily ball game is like any other big league game, except you get to see a lot of young men trying to make it to "The Show," as the majors are called by those aspiring to join in it.

No, the joy of spring training comes from watching what happens on the practice fields that surround the game stadium. There are literally hundreds of young men on those practice fields (which are generally no different than the ones around America used for knothole games) for the chance to remain in baseball at some minor league level. They aren't playing for money. They are playing for the love of the game and the remote chance they will make it to the big club someday.

Find the kid trying to impress his Single A coach that he's good enough to play Double A ball and you'll find the essence of baseball.

The hearing was held the next morning, St. Patrick's Day, in the hospitality tent behind the clubhouse of Ed Smith Stadium, the winter home of the Cincinnati Reds (or Greens as they were called for only that one day of the spring training season). Usually reserved for entertaining the Reds' television and radio advertisers, the mood in the tent was normally light and quite festive, but on this particular occasion, there were no hot dogs or complimentary draft beer in the tent—and very few smiles.

Only Thompson and O'Toole sat as the Congressional panel, but the audience was filled with more television, radio and print media than was normally expected at any spring training event. The presence of so many television cameras fighting for position added to the intensity of the hearing. As each panel of witnesses came to testify, a new buzz emerged from the tent.

Congressman Kevin O'Toole, a former college baseball player, had the reputation of being the most outspoken Member of Congress regarding the abuse of performance enhancing drugs in major league sports. A senior member of the House Committee on the Judiciary, O'Toole was in his late-60's. His red hair had a light sprinkling of gray running through it. The gold, wire-rimmed glasses he wore accentuated his ruddy cheeks and other Irish facial features. Short in stature, Thompson imagined that O'Toole was still fit enough to try and turn a double play from the short stop position he had played in college.

A report issued by baseball only months earlier naming several All Stars and future Hall of Famers who had used performance enhancing drugs such as steroids and human growth hormone. O'Toole used the report as the basis for conducting a series of hearings on the issue, culminating in this final one in front of the hometown cameras. At the morning hearing, O'Toole had thrown his ire at several players like an intimidating brush back pitch.

O'Toole set the mood for the hearing when he interrupted the first witness, a player who had been suspended from baseball for violating baseball's drug policy. That player tried to testify that he had repeatedly, albeit mistakenly, taken an oral growth supplement given to him by a personal trainer who had told him it was flaxseed oil.

"Hold it right there," interjected O'Toole. "Are you telling this Committee that you thought the clear liquid you were dropping under your tongue was flaxseed oil?"

"Yes, sir," replied the player, somewhat stunned that O'Toole had interrupted his prepared statement.

"That is absolutely absurd," barked O'Toole. "Steroids in a clear oral form are bitter to the point that they make you nauseous when drops are placed in your mouth. You better check your written testimony, sir. Before you proceed, I remind you that you are under oath. I'll have no problem finding your pampered butt in contempt of Congress if you dare commit perjury to this Committee again."

As if O'Toole had just thrown an unhittable slider across the corner of the plate, the player sat in stunned silence before nodding at the angry Congressman and then picking up where he had left off. Interrupted a second time, the player and O'Toole had a hot exchange regarding baseball's policy and the practicality of banning substances for which no detection test existed.

As the hearing continued, O'Toole asserted that if any player was found guilty of using steroids, he would personally and single-handedly pass legislation banning that player from professional sports. If careers were ruined, reputations forever tarnished and stars labeled as cheaters, so be it. Both justice and the game would be well served.

For his part, Thompson did make several points as players testified. A baseball fan at heart, Thompson was very familiar with the issue. He had convinced himself that he didn't want to overshadow O'Toole in his own district. The fact of the matter was, in this hearing, Thompson was the young rookie learning at the feet of the seasoned veteran.

So Richard Thompson mostly sat and learned as O'Toole ripped witness after witness. "Players need to fear getting caught," O'Toole said, addressing himself to the union representatives and club owners in attendance (as well as those who would quickly learn of his remarks secondhand). "As owners you don't want the confrontation. And, as the player's union, you don't want your rank-and-file humiliated. But, let me tell you this: if you don't get together and come up with a much tougher testing protocol, Congress will. Baseball is America, and if you can't stand up and protect the integrity of this game, we will do it for you. And, at that point, I can guarantee you that neither side will like it."

"At that point, gentlemen, players will have more to worry about than their careers and owners will have more to worry about than baseball's exemption to the anti-trust laws. People will go to jail. I can assure you that it won't be just reporters or locker room boys who refuse to give up their sources to a grand jury," O'Toole said.

O'Toole was making reference to John Gustine, Joyce Lang and Greg Graham. The first two were reporters from California, with *The Los Angeles Journal,* who were awaiting sentencing for contempt of court, for refusing to reveal their leaks to the judge conducting a grand jury investigation on steroid abuse in professional sports. Greg Graham was a personal trainer who was facing a similar fate from the same judge, for failing to cooperate with the grand jury.

After the hearing, O'Toole was surrounded by reporters. His post-hearing press conference, against a back drop of blue sky, fluffy clouds and palm trees, was carried live on ESPN and CNN. Surrounded by curious fans on the grounds of the spring training complex watching the pre-game warm-ups, O'Toole continued his assault on players and owners alike. Except, this time, acting as a mentor to his young colleague, O'Toole brought Thompson into the media mix to share the spotlight with him.

There, Thompson had the sound bite of the day. Following the hearing, one of the players who had testified, Donny Alberato, had blasted the hearing as a "circus side show." He had gone on to issue a warning of his own, suggesting that the Congressmen, who had conducted the hearing had better watch out or their constituents would revolt against this apparent waste of tax dollars. A sports reporter asked Thompson for a response to these comments. In reference to rumors that Alberato's hat size had increased due to steroid use, Thompson quipped, "I don't think I need to take political advice from a man who needs zippers on his t-shirt to get them over his head."

The reporters all laughed, but Thompson realized he had probably gone beyond the bounds of decorum for a United States Congressman. So he added: "These hearings are about the integrity of the game. Steroid use undermines the integrity of the game just as much as gambling. If you're going to let Alberato into the Hall of Fame, then you have to reconsider the bans on Pete Rose and Shoeless Joe Jackson."

As the pair of Congressmen continued their assault on steroids to the media, the three owners who had testified huddled around a speaker phone in the executive offices of Ed Smith Stadium. On the other end, a top league official from baseball's corporate office verbally demeaned the owners for their lackluster performance at the hearing.

"I lived up to my end of the bargain," said the official in a stern voice. "I let you guys try to handle this your way and you blew it. You are the owners of the greatest enterprises in the country and you came off like a bunch of pussies. Starting right now, we're in charge of this problem and we'll handle it as we see fit. Baseball will not die over this issue. We will prevail, no matter the cost."

Similarly, behind the closed door of the visitor's training room, the players' union representative chided Donny Alberato. "Listen, Donny," he said to the All-Star first baseman, "you keep saying that you've never juiced."

"I didn't," interjected Alberato.

"I don't give a flying fuck if you did or didn't," said the union representative as he looked at the muscles bulging out from Alberato's t-shirt. "It's none of my business. But, I'll tell you one thing that is my business. If this grand jury thing goes against you, you're done. Kiss your sweet ass goodbye, along with your pension. We're not standing by you."

That was the morning business. By noon, most of the media who had come for the hearing had drifted away and it was time for the two Congressmen (and their volunteer staffer for a day) to have some fun. The sky was royal blue with only a few white clouds coming in off the Gulf of Mexico to occasionally hide the sun. As Thompson looked skyward at the perfect day for baseball, he took a deep breath to smell the salt air blowing in off the Gulf.

Life is definitely good, Thompson thought to himself.

O'Toole was on the field preparing to throw out the ceremonial first pitch of the game and Thompson was going to be behind the plate to receive it. Thompson and The Fat Man sat in the dugout, drinking it all in like a game day cold beer. The festive atmosphere of the annual St. Patrick's Day classic was in the air. Irish folk musicians played *O Danny Boy* in the stands while patrons bought baseball caps emblazoned with the classic Cincinnati Reds' "Wishbone C" in green rather than red.

O'Toole and Thompson wore light green jerseys over their crisp business shirts, ties, and suit pants. As game time approached, they both stood on the steps of the dugout, and several fans yelled greetings from the stands to the popular O'Toole. One fan in a striped shirt, who had been in the background at the post-hearing press conference, even handed O'Toole a green beer to sip before going out onto the field to do the ceremonial honors.

"These are my people," O'Toole said to Thompson, as he raised his green beer to the crowd. "Erin go Bragh," he shouted before downing the beer in a couple of quick gulps. He belched after the downing of the beer. "Damn, the wife must have put garlic on my salad last night."

The Fat Man was over to one side, explaining to one of the young prospects why the stadium announcer said a player's name twice when he was being introduced to the crowd. "Paul Sommerkamp started it when he used to announce games at old Crosley Field in Cincinnati."

"Why was that?" asked the young player, genuinely excited that any fan was talking to him as if he had already made the final squad.

"Well, the sound system was so bad at Crosley that, when he said a player's name once, fans keeping score at their seats couldn't hear the name over the cheers. It was especially bad when Big Klu, Ted Kluszewski, was introduced at the game. So he'd say the name once…wait for the crowd to calm down and say the last name a second time."

"Ted Kluszewski," said the rookie in his best announcer voice, then paused and repeated, "Kluszewski."

"You got it," said The Fat Man laughing with his new friend.

When Thompson and O'Toole were finally introduced by the public address announcer, they trotted out to the mound and the plate to the polite applause usually given to those who are bestowed with such duties. O'Toole hammed it up for the locals, waving in all directions to his loyal constituents. The announcement was made that the pitch was about to happen.

Donny Alberato leaned against the fence next to the dugout, talking to a gray haired man who seemed to be his agent, but all the while staring at O'Toole. The massive muscles in his arms stretched the sleeves of his blue and gray pin stripe jersey to their limits.

O'Toole was clearly in his element and having a great time. Grinning from ear to ear, he rubbed up the ball with both hands, as if somehow he would make this ceremonial toss one for the ages. O'Toole's grin suddenly disappeared as he looked in towards Thompson, waiting for a sign.

At first, Thompson thought that O'Toole was yucking it up for the crowd. He played along, by getting down to a half crouch, giving O'Toole the one finger down sign for a fast ball, and elaborately pounding the leather pocket of his glove. But O'Toole just stared in at Thompson, motionless.

Still trying to play along with O'Toole, Thompson acted as if the first signal had been waved off. He gave the two fingers down sign, calling for a curve ball, like the older of the two somehow had the ability to put enough spin on the ball to make it curve. Thompson smiled a big toothy grin. O'Toole continued to stare blankly at Thompson.

Thompson pounded his glove again, trying to snap O'Toole out of his trance.

Suddenly, O'Toole's eyes rolled back into his head and he made two half stutter steps to his left, before collapsing to the ground.

Thompson was the first to reach O'Toole, quickly followed by the trainer for Los Angeles. "No pulse," screamed the trainer at his colleague from the Reds, "he's got no pulse." Thompson stepped back from the mound in disbelief at the surreal scene transpiring around him.

A paramedic ran in from the outfield, leading the ambulance which was parked just beyond a gate in the outfield fence. A doctor who was attending the game jumped over the railing from the third base side and rushed to the mound.

O'Toole's jersey and shirt were ripped open as the doctor began CPR. The doctor yelled for the paramedic to charge the defibrillator carried in the ambulance. Once in his hands, he vigorously rubbed the paddles together before shouting "clear." O'Toole's body jumped as they shot 1,000 volts into his chest in a vain attempt to jump start his heart.

Despite repeated efforts, Kevin O'Toole would never again regain consciousness.

The crowd was aghast. People cried in disbelief. Others simply stood and stared in shock. Still others simply looked on with blank looks on their faces ... Donny Alberato from the visitor's dugout ... the owners from their front row seats.

In any event, no one left their positions until Congressman Kevin O'Toole's lifeless body was placed on a stretcher and removed from the field in an ambulance for the trip to Sarasota Memorial Hospital. Reporters in the press box called their news desks about the breaking story they were observing.

Everyone was stunned.

That is all except one fan who slowly, but deliberately, walked out of the stadium to his waiting rental car. He gently placed a backpack of autographed baseball cards onto the seat beside him like they were some sort of precious commodity and calmly drove out of the parking lot.

Chapter 1

Congressman Richard Thompson generally began each weekly legislative staff meeting at his Washington, D.C. office with some story about the history of the Capitol or some amusing anecdote about one of the Members who had served or was currently serving in Congress. The tradition started by accident when, at his very first staff meeting on the Hill, he told the story of the great Florida Democratic Senatorial primary race of 1950 between incumbent United States Senator Claude Pepper and his former supporter turned opponent, George Smathers.

It was a brutal campaign. As Pepper had led the "Dump Truman" effort in the 1948 Presidential election, Smathers was running with the personal support of President Harry S. Truman. Some say the President had called him personally to ask him to run. Yet, even the support of President Truman couldn't protect Smathers from the vicious nature of the campaign trail. Pepper's loyal base of rural voters were ferocious in their support for him. At one stop, Smathers claimed a woman spit tobacco juice in his eyes as he attempted to address the crowd.

Smathers fought back. *Time* magazine reported Smathers, playing to the poor (and oftentimes illiterate) voters of the rural communities of Florida, told crowds: "Are you aware Claude Pepper is known all over Washington as a shameless extrovert? Not only that, but this man is reliably reported to practice nepotism with his sister-in-law and he has a sister who was once a thespian in wicked New York. Worst of all, it is an established fact that Mr. Pepper, before his marriage, habitually practiced celibacy."

Until his death in 2007, Smathers claimed he never gave the speech and offered a cash reward to anyone who could prove otherwise. He did, however, admit he referred to the fact Pepper had visited the Soviet Union in 1945 and had declared Joseph

Stalin "was a man America could trust." For that comment, Smathers called Pepper a communist and referred to him on the campaign trail as "Red Pepper."

Smathers defeated Pepper in the primary by some 60,000 votes and went on to win election to the United States Senate in the general election. In the Senate he became close friends with a young man named John F. Kennedy and was the best man at his wedding. Pepper came back, as many great politicians do and was elected to the House of Representatives from Miami in 1963. He served in Congress until his death in 1989. He was so beloved that Congress paid him the ultimate honor at the time of his death by allowing his body to lie in state in the rotunda of the Capitol.

The kids on the staff liked the story so much they began asking Thompson about other stories and lore of the Capitol. In order to keep them at bay, he agreed to start each meeting with such a story. Teaching them Congressman Gene Snyder, who served Kentucky for over twenty years, from 1963—1986, was a master of the Jefferson Rules of Procedure might actually get them to pick up the book every now and then instead of calling counsel's office when they had a rules question.

Today's meeting, however, did not start with any amusing story. The mood in the room was quite somber, as Thompson was still feeling the sting of watching his colleague, Kevin O'Toole, die in front of his eyes.

Richard Thompson had a reputation as a man who lived life with passion. This meant his highs were very high. Unfortunately, as it is for most people with this personality trait, the lows are cavernous. This day, Richard Thompson struggled with the depth of his emotional divide.

Now he was in office, Thompson had changed his appearance in not-so-subtle ways to reflect the stature of his new position. The sport coats and penny loafers on his 5'10" frame had been replaced by tailored suits and French cuffed shirts. The glasses were gone and contact lenses in their place. Most noticeably, he had started to keep his sandy brown hair cut tight around the ears and collar. The new hair cut had reduced the references of him resembling Bill Gates, which he had to endure during the campaign.

"All right, so we will have the Department of Defense Appropriation starting on the floor on Wednesday," said Thompson quietly about half way through his legislative staff meeting. "When do we think the amendment on Ft. Knox will make its way to the floor?"

"Hard telling right now, Congressman," replied Thompson's Legislative Director, Bobby Richmond. "The DOD Appropriation usually takes a week or two to get all the way through. The Rules Committee will take it up tomorrow and decide exactly how many amendments will be allowed. I'll have a better idea then, but I expect the amendment will get called up early next week."

"Right." Thompson thumbed through the detailed summary Bobby had prepared. "I just promised Congressman Singleton last week I would go to the well and support him on this one. He said he's already been given a silent nod from the folks on Rules they are going to allow his amendment and give him an hour of debate on it. Call Aimee over in Singleton's office and see who's running the floor on the amendment. Make sure I get some time in the half-hour for debate in support."

"How many minutes do you want?" asked Bobby.

"It's a Kentucky issue, but I'm not on the committee," replied Thompson. "I'll be lucky if I get a minute."

"Yes, sir," said Bobby. "I'll prepare a one minute for your live speech and five for entry into the Record."

Unlike the Senate, where debate is unlimited and unstructured, debate in the United States House of Representatives is governed by rules which are very structured. House rules limit the number of amendments which will be considered on a given bill and impose strict time limits for debate thereon. Before a bill goes to the floor of the House, it must go to the Committee on Rules which sets the parameters for amendment and debate. It's not unusual for one amendment on a bill to get only a half hour for debate, split equally between supporters and opponents. With 435 Members, splitting those 15 minutes is often like divvying up a pizza into slices of eight when there are a dozen who want to eat.

"Sounds good to me," said Congressman Thompson. "When you call Aimee, ask her what issue they want me to hit on for the one minute portion."

All Members of Congress handle their staffs differently. The weekly staff meeting is generally one regular activity in every Congressional office. The Member gets a briefing on what is coming up on the floor that week, what's happening in the committees he serves on and what type of mail and calls are coming into the office. Always, of course, they talk politics.

Having been a staffer once himself, from the beginning Thompson wanted to be known as one of those Members who treated his staff with respect and dignity. Every year, *Roll Call*, one of the newspapers on the Hill, lists the worst Members to work for in what they refer to as the Simon Le Greed Caucus. Thompson had known one of those caucus Members when he had worked on the Hill. In staff meetings, staffers couldn't smile or they'd be yelled at for making fun of their boss. Nor could they frown, or he would yell at them for not appreciating the job he had provided for them. So they would sit in meetings like expressionless zombies fearing the wrath of their leader. When the Congressman was caught up in an FBI sting, all his former staffers smiled appropriately.

Another Member was known to throw his telephone receiver at staffers when he didn't like the information he was being given. The weekly meeting was held with staffers sitting in a semicircle around the Member's desk, the radius of which was determined as being just beyond the reach of the fully-extended phone cord.

"Thank God the old SOB retired before the advent of cell phones," Thompson had once told his young staff while tossing his cell phone from hand to hand. "He could have killed somebody with one of these."

Thompson paused and, through his self-imposed melancholy, looked around the room at the young faces eagerly staring back at him. He couldn't help but smile and wonder if that's how he had looked when he was a young man on the Hill working for his mentor, the late-Congressman Garrett Jackson. He swore from the day he arrived he would not be one of those Members who would douse their youthful idealism with the butt end of a flying telephone receiver.

Josh Barkman was his Chief of Staff.

A young, baby-faced, go-getter, Barkman had been Thompson's press secretary/political director during the campaign. His curly blond hair matched his preppy D.C. uniform—khaki slacks, blue blazer, button-down shirt, red power tie and penny loafers. His political skills on the campaign trail convinced Thompson he needed to be the one running his Washington operation following the election. He was young, but he had good instincts.

Thompson had met Bobby Richmond, his Legislative Director, during the last campaign, but it had not been under the best of circumstances. The young African-American had worked for the House Rules Committee and helped Thompson blow the cover off Congressman Marcus Lackner's illegal scheme to run guns to anti-Castro rebels in Cuba. Still, he liked the kid's passion and had a good feeling about his abilities.

"So what else is up this week?" asked Thompson. "What are we doing in the Judiciary Committee?"

"Nothing on the schedule," interjected Molly Kemen. A young blond lawyer in her first year or so out of law school, Kemen was handling the Congressman's primary committee assignment. She was from Ashland, Kentucky, in the eastern end of Thompson's district and spoke with a heavy southern accent. "With O'Toole's death, they have cancelled everything this week. The staff director said we will get back on schedule next week."

"Are we going to continue the steroid hearings?" queried Thompson.

"I'm not sure," replied Kemen. "That was O'Toole's signature issue. No one is sure if the new Chairman of the Subcommittee will have the same passion for it."

"Well, with Kevin gone," said Thompson, "it would be a shame to see it die on the vine."

"Do you want to take it?" asked Kemen.

"No, I don't think so," Thompson replied.

"Really?" said Kemen, with more than a little disappointment in her voice.

"Tell the new Chairman's staff I will help out where I can," he said, "but I don't want it as one of my signature issues."

"Understood. I'll nose around and see what his plans are," said Kemen.

"Thanks," Thompson said.

"Speaking of O'Toole, the Special Order on the Chairman is going to be Tuesday night after regular business," said Thompson's Chief of Staff. "I called the Majority Cloak Room and told them you wanted to have some time."

"And they were all right with a Republican eulogizing a Democrat?" Thompson tried to joke, but the tone in his voice gave away his angst.

"Yes, sir," said Josh. "They know you are still pretty shook up about what happened. I think they appreciated that you want to talk about the Chairman. Do you want me to prepare something?"

"Yeah. Prepare ten minutes or so for me to put into *The Record* about his career and such. But, when I talk live on the floor, I think I'm just going to shoot from the hip. I want to do a couple of minutes live about his passion for baseball. I'll probably get into his views on steroids, but just a little bit. I really want to capture how much he truly loved the game."

The Record is *The Congressional Record*, a daily journal of every word said on the floor of both the House and the Senate. Well, almost every word… Many times Members will speak from the hip, but the words which appear in the Record are those which are "revised and extended" in the written speech given to the body's clerk.

Thompson turned his chair in towards his computer pulling up the week at a glance view of his schedule. "Who is on the schedule? Is there anyone interesting coming in this week?"

"It's spring, sir," Josh laughed. "You should remember from your staff days, the National Association of Everybody is in town each and every week for the next month or so. Thirty-some realtors will be by on Wednesday and the Greater Cincinnati Airport board members are in town. They are having you speak to them at breakfast on Thursday morning."

"Greater Cincinnati **Northern Kentucky** International Airport," corrected Thompson. He sometimes had to remind his young Chief of Staff that the Greater Cincinnati, Ohio airport is actually located in Thompson's 4th Congressional District, which is centered in the three counties which comprise what is commonly referred to as Northern Kentucky.

"And Cooper is coming by on Wednesday morning before your committee meetings," said Josh referring to Kentucky lobbyist John Cooper, an old friend of Thompson's.

"Is he coming up with the bankers?" Thompson asked, referring to one of Cooper's stable of top Kentucky clients.

"No, sir," said Josh with some reluctance in his voice. "You may not believe me when I tell you what organization he registered to lobby for late last week."

"Try me, Josh," replied Thompson.

"Baseball," said Josh.

"Baseball?" Thompson replied incredulously.

"Yes, sir," said Josh. "Apparently, they are concerned you might get interested in taking up the steroid issue where Congressman O'Toole left off."

"I just told you. I have no desire to take on that issue," said Thompson.

"I didn't think so," interjected Kemen, "but the committee may be looking for someone to take the lead now Congressman O'Toole is dead."

"And they hired John to make sure it wasn't me?" laughed Thompson.

"Apparently so," said Kemen.

"Good," said Thompson. "I hope John got his fee up front. Is there anything else on the schedule?"

"Just the regular line up of fundraisers and receptions," Josh replied.

"Just try to keep Thursday evening free. I want to get a good night's sleep before I fly home on Friday afternoon. I don't get to see Ann and the kids during the week, so I want to try and be fresh for the weekend."

"Such as it is," said Josh. "You and Ann have a black-tie affair on Saturday night."

"Saturday nights are part of the job," replied Thompson. "Just don't schedule anything for me on Sundays. That's family time. Period."

Thompson hoped he had made the edict about Sundays authoritative enough. The fact of the matter was since taking office some six months earlier, his relationship with his wife and children had been strained. If he could make the staff believe his family life was stable, maybe he could convince himself.

For Richard and Ann Thompson, the tension of entry into public life was exacerbated by the amount of time they were forced to spend apart. Whoever opined absence makes the heart grow fonder, obviously wasn't a married politician.

Thompson paused to end the meeting. He stood up from his chair and looked around the room in an authoritative manner signaling the dismissal of his newly assembled crew. "All right, thanks, folks. Let's have a good week."

As the rest of the staff quietly made their way out of the office, Josh remained behind.

"I think we put together a pretty good group of folks," said Josh. He was proud of his efforts to quickly assemble a group of young staffers following Richard Thompson's special election victory only months before. The election was termed a "special" election, because it fell outside the regular even-year, election day for Congress. The sitting Member, Garrett Jackson, died in office and a "special" election was called by the Governor of Kentucky to fill Jackson's unexpired term.

"They are starting to gel," replied Thompson. "They have a lot of passion. Let's hope we can keep them here at least through the next election cycle."

"I asked them each for a commitment at least through the election," said Barkman.

"I would never hold them to it," said Thompson. "If the right job came along, I would be happy for them to move up."

"They know , sir," replied Josh. "That's why I think they will stay. They respect you."

"I'm even getting used to them calling me 'sir' and 'Congressman' instead of Rick," said Thompson.

"They have respect for the office, too, Boss," said Josh. "Did you ever call Congressman Jackson 'Garrett' in front of anyone?"

"No. I still have to get used to sitting in his chair." He paused. "I guess I feel like the first guys felt."

"How do you mean, Boss?" asked Josh.

"The first Members were frontiersmen," explained Thompson. "They were explorers and settlers. They came from farms and backwoods to Washington to work in the ornate surroundings of the Capitol. I read one time most of them felt quite out of place in their new settings."

"Well, you are here now," replied Josh. "You had better get used to it."

"I'm working on it," Thompson said.

"Speaking of working on it," said Josh, "we need to get to work on getting the chance to continue that honor. I've started to schedule some PAC fundraisers."

"God, we just finished winning a special election," said Thompson. "Can't I get some time without calling people for money?"

"You know the game, Congressman," replied Josh. "Griffith keeps telling us it is your first re-elect. The opposition knows if they don't beat you next year, you will have the seat until you are caught either with a live boy or a dead woman. You have received a lot of good press over these steroid hearings and we need to take advantage of that fact. Griff made me swear we will start the fundraising now to make some Democrat back home think twice about running against you. They need to know if they are going to run against you, it's going to cost them a couple of million bucks."

"You know what?" asked Thompson.

"No. What, sir?" replied Josh.

"You are starting to talk a little too much like Griff," said Thompson of his friend, alter-ego and campaign guru, Michael Griffith. Griffith was known in political circles for being the man who could win the election deemed unwinnable by others. He didn't want to admit it to the two of them, but he liked the idea Griffith had taken the young man under his political wing.

"Kind of scary, isn't it?" Josh laughed.

"Yeah. Still, I would just like to go one week without asking someone for campaign contributions." Thompson paused reflectively, hoping Josh would give him a break and tell him not to worry about it. When such a reprieve didn't come, he continued. "Keep scheduling me some time over at the National Republican Congressional Committee each week and I'll make calls from there."

"Just as long as you are making calls and not hanging out in the basement grill playing gin with Charlie, Sport and the Sarge," replied Josh, referring to three lobbyists who were friends of Thompson's from back in the days when he was a staffer on the Hill.

"Funny boy," said Thompson. "You are listening to my wife too much."

"Well, she did call me this morning," replied Josh.

"Great," said Thompson. "She's talking to you more often than she is to me. You do still work for *me*, right?"

"She's worried about you, Boss," said Josh. "She says you are still pretty shook up over the whole thing in Florida."

"I admit it," said Thompson. "I've not been in the greatest of moods since Florida."

"We have noticed it around the office," Josh replied. "You are always singing some song reflecting your mood, but you've mostly quit doing that since O'Toole died. The only songs I've caught you singing lately are those Zevon songs about death and mortality."

"Sorry," said Thompson. "I really hadn't noticed."

"Well, I've noticed," Josh said. "I know it's been tough on you, but you have to quit singing the lyrics to *I'll Sleep When I'm Dead* in front of the staff."

"Fine," snapped Thompson. "Just to keep you and the staff happy, I'll try to break into *Monkey Wash Donkey Rinse* the very next chance I get."

Thompson had to admit his wife's worries over his mood were justified. He had fought bouts of depression before, but it was going to take Thompson a long time to shake the melancholy he was feeling over O'Toole's death. His emotions were wrapped up between the loss of a colleague and the selfish reflections of one looking at some future legacy through that colleague's mortality. Still, he didn't mean to snap at his young Chief of Staff.

"Sorry, Josh. The whole day was such a contrast in emotions," said Thompson. "The steroid committee hearing went great. The Chairman really hit a home run on his opening statement. Then, Donny Alberato was called up to testify."

"Alberato…the first baseman for Los Angeles?" asked Josh.

"Yeah," said Thompson. "Alberato testified he had never used steroids and O'Toole about lost his mind. He started talking about how Alberato looked in his old baseball cards versus his new ones. He asked him to explain how he went from a size 9 cleat to a size 13 in three seasons…how his hat size increased over the same period."

"What did Alberato do?" asked Josh.

"Alberato was pissed. I thought he was going to get up from the hearing table and take a swing at O'Toole."

"Alberato is big," said Josh. "But, O'Toole…well, there was a lot of big fight in that little Irish dog."

"Yeah, but have you ever seen Alberato's arms?" Thompson asked the young man.

"I have," Josh replied. "He's huge. Those guns can't be real. They had to be made in a lab."

"Anyhow, it was pretty intense," said Thompson. "There was more press around there than I have ever seen at a hearing here on the Hill. The photographers were scrunched together so tight in front of the witness table they had to take turns at steadying their cameras to take pictures." He got up from his chair and walked to the window, pausing in reflection. "I stayed pretty quiet during the hearing."

"Good call," said Josh. "Never steal the Chairman's thunder at his hearing in his home city."

"It was more than that, Josh," Thompson replied. "He was good. Damn good. For the most part, I just sat back and watched a master at work. He controlled the pace of the hearing like a mechanic controlling the timing on a Mercedes."

"He had that reputation," Josh said.

"But, he didn't exclude me either," said Thompson. "After the hearing...when he held his impromptu press conference...he brought me into the scrum. He could have grabbed the entire spotlight."

"But, he didn't," replied Josh.

"No, he didn't," said Thompson. "He put his arm around me and included me like I was one of his oldest colleagues and best friends."

"Where you got the sound bite of the day," said Josh.

"Well, they started talking about the Hall of Fame and the integrity of the game," said Thompson.

"And you got pissed off, didn't you?" asked Josh.

"Yeah, I got pissed off and said if all the talk about integrity of the game is really important, then you can't let steroid users like Alberato into the Hall of Fame."

"And..."

"And, if you are going to let steroid users into the Hall, then you have to let Pete Rose and Shoeless Joe Jackson into Cooperstown."

"Lead quote on *Sports Center* that night," said Josh. "That little quote created more emails and phone calls than anything you have done up here so far. Some were even on your side."

"Come on, Josh. Steroid users like Alberato have done far more to hurt the integrity of the game than Pete and Shoeless Joe."

"Not according to fans in Los Angeles," said Josh.

"No, but a reporter for *The Journal* loved me," Thompson quickly quipped. "He quoted me in his story the next day."

There was a pause as Josh realized he might have pushed his boss a little too far. Thompson renewed the conversation by changing the topic.

"Then the press conference was over and the whole mood changed."

"Was it time for the ballgame?" asked Josh.

"Yeah," said Thompson. "It was time for the ballgame."

"I know you don't want to hear about it," said Josh, "but I saw the pictures. You were having a catch with a couple of the Reds' players?"

"I met up with The Fat Man and they pretty much gave us free reign to go wherever we wanted. We had some time before the start of the game, so for a while we were just hanging out on one of the practice fields right behind center field of Ed Smith Stadium. A couple of the players were warming up. Someone gave me a glove and I just started tossing."

"Cool," said Josh. "That made *ESPN*, too."

"God, we were on cloud nine," said Thompson. "I mean, a few minutes later we were in the Reds' dugout. Then, the Chairman took the mound to throw out the pitch…"

Thompson looked down and paused.

"Pretty tough, huh, Boss?" asked Josh.

"The look on his face was piercing," said Thompson. "It was like he knew something was happening to his body, but he couldn't do anything about it. Now when I look back on it, I wonder if he was looking at me to make it stop."

"I can't even begin to imagine," said Josh.

"Josh, I looked him square in the eye as he died. And there wasn't a damned thing I could do about it."

"Well, Boss," said Josh, "at least the last person he saw was a friend. Think of it this way, if you love the game as much as he did, dying of a heart attack on the mound is the way to go."

"Good line," said Thompson. "I think I'll steal it on Tuesday night."

"I'll put it in your remarks," said Josh. "You better get ready for the day."

Josh had started out of the room when he remembered there was one thing left on the morning's agenda which he had forgotten to discuss with his boss. He turned.

"Oh and there is one other thing. Someone wants to see you before you head home on Friday."

"Who's that?"

"FBI Agent Leo Argo."

Chapter 2

When A.B. "Happy" Chandler replaced Judge Kennesaw "Mountain" Landis as Commissioner of Baseball in 1945, he made a critical decision that would seal his doom with the club owners. Chandler's grave error in judgment did ***not*** involve his discussion with Brooklyn Dodgers owner, Branch Rickey, which allowed Jackie Robinson to integrate the game. Instead, it was one of his first decisions as Commissioner, in which he commanded the offices of baseball be moved from Chicago to Cincinnati. The Reds were then the smallest market in baseball…a National League town where American League teams, owners and writers rarely traveled. Most importantly, it was not New York, which, at the time, had three major league clubs.

Chandler had not realized he needed the writers in New York to back him and the changes (like integration) which he wanted to implement. Placing his office in Cincinnati so he would be closer to his home in rural Versailles, Kentucky, had the practical, if unintended, effect of alienating him from those metropolitan writers.

So in 1951, when Chandler was replaced by the man passed over in favor of Chandler years earlier, Ford Frick, baseball's offices were promptly moved to New York City, where they remain to this day. Frick is otherwise known as the man who put an asterisk in baseball's record book when Roger Maris broke Babe Ruth's single season home run record.

On the 49th floor of the Majesty Building in New York City, overlooking the Hudson River, a small group of men were meeting with the intensity and deliberation normally afforded to the scheduling of advertising during a playoff series. More intensity, in fact, was being shown to the topic at hand, for, after all, this topic—steroids—would eventually affect those most precious advertising revenue dollars.

The man behind the impressive modern glass-top desk was Colin N. Korey, Special Assistant to the Commissioner of Baseball. At thirty-nine, he was an experienced executive but, by the standards of the baseball establishment, considered young to be in such a powerful position. A tall, good-looking man, with flowing sandy blond hair, Korey was responsible for many of the innovations baseball had implemented over the past five seasons which had increased attendance at ball parks. He was a lanky man, but his thin frame was hidden by the custom-made shirts and suits which he regularly wore.

The success he had obtained at putting money into the hands of owners earned him a meteoric rise in baseball's hierarchy. Observers in the media often editorialized Korey was the *de-facto* commissioner. Most owners felt Korey was far too young to be granted so much clout. They shared a fear—never publicly uttered—that Korey was rapidly gaining excessive power over the teams and owners themselves.

Such whispers were not helped by Korey's abrasive personality and cut-throat attitude. Around owners, Korey carried himself with the polite arrogance of a man who knew he had the complete confidence of the Commissioner on whatever assignment he was given. He was somehow able to intimidate men and women of success and wealth far beyond his own.

No one ever got too close to Korey. He was a complex personality wrapped in a cold exterior. Korey's father, a former major league baseball player, raised his son with all the warmth of a Little League dad who yells at the manager to put his son in the game. He warned Korey if he did not achieve success by age forty, he would never obtain it. Korey played baseball in college with little success. When he realized he would never make it as a top notch ball player, he switched gears to the operations side of baseball.

With a background in general business administration, Korey began his climb up the ivy-covered ladder of baseball. Through a series of A ball, Double A and Triple A executive positions, he developed a hard exterior which gained him accolades from the owners for whom he worked. By the time he was thirty-one, Korey had already been named Minor League Executive of the Year by one of the industry rags.

His tough business exterior helped to turn each franchise he touched into a money maker, but the persona he created for himself was more than that. At his father's urging, he developed a calculated air of superiority which rubbed players the wrong way. "If you want to be somebody in management, carry yourself with more pride and arrogance than the best ball player on your club," his father had told him. "Make sure they know you are better than them."

When Korey was hired by baseball's home office, his dad told him to treat owners the same way he treated players. This time, however, he had to get the blessing for such behavior from the Commissioner, not some minor league club owner. When his pit bull approach won a vote of the other owners over a renegade club, the Commissioner promoted him to "special assistant." His promotion to the inner circle gave Korey carte blanche to treat owners however he damn well pleased.

From that day forward, just as his dad counseled, he treated owners like he treated players. It didn't win him any friends, but Korey didn't care about friendship. His attitude worked and that was all that mattered.

Like it or not, Korey had become the man the Commissioner went to when a successful result was more than just the desired outcome. He went to Korey when success was necessary. With opening day looming and steroids in baseball on the front pages of every newspaper in the country, success was necessary.

As the meeting convened, Korey sat stoically in his high back leather chair, looking down at the other two men sitting opposite him. Korey had maintenance cut a couple of inches off the legs of the guest chairs so whoever sat in them had to look up to him. On his left was Bill Pappard, the general partner who owned the controlling interest in the Los Angeles ball club; on his right was M.T. Stacy, baseball's head of security. Stacy had been hired personally by Korey and reported directly to him. Short and muscular, Stacy had a head which seemed just a bit too large for his body. His short graying hair and receding hairline emphasized his moon face. Odd looks aside, he was Korey's right hand.

The mood in the room as the trio exchanged pleasantries indicated to Pappard Stacy's loyalty was clearly to the Commissioner.

"Gentlemen," said Korey. "We have a problem of major league proportion."

"Goddamn right we do," Stacy replied in his thick Brooklyn accent.

"My team should be coming out of spring training talking about our starting rotation," said Pappard as he looked around at the well equipped but fairly sterile office. Other than a photo of Korey's father in his major league baseball uniform, there were no personal effects on the desk or walls. "Instead, I'm spending all my time answering questions about Donny Alberato and what his soon-to-be-sentenced trainer was injecting into his ass."

"The Los Angeles press is brutal," said Korey.

"*The Journal* assigning Gustine and Lang to the story hasn't helped you any," said Stacy.

"Yeah," said Pappard. "I'm used to dealing with John Gustine. He's been covering us for years. I've had dinner with him a million times on the road."

"And you still can't control him?" Korey asked.

"Gustine I can control. He's not the problem," said Pappard. "Now, I have to deal with that bitch Joyce Lang. She's a real honest to God reporter—or at least she thinks she is. I hate sports reporters, but I can deal with them. I can't deal with him teaming up with a real one. Having her breathing down my neck is just too damned much."

"Calm down, Bill," said Korey coolly. "M.T., don't you have some dirt on her?"

"You bet I do," said Stacy. "She's a real freakin' whack job. There are rumors all over Los Angeles about her and what she'll do to get a story."

"What do you mean by that?" asked Pappard.

"She's a news slut," said Stacy. "She gets her stories out of the police department by providing…let's just say certain personal favors…for the detectives."

"You have to be kidding me?" Pappard laughed.

"Not in the least," said Stacy. "The other reporters in L.A. hate her because of her tactics, but *The Journal* doesn't seem to mind. They get their story ninety percent of the time."

"Wow," was all Pappard could muster up, unsure if he really wanted to know how Stacy got his information.

"Not to worry," said Stacy. "If she gets too close, we will hit her hard. I have a couple of reporters out on the coast ready to take her down. There is this detective she's close to who's one of her major sources of leaks. I think I can pin one of the leaks in a big murder case directly to the two of them."

"Pictures?" asked Korey.

"Not yet," said Stacy. "I'm working on it."

"How about Gustine?" asked Pappard.

"Not much there," replied Stacy. "He's clean. He's just one of those old-style sports reporters who believes God put him on this earth to protect the integrity of the game. Players like him, they think he's tough, but fair. They talk to him a lot so he has a lot of sources."

"Alberato hates him," interjected Pappard.

"Yes, he does," confirmed Stacy. "Alberato apparently dared him to come within 15 feet of his locker and started keeping his posse around to make sure Gustine stays away. There was a bit of a shoving match last season."

"We took care of that for this year," said Pappard. "Donny can only have one guy in the locker room at a time and we have moved him to a special corner where it's harder to get to him. When he's having one of his classic hissy fits, we can keep people away."

"Well, that may stop shoving matches. It still doesn't stop Gustine from writing about Alberato." Korey calmly shifted his gaze to Stacy. "M.T., you will have to figure out how to deal with Gustine. Lang can be discredited, but this Gustine guy is a real threat—especially if he believes in his mission. He could be the one who brings us down."

"Understood," was all Stacy had to say in response.

"What about Congress?" asked Pappard. "That hearing in Sarasota was a public relations disaster for us."

"In more ways than one," said Korey. "You guys blew it. The Commissioner told you guys not to do it. But you insisted and you blew it."

Korey paused and made direct eye contact with Pappard, forcing the owner to look away. Stacy smiled at the silent exchange which showed that, despite the sudden change in the tone of the meeting, Korey was still in complete control.

"But," Korey continued, "all in all, for a one day story, it couldn't have worked out better for baseball. That dead Congressman took us off the front page pretty quickly."

"That's cold," said Pappard, in a tone of voice suggesting he was actually offended by Korey's comments. The death of Congressman Kevin O'Toole meant nothing to Pappard personally, but he had enough "old money" in his upbringing to make him recoil when someone was especially crass in his presence.

"Don't get all sanctimonious on me, Bill," said Korey. "I saw how he chewed you up and spit you out in Florida. You were happy his death knocked your pitiful ass off the front page headline the next day."

"I don't like where you are going, Colin," said Pappard. There was fire in his eyes, but there was something about his voice and his body language that gave away the fact Pappard was overmatched. He wasn't used to this kind of vulgar directness. Korey sensed it immediately.

"With all due respect to you and all the other owners, fuck you," said Korey.

"Excuse me?" said Pappard, dropping his eyebrows, leaning forward in his chair and looking intently at Korey.

"You heard me," repeated Korey. "Fuck you."

"You can't talk to me like that," said Pappard. His voice was clear, but he was shaken and his eyes kept darting back and forth between the floor of the office and the Manhattan skyline outside the window. For some reason Pappard could not look Korey in the eye.

"The hell I can't," replied Korey with a force that shocked even Stacy. "You have yourself and baseball in a position you can't get out of by yourself. I'm your fixer. I can talk to you any damn way I want to talk to you because you need me and you know it."

Stacy inwardly smiled as Pappard sputtered, trying to interject, but Korey would not allow him to do so.

"The owners don't like me. I know that. You will respect me, though. You will respect me because, at the end of the day, I'm the guy who will preserve the game and your precious profits. You will respect me because I know somewhere deep inside your soul, in a place you don't admit exists when you go to church on Sunday, you smiled when O'Toole collapsed on the mound."

Pappard sat in stunned silence.

"Now get out of my office and let me do the job the Commissioner hired me to do," said Korey.

Pappard stood up with as much dignity as he could muster, leaving the room without acknowledging the presence of either Stacy or Korey.

When the door of Korey's office closed, Stacy smiled and said, "I think he'll need to stop by the men's room to look in the mirror for what's left of his ass."

"Don't worry about him," said Korey to his trusty aide. "He's just an old drunk."

"He doesn't look it," replied Stacy.

"Yeah, I know," said Korey. "He covers it well. I never knew he was drunk until I saw him sober one day."

Stacy laughed. Korey remained grave.

"He's right though," said Korey. "The stupid bastard doesn't know it, but he's right."

"About what?" asked Stacy.

"Congress," said Korey. "That's our real issue. The payroll can deal with trainers and ball players and owners and reporters. Congress, now that's going to be much trickier."

"How so?" Stacy responded.

"They live under the impression they are as big as we are," said Korey. "Sometimes they are and it's always the owners' fault. The owners fold whenever Congress gets involved. You realize we have never expanded teams to new cities unless Congress forced us to. They are afraid of Washington."

"Shouldn't they be?" asked Stacy. "You know, shouldn't they be afraid of Washington, at least to some extent? You have guys like O'Toole. He was clean and we could never get to him."

"Maybe," replied Korey. "If anyone was going to go after us in Congress, it was him. Now, he's out of the way. The new subcommittee chair won't go there by himself. He's too timid. If he wades back in, he'll want someone to go with him."

"Agreed," said Stacy.

"How about that other guy?" asked Korey. "You know the one…the guy who made the wise-ass comment about letting Rose and Shoeless Joe into the Hall."

"He's a freshman in the minority party," said Stacy. "I don't think he'll be a threat."

"Don't assume anything," said Korey.

"I'm not," said Stacy. "I've already hired a lobbyist from Kentucky in case we need to leak information and blame it on somebody."

"Good thinking," Korey replied.

"Don't worry, Mr. Korey," said Stacy, proud of the compliment he had just received. Korey didn't give them often. "I'll find out what kind of dirt he has under his fingernails."

"We have gone this far on controlling this mess," said Korey. "Let's not let it slip on some first-termer from…."

"Kentucky," said Stacy, completing his boss' sentence. "Understood."

"Now, the most pressing issue," said Korey. "What are you going do about the Alberato situation?"

"I don't know what I can do right now," replied Stacy.

"Well, you better figure out something," said Korey. "And do it in a hurry."

"Pappard swears Alberato is clean," said Stacy. "I've looked at the reports myself and we have cover."

"Do you actually believe the report?" asked Korey.

"No way," replied Stacy. "He's a juicer. No doubt about it. I just can't prove it. Other than a couple of baseball Annies who claim to have injected him on the road, there is nothing out there."

"Except Graham…" said Korey.

"The report gives us cover," Stacy replied, "but Greg Graham was Alberato's trainer. He did the juicing. If someone gets him to talk, he could blow the whole thing up. Worse yet, apparently nobody knows where he is. He's gone underground."

Korey paused and looked at Stacy with a piercing stare. "I want the payroll on this as soon as possible."

"Understood," was his reply.

As Stacy turned to leave the room, he turned and looked at Korey, who already began to read the report Stacy previously placed on his desk about potential security threats on opening day. "Happy Birthday, Mr. Korey," he said in an upbeat tone.

Korey did not look up.

Chapter 3

Far from the friendly confines of the basement workout room in a plush Hollywood home, where trainer Gregory Graham used to count reps for his wealthy top client, baseball superstar Donny Alberato, a gray haired man approached the door of a small store-front gym near Huntington Beach. The gym was off the beaten paths of downtown L.A., where the man would normally travel in his daily affairs. It was in one of those gritty neighborhoods that made the hairs on the back of your neck stand up in broad daylight, nervous about who might be behind you. Most of the other stores in the strip were empty except for a hair salon at one end and a liquor store on the other. Both businesses had steel bars in the windows. Gang symbols were spray painted on the sidewalk to mark the territory.

At the door of the nondescript store front and, per instruction, he knocked to be granted entrance. Upon hearing the sound of the door being unlocked, he entered the store. He wasn't a typical "suit" by any means, but immediately he felt out of place in the dark, smelly room.

He clearly didn't look like anyone else in the room. He was taller than most of them. Their squatty, muscle bound bodies stood in contrast to the paunch he carried above his waist. What the man noticed most was all the men had little, if any hair on their heads. Whether it had fallen out due to steroid abuse or not, it was a stark difference to his long gray hair which had been slicked back to form a duck tail near the collar of his silk, lime green, short sleeved shirt.

He was nervous. Something about standing in a business where the windows have been painted over to block the view of the outside world made him feel uneasy. Hip-hop music from a boom box filled the room with a bass vibration that rattled his chest.

Inside, the space was basically an empty shell with bad fluorescent lighting, a beat up linoleum floor and holes in the walls reflecting the spots from which the previous tenant's fixtures had been removed. There was a single dividing wall across the space, about three quarters of the way back, which had at one time separated the retail space from a storage area.

About 20 feet from the front door, a grotesquely muscular man face up on a weight bench grunted expletives as two men, standing on either side of him, spotted the weight laden bar and counted out his repetitions. A little further in and to the right, a young African-American man, with a body which appeared to be chiseled in black granite, stood in front of a full length mirror, pumping two dumbbells up and down as if he were running in place with them—staring at the mirror to view the flexes in his well-defined upper body as he did so. On the other side of the room, opposite him, a heavily tattooed young woman in tight lycra shorts and a sports bra did sit ups on an incline bench raised to its highest level, yelling a guttural count with each successive trip up the board.

The aroma in the room was more than the distinctive bitter smell of a perspiration soaked locker room. It reeked of testosterone. Not the kind the people in the room were obviously injecting. It smelled of the more poetic testosterone which often defines exceptionally muscular men and women. While the man entering the room was repulsed by the smell, the others already there had grown accustomed to it, as if it were some sort of perfume which engulfed their image like a fine, sweet fragrance.

At first, no one appeared to notice him. As he stood just inside the front door, one by one they each silently recognized the newcomer's presence.

He decided to approach the guy in front of the mirror.

"Is Greg Graham here?" he asked just loud enough to be heard over the blaring music.

The guy in front of the mirror stopped his routine, readjusted the leather half gloves on his hands and stared at the man for a moment, looking him up one side and down the other like the outsider he was. With a disgusted grimace on his face, he nodded his head in the direction of the closed door at the back of the room before resuming his routine.

Compliantly, he approached the door and knocked. "Greg," he said in a voice he hoped was loud enough for whoever was on the other side of the door to hear, but low enough not to bother the men and women in the room, who were obviously as uncomfortable with him as he was with them. "Are you in there? It's me, Murph."

As Greg Graham opened the door, the smile with which he greeted attorney Adam Murphy was half welcoming and half suspicious. "C'mon in, Murph. Grab a chair." Graham glanced out into the front part of the space before closing the door, which had the effect of muffling, but certainly not silencing the music.

As Murphy entered, he noticed a young man carefully removing himself from a dilapidated training table in the middle of the room. He was pulling his shorts up above his waist at the same time. The young man glanced up at Graham who silently gestured him out of the room. After another two second blast of music, the door clicked closed behind him.

Graham eyed Murphy while wrapping duct tape around an empty sports drink bottle. As Murphy looked at the collection of vials and syringes on the shelves along the left hand wall, he could easily guess what Graham was hiding in the bottle. He ran his hands through his flowing gray hair in disbelief. When Graham tossed it in the garbage can, the contents hidden by the tape made an evil rattling sound.

There was a framed picture on one wall of Graham and Alberato comically striking muscle poses on the field at spring training, inscribed: "To Greg, the best damn trainer ever, Don."

"Jesus, Greg," said Murphy. "Where the hell did you find this fucking place?"

"A friend of mine owns this strip of stores," replied Graham. "It's a sort of tax write off or something."

"When I heard you had gone underground, I didn't envision this," said Murphy.

"After the raid, I had to go low key," Graham said.

"Low key and apparently low rent," Murphy replied. "Our friend asked me to come by and talk to you."

"Our friend?" said Graham. "We're not using names here?"

"Well, I'm not sure, Greg," said Murphy. "After the raid, we're not sure what's going on."

"What?" asked a pissed off Graham. "You think I'm wired? Fuck you!"

Murphy looked at Graham as he turned away. Graham's mousy brown hair and diminutive height would fool anyone about the solid body hidden beneath his gold running suit. A collegiate wrestler, Graham's body was tight, but not over the top. He obviously didn't personally use the stuff he was shooting into kids like the one who had just left the training room.

"Come on, Greg," pleaded Murphy.

"Don't 'come on Greg' me," said Graham. "It's my ass on the line right now. Not yours—and certainly not Donny's."

"We know that," explained Murphy.

"You are his lawyer," said Graham. "You know what I'm up against here. I'm looking at jail time."

"Maybe not," said Murphy. "I've been following the case. You may beat the rap."

"Oh, I'll beat the rap," said Graham. "They have no hard evidence on me. I've been too damn smart in setting up my distribution line. It's untraceable. But even if I beat it, I'm still looking at a year or more on the contempt charges for refusing to cooperate with the grand jury."

"I know," replied Murphy. "Our friend knows, too."

"A year, Murph, a fucking year," Graham shouted with deliberate over-enunciation. "Our friend keeps on hitting home runs with baseball groupies following him around like puppy dogs. You keep waltzing around Los Angeles practicing law and going to movie premieres with your clients. And I go to the slammer for a year."

"Calm down, Greg," said Murphy.

"It's hard to be calm right now, Murph," said Graham. "I'm done."

"You are not done," said Murphy. "You've just got some tough times ahead of you."

"I'm done," Graham reiterated. "No one's returning my calls, least of all my high paying clients. Look at what I'm doing to pay my fuckin' legal fees and child support. I'm mixing HGH cocktails for muscle bound goons and shooting testosterone into tattooed lesbians."

"That's why I'm here," said Murphy. "Our friend wants to help."

"Our friend," repeated Graham with a sarcastic tone, "wants to help."

"Yes he does," said Murphy.

"I'm touched," said Graham. "I really am."

"Greg, think about it. Of all your clients, he's got the most to lose, right?" asked Murphy.

"Probably," Graham acknowledged.

"Then," said Murphy, "on a purely personal level, you've got to assume he's more willing than any of your other clients to help you out."

"All right. I'll buy that," said Graham.

"But," said Murphy, "before we can help, we have to know what's going on with you and your case."

"In other words, you want to know how far I'm willing to go on this thing," said Graham.

"Look, Greg, this meeting is as uncomfortable for us as it is for you," said Murphy.

"You and your uncomfortable friend need to realize I made him a bigger star than he could've ever imagined," said Graham.

"And he appreciates what you've done," said Murphy. "He knows the risks you've taken and what you are looking at."

"Then why did you come here to call me a rat?" asked Graham.

"I'm not saying you are a rat, Greg," Murphy replied.

"Exactly, what are you saying, Murph?"

"All right, I'll cut to the chase," said Murphy.

"Please do."

"Straight up, our friend is concerned his name may be on some of the things they confiscated in the raid," said Murphy. "You know, like computer records and stuff."

"I told you guys a hundred times. None of that was on my computers. You know how we operated. There were always multiple shipments to different people before the juice reached you."

"And what about your suppliers?" asked Murphy. "Are there any traceable connections there?"

"All overseas," said Graham. "I had it shipped to Mexico and brought back over the border by mules. To the overseas folks, my big clients are just numbers."

"And were those numbers on anything confiscated?" Murphy asked.

"No way would I write those down. Those were all in my head."

"Your head?"

"Yeah, my head. I have a system on how I identified each shipment and who it went to. There are numbers on the invoices, but unless you know the formula on how to break my code, the numbers are useless. Tell our friend everything is up here. And as long as he abides by our agreement, it will stay up here," Graham said pointing to his temple.

"Great," replied Murphy. "There is absolutely nothing linking the two of you to the juice."

"Nothing," Graham replied. "And as long as I have a retirement account waiting for me when I get out, there never will be."

"Retirement account?" asked Murphy. His voice sounded quizzical, but Murphy had been expecting the topic of money to come up sooner or later.

"Let's not play games here, Murph. There is only one thing linking our friend to the juice. And that's what I've got up here," said Graham, again pointing to his temple. "As long as I know I'll be taken care of when I get out, what's up here will never come out."

"Don't worry, when you get out of prison, you will be a wealthy man," said Murphy

"Wrong answer," said Graham. "I want to be a wealthy man before I go in."

Graham reached in his wallet and handed Murphy a slip of paper with a bank name and account number on it.

"This is my bank in the Cayman Islands," said Graham. "The account is set up and waiting for its first big deposit. The fee for my silence is ten million dollars."

Murphy gave Graham a standard "you must be crazy" look he had learned at a legal seminar on how to negotiate. But he wasn't there to drive the price down, so the tone of his voice did not match the expression on his face. "That's a lot of jack," he said simply.

"Damn straight it is," said Graham. "But, it's only a fraction of what he makes a year. Consider his next credit card commercial to be a down payment. I want half of the money in the bank now and the other half when I get out."

"And then?" asked Murphy.

"And then I disappear," said Graham. "No one ever sees me again. Not you. Not my ex-wife and not any *Journal* reporters looking to do a story on the steroid abuse of Donny Alberato."

Graham paused and stared at Murphy.

"That's right, Murph," Graham continued. "You don't think those reporters over at *The Journal* will find me? They will. Indictment or not, a story from those two will end Donny's endorsement deals forever. You won't be able to get him a deal to be the spokesman for a local plumber, let alone a national credit card company. Ten million keeps me out of their stories, too."

"That's a lot of money," said Murphy. "I'll need to talk this over with Donny."

"You do that," said Graham. "You need to realize the window of opportunity is getting shorter with each passing day. My lawyer tells me I should expect to get sentenced on the contempt charge within the next month or so. If I reverse course between now and then, it'll have a big impact on where I am six months from now."

The overt threat was a little more than Murphy had been expecting. Graham seemed jumpy and jumpy was not good. Reassuringly, Murphy said, "I think you will be pleased with our response."

"I goddamn well better be," said Graham. "I won't go down alone."

"I understand," said Murphy as he turned and left the small training room, closing the door behind him.

As he walked through the weight room Murphy noticed the African-American and the woman had left the make-shift gym. He paused and nodded at the three men who remained lifting weights. As he exited the building he squinted at the bright sunlight of day. His head jerked only slightly when he heard the sound of the door locking behind him.

Chapter 4

The movements performed daily on the dark marble floor in front of the elevators in any of the Congressional office buildings are a timed waltz of the egotistically challenged and power deprived. Over-eager young staffers and aggressive lobbyists mingle on the polished marble floors hoping to get a nod from a Congressman or Congresswoman inviting them to ride on the elevators designated exclusively for those who wear the badges on their lapels identifying them as Members of Congress. A short ride up a couple of floors with the right Member is important to those who score the value of their days in such experiences.

In his younger days as a staffer, Richard Thompson thought the practice was demeaning. He was loyal to his boss, Congressman Garrett Jackson and did not need to ride on an elevator with another Member to find a better job or to establish his own self-value. Now he was one of the objects of affection of the gathered masses, he found the ritualized fawning absolutely repulsive. That grown men and women would make eye contact simply for the chance to take a brief, power-driven elevator ride said as much about those seeking the ride as it did about those who returned the nod.

Still, during the busy days of spring, the "Members Only" elevator and the special lapel pins for Members and their wives allowing them the ability to walk past the security lines at the entrances to the House office buildings and go straight to those elevators may be the most important perk on the Hill. On the day when Thompson was sworn in, his wife, Ann, used her spouses' identification badge to walk past the long line of people waiting to go through security. She overheard someone ask a Capitol Hill Police Officer how much money she paid to be able to walk into the office without going through the line. "About two and a half million dollars," was the officer's response, referring to the amount of money someone has to raise in order to be elected to Congress these days.

Barry Goldwater wrote that a conservative "recognizes that the political power upon which order is based is a self-aggrandizing force; that its appetite grows with eating. He knows that the utmost vigilance and care are required to keep political power within its proper bounds."

In other words, absolute power corrupts absolutely.

In the first week of his career as a Congressman, his old lobbyist friend, The Sarge, set up a lunch for Thompson with a former D.C. power broker who, while working at the White House, was convicted of obstructing justice before spending more than a year in jail.

"Power is a two-faced friend," the man warned Thompson. "When I was at the White House, I was one of the 'gate-keepers.' On my issues, I controlled the President's schedule. To get to see POTUS, you had to go through me. I controlled that access with more concern about my own agenda than his or the country's for that matter."

Thompson listened intently.

"Without a doubt, at the top of my game, I was one of the most powerful men in D.C.... hell, maybe the world. And, I can assure you, I knew it."

"So what happened?' asked Thompson.

"Son, there are no right answers in life, only right questions. Well, when I came to this town, I came for the right reasons. I asked myself the right questions. Things changed pretty quickly and I was caught up in the power game. Eventually, I started to believe I had real power. Then one day, I quit asking myself the right questions. I started to believe our mission was more important than the law. I started making decisions based upon my perception that I, personally, somehow had power and the wisdom to use it properly even if some law said I couldn't. And I was caught."

"I remember the hearings," said Thompson.

"Worst time of my life," he said. "Congress was investigating me and I was taking the Fifth before a special grand jury. All of a sudden, the most powerful man in the world couldn't get a phone call returned."

"I remember. It got worse," Sarge interjected.

"I didn't think it could get any worse, but it did. Indicted. Convicted. Sentenced."

"I can't imagine how you handled it," said Thompson, trying to show sympathy and not knowing what other emotion to show in response.

"My first night in a jail cell was about as rock bottom as it could get for me."

"It must have been horrible," said Thompson.

"Seventeen months and four days is a lot of time for reflection, son," warned a man who spent a precise amount of time in dark reflection. "I re-started my life as a divorced convicted felon without two dimes to my name."

"That's why I set up this lunch," said the Sarge, an old Vietnam era pilot who now lobbied for the defense industry on the Hill. He was one of the first people Thompson met when he was a staffer for Congressman Garrett Jackson. He had come to know and trust The Sarge over the many nights of playing cards in the basement of the Capitol Hill Club. "He was like you one time in his life. He was one of the true believers."

"So how do I keep it from happening to me?" Thompson asked.

"Remember there are no right answers, only right questions. Keep asking yourself all the right questions and you will be fine. When you start thinking you know all the right answers, that's when you are in trouble."

Richard Thompson remembered that lunch as he made his way through the masses and stepped into the "Members Only" elevator. He reminded himself , despite having elevators designated specifically for his personal use, being a Freshman Member of the United States House of Representatives was only glamorous if he allowed it to be considered as such.

Either hard work or privilege has placed a newly elected Member of Congress in the position to be elected in the first place.

For Richard Thompson, it was certainly not privilege. He grew up in a small town in Kentucky, the youngest of five children in a working class family. His parents helped him through college, but he still delivered pizza on the weekends to make ends meet.

After college, he landed a job on Capitol Hill working for his mentor, Congressman Garrett Jackson, during the day while he went to law school at night. During that time, he met his wife, Ann and they started a family. Following years on the Hill, he returned home with his wife and two kids to practice law with a small firm in Northern Kentucky.

At the law firm, Thompson had all of the perks of private sector success—a nice office, a large and well-seasoned support staff and an expense account. In between cases and clients, he put his life lessons to work to win an election to Ludlow City Council and then, in a huge leap, to the United States Congress.

It was not privilege for this Member. No, Thompson had put himself in the position to be elected. His own sweat and blood put his name on the ballot.

Having been a staffer as a younger man, Richard Thompson was ready on day one for his first trip to the Hill as a Member.

The exuberance a new Member feels following their election is usually tempered when they arrive on Capitol Hill, see their first office spaces and review the budgets they have to work within to run that cramped space.

The budgets offered to each Member require them to hire small, underpaid staffs. But that's okay, because the three room office suites are even smaller than the budgets which support the operations are supposed to take place within them. One room houses the Member's personal office, leaving the other two small rooms to house a nine or so person support staff and a reception area. There is a small restroom in the suite that usually has been converted to a copy center or a computer server room.

The physical set up is likely to be even worse when the freshman is, as Congressman Richard Thompson was, a Member of the minority party—especially one who was elected through a special election.

The privileges of Members in the United States House of Representatives are based entirely upon their seniority therein.

Committee assignments, office space, even parking spaces are all based upon a Member's rank in seniority. Elected in a special election following the regular election, Richard Thompson ranked dead last of the 435 Members of the House. Even the non-voting Members from U.S. territories had better offices and parking spaces than Thompson.

So United States Congressman Richard Thompson started his career on Capitol Hill from an office on the top floor of the Longworth House Office Building. Inasmuch as these spaces normally house the staffs of Members of Congress whose offices have been moved because they have either passed away or have had their floor privileges stripped due to criminal charges pending against them and are spending their days awaiting trial, the suites on the top floor are often referred to as the "dead and indicted" rooms.

Thompson lucked out on his committee assignment and landed a seat on the House Committee on the Judiciary. The Rules Committee Ranking Member, Marcus Lackner, had been forced to resign while facing an FBI investigation into union corruption in his South Florida district. A member of the Judiciary Committee had filled his spot, leaving the plum committee assignment open when Thompson was sworn in.

If the assignment to the Judiciary Committee was great, the timing of his appointment to the Subcommittee on Oversight was even better.

Oversight is usually the worst subcommittee assignment on any committee because it looks at issues in a willy-nilly fashion, with no particular relevance as to how they are germane to the main committee's jurisdiction. Nevertheless, the week following Thompson's election, the Subcommittee on Oversight had begun to hold hearings on steroid abuse in professional and amateur athletics. On his first days on the Hill, the young Congressman was participating in hearings which were getting national attention.

Kevin O'Toole had been the Chairman of the Oversight Subcommittee and had quickly taken a liking to the young man from Kentucky. Likewise, Thompson had bonded quickly with the senior Democrat and was thrilled when the Chairman allowed

Thompson to volunteer to be the Republican accompanying the Sub-Committee to Florida for the field hearing exploring steroid abuse in sports.

It seemed surreal that Thompson was now sitting in the Speaker's Lobby going over the notes he had prepared for the Special Order to eulogize O'Toole.

Special Orders is the time on the day's schedule following regular legislative business and votes when Members can go to the floor of the House and speak on whatever topic they desire. When *C-SPAN* started televising the daily business of the House of Representatives, Newt Gingrich saw it as a way to televise daily attacks on the Democrats to a national audience (and an empty chamber). During one such tirade, Speaker of the House Tip O'Neal was watching from his perch at the Dubliner Irish Pub, just down the street from the Capitol. The Speaker was so enraged (and apparently tipsy) that he charged back to the Chair of the House and ordered the cameras to be focused on the empty chamber. From then on, as specified by a rules change, cameras for Special Orders alternated back and forth from the person speaking to the usually empty floor.

Today was different; a quorum call had been made about 25 minutes earlier so all Members could make their way to the floor to pay tribute to their fallen colleague. On this particular occasion, the House chamber would be far from empty.

Leadership was going first and Thompson was sitting in a chair by the window of the Speaker's Lobby, reading his speech one final time before going to the floor.

Thompson found the Speaker's Lobby to be one of the more tranquil places in the Capitol. Located in the hallway just behind the Speaker's chair, the lobby is an ornate room nearly the width of the House floor itself and is reserved for Members and their invitees as a place where they can relax before entering the squared circle known as the House floor.

In the distant past, when a Member's only "office" was a desk on the House floor, the Speakers Lobby had been a convenient location to meet with constituents and others wanting a moment of a Congressman's time. Then, it was simply a hallway, with leadership offices against the wall that looked out over the National Mall. The pillars today mark where the walls had once stood dividing the offices. In fact, the architectural effect of the paintings on three separate ceilings coming together as one, make the Speaker's Lobby seem a bit misplaced and disorienting.

Disorienting, or not, Thompson loved the room for its windows.

The Speaker's Lobby offers one of the most scenic views in Washington, peering down the Mall towards the Washington Monument and the Lincoln Memorial. During the day, the view is beautiful. At night, with the monuments lit against the black sky, it's positively breathtaking.

Tonight, as Thompson turned in his overstuffed leather chair and peered down the darkness of that famed trail, he reflected on the Members who had graced this space. He caught himself humming Warren Zevon's *Numb as a Statue*.

Damn, Josh is right. I have to start singing some John Prine soon or no one will want to be around me anymore.

He looked at the portraits on the wall of all the Speakers. Sam Rayburn, Henry Clay, Uncle Joe Cannon and Newt Gingrich —all had used this room for reflection. He first met Kevin O'Toole in this room, also.

He was thinking about the brief friendship he had with Kevin O'Toole and the legacy which O'Toole had left behind, when he heard a familiar voice.

"Good evening, Congressman Thompson."

"Evening, Leo," said Thompson, rising at the sight of burley FBI Agent Leo Argo. Although Thompson had only met Agent Argo in the final days of his special election, Thompson greeted the smiling Hispanic man with the familiarity of a life-long friend.

Argo had been the lead agent running an FBI investigation of gun running, anti-Castro union bosses in southern Florida. To his great surprise, then candidate Richard Thompson had been enlisted to participate in a "sting" directed at establishing the involvement of Congressman Marcus Lackner in those illegal activities. The investigation had resulted in the aforementioned resignation of Lackner and had almost resulted in the death of Thompson.

"You are looking prosperous," said Argo as the pair separated from their embrace. "How's your lovely wife?"

"She's doing great," replied Thompson. "She'll be happy to hear you dropped by. You know you are her absolute favorite law enforcement officer."

"Yeah. I usually get that admiration from the wife when I shoot somebody trying to kill her husband," said Argo. He was referring to the fact that, just a few months earlier, Argo had shot a man who had attempted to kill Thompson in the course of the sting operation.

"So what brings you down to the Hill?" asked Thompson. "The re-authorization for the Department of Justice won't be up for a couple of months. If you are here to lobby me on something in the bill, I'll probably forget it before it gets to the floor."

"Things a little frenzied in your new job?" asked Argo jokingly.

"Frenzied isn't the word, pal," replied Thompson. "You know, when I was a staffer on the Hill, I always thought the Member had it pretty good, what with everyone he has to keep him up to date and all. Being a Member is a bitch. I'm having trouble remembering my name at the end of the day."

"I guess you are becoming pretty attached to your beeper," Argo added.

"I couldn't live without it," Thompson replied. "It lets me know when goons like you are trying to hunt me down for more money for their agency."

"No, don't worry, the Director will be calling on you himself when our authorization comes up before the Committee," Argo responded. "He has this idea you will be pretty friendly to the Bureau."

"Will I have a choice?" asked Thompson.

"Probably not," laughed Argo. "He has your wife's cell number. Either you are with us or he calls Ann."

"Thanks," said Thompson in mock appreciation. "So why are you here?"

"I'm here on an investigation today."

"Don't even think about it, brother," interrupted Thompson.

"What..." said Argo in a surprised tone.

"I'm not going to put on a wire for you again," Thompson said. "If you need a Member to put a target on his back, go find a Democrat this time."

"No," laughed Argo. "Don't worry. This time you are just a witness."

"Witness?" asked Thompson. "To what?"

"To the death of Congressman Kevin O'Toole," replied Argo.

"What in the hell are you investigating? I thought Kevin died of a heart attack?"

"He did. But, he was a United States Congressman. We're going to take a look at it simply as a matter of course."

Thompson frowned, showing his displeasure he had to go over the details once again. "I've already gone over this a million times for everyone in the press and all the folks up here. I really don't relish telling it again."

"Sorry," said Argo. "It's standard operating procedure. You were on the field in Sarasota when a Federal official died. I need to get a statement from you about what happened."

Argo pulled his Dictaphone from his suit coat.

Thompson spent the next fifteen minutes going over the events of the fateful day at Ed Smith Stadium in Sarasota. Argo occasionally interjected a question to clarify a point, but, for the most part, Thompson just narrated the flow of events. As he came to the point where O'Toole collapsed on the mound, Thompson paused as his voice became overcome with emotion. He turned and gazed out the window of the Capitol.

It was an awkward moment for Argo, who turned off the tape recorder and quietly thanked Thompson for his time before turning to leave.

Thompson continued to look out the window.

Thompson had learned many lessons from watching his old boss, Garrett Jackson, operate on the Hill. Jackson was the king of local politics. He knew he was elected by his constituency and focused on the issues important to them. He made one exception. Each session of Congress he would tackle an issue of national importance in which there might or might not be any interest back home.

As Thompson stared out the window of the Speaker's Lobby down the Mall, his melancholy ended. He felt a sudden rise in his mood as he intuitively knew he had come upon his issue of national importance.

Almost instinctively, he started singing his favorite John Prine song, *Clay Pigeons*, to himself:

And get along with it all,
Go down where the people say y'all,
Sing a song with a friend,
Change the shape that I'm in,
And get back in the game,
And start playin' again.

Chapter 5

In the dark confines of a small apartment in Suwannee, Georgia, a middle-aged man sat in front of his flat screen computer monitor, adjusting the image back and forth from streaming *C-SPAN* coverage of the Special Order on Congressman Kevin O'Toole to an eBay auction on a mint condition, gold bordered, rookie baseball card of Donny Alberato.

He had been out of town recently and missed several very important baseball card auctions. To miss out on this card would be a serious blow to his enterprise: the card, though not serial-numbered, was actually only one of ten copies of that particular variation printed in Alberato's rookie year. The item description on eBay did not point this out and it was apparent from the level of the bidding neither the seller nor any of the other active bidders realized just how rare the card was.

As he paced around his living room considering his strategy, his shoulders slumped with a rhythm as steady as his gait. His long face separated his reddish beard from his receding hairline. His nose stood out in the center of it all as his most distinguishing facial characteristic. Although he owned several different shirts, when doing his business he always wore his favorite striped one.

Despite the fact he had the means to live well beyond his minimalist lifestyle, the apartment was devoid of the numerous little domestic details that would otherwise have given insight to the personality inhabiting the space. As no one ever visited the man, it really didn't matter. Even his own neighbors could not see past the semi-opaque stick-on insulating film covering his windows.

In the living room of the apartment, a tapestry of Jesus reaching out in the water to Peter hung neatly against the wall over the couch. A larger tapestry featuring Elvis in Hawaii hung on the opposite wall.

On the one extravagant furnishing in his home, his computer desk, sat his most cherished possession, his computer. Also, on his desk was his *Last Will and Testament*. In case something ever happened to him, he wanted to make sure everyone knew immediately his church would get all his worldly possessions, including his extensive collection of autographed baseball cards (and Elvis tapestry).

He personally hadn't been to church since his mom had died three years ago. Churches made him so nervous he would start sweating when he even saw one from a block away. But, nevertheless, the church was the motivation for all he did in life.

No, there was nothing extravagant in his apartment. He spent all his mom's trust fund money on baseball cards and donations to television evangelists. His living expenses were paid through special jobs and assignments he did for a limited number of businesses—an independent contractor of contractual oddities, if you will.

He clicked *C-SPAN* up to the screen.

"The Chair recognizes the Gentleman from Kentucky for such time as he may consume," said the woman sitting in the Speaker's Chair.

"Thank you, Madame Speaker," replied Richard Thompson as he handed a written speech to the House Clerk. "I ask unanimous consent to have my entire written statement placed into *The Record*."

"Without objection...so ordered."

Thompson took a moment to soak in the feel of the floor of the House of Representatives. He thought to himself how much smaller the room was than it appeared to be on television. The dark colors of the room gave it an intimacy which surprised many on their first trip to the chamber.

Positioned in front of a large American flag, the Speaker's Chair is the central point of the House floor. The desks of the reading clerk, parliamentarian sergeant at arms and other House officers are located just below the chair. Podiums from which Members can speak are just in front of those desks. Portraits of George Washington and the Marquis de Lafayette sit on either side of the Speaker's chair.

Thompson looked up at the busts of the great lawgivers tht encircled the very top of the room. Some, like Mason and Jefferson, are recognizable to American history buffs. Others, like Hammurabi, are more obscure. Directly in front of him was the bust of Moses, the giver of all laws, which faced the Speaker's desk.

Thompson took a deep breath before he began.

In New York, M.T. Stacy used a remote to increase the volume on the custom mounted plasma television screen, as Colin N. Korey leaned back in his black leather chair. "This is the one that worries me, M.T.," Korey softly mentioned to Stacy. "He's the one."

"Many of my colleagues have come to the well today to talk about Chairman Kevin O'Toole and his dedication to the people of his state and this country," Richard Thompson said to the gathering of Members sitting in the leather chairs on the floor of the House chamber. "I'm the newest Member of this distinguished body and I really didn't know him well enough to talk about the many years he spent in this chamber loyally serving the people of Florida and America.

"No, I really can't talk about Kevin O'Toole's love of country, but I was on the field with the Chairman at spring training when he passed into the Hands of The Father. From that half of a day we spent in spring training at Sarasota, Florida, what I can talk about is Kevin O'Toole's love of baseball."

The online bidder in Georgia quickly maximized the eBay auction window to full screen so he could check the amount of the current high bid and the time remaining on the auction. He clapped his hands repeatedly in excited recognition of his growing anticipation before clicking the screen back to the *C-SPAN* speech.

"Everyone knows Chairman O'Toole attended Notre Dame for his undergraduate degree." Thompson paused for effect and smiled that big smile he was prone to do when he needed it for effect. "With a name like O'Toole, where else could he actually go?"

Thompson waited while a light chuckle emitted from the chairs where the other Members were sitting. *At least they are listening*, Thompson thought to himself.

"What most of you may not know is that he attended Notre Dame on a baseball scholarship. He was an accomplished second baseman and a prolific hitter. They say he could turn a double-play faster than anyone in the college ranks. In his junior year, he led the Fighting Irish to a conference championship by batting .321 and stealing 14 bases."

"So the bum knew how to play," mumbled the man at the computer. "Whooptie freakin' doo!"

"Going into his senior year, most of the leading scouts of the day listed him as one of the nation's top 10 professional prospects."

The man at his computer quickly minimized his *C-SPAN* screen again and brought the eBay screen back to full view. With 5 minutes and 37 seconds left, the bid on the Alberato card was at $15.75, very low for the gold edged rookie card.

"Ah ha, the high bidder is 'Cardguy76'," he said aloud to himself, in a tone a military general might use to speak to an officer of lower rank. "We have battled before. You never go beyond eighty-five percent of book value. Let the game begin. That card will be mine!"

He clicked *C-SPAN* back up on the screen, where he watched Congressman Richard Thompson continuing his speech.

"...Unfortunately for young Kevin O'Toole, early in his senior year, a pop fly on a wet field led to a torn ACL. On our recent trip to Florida, Kevin told me about that game...and how it ended his thoughts of a career in professional baseball. With the encouragement of his parents, he decided to forego a long rehab. Instead, he pursued his masters in business rather than a life in the majors."

"I bet he turned a deuce so quick because he used greenies," Stacy said snidely. Korey quickly shut him up with a disapproving glance.

"…What would eventually be good news for the United States Congress and the American people, was bad news for baseball—in more ways than one."

The man in the apartment brought the eBay screen back to full view, leaving the *C-SPAN* audio on in the background. It was time to start preparing his bid. He opened yet another instance of his web browser and logged into eBay using one of the seventeen names under which he purchased sports cards. He chose GeorgiaSniperBidder, which, according to the cross-referenced Excel spread sheets he had been maintaining for years, had never been used before to do battle with Cardguy76. With 2 minutes and 48 seconds, he typed in a bid of $52.78 on the gold bordered Alberato card, yet, he didn't actually go ahead and place the bid. No, he stopped short of the "Confirm Your Bid" screen, minimized and watched the time count down in the original eBay window he had opened first. He would wait until only seconds were left in the auction and place the bid at the very last moment, topping the current high bid and essentially blocking out any chance for the previous high bidder to react and take the price higher. In the parlance of online bidding, it's called placing a "sniper bid" and it is one of the mainstays of the proficient eBay shopper.

Meanwhile, Thompson's voice continued over the *C-SPAN* feed.

"…Like Kevin O'Toole, I am one of those people who believe America needs baseball. We need moms and dads walking hand in hand with kids to smell the newly cut grass on a hot summer day. It is part of our very nature to want to find the perfect seat on the third base side and eat an overpriced hot dog, while explaining to our kids the technical intricacies of the 'infield fly rule.'

"We sit and explain to them how Teddy Ball Game could read the spin on a pitch better than anyone who ever played the game. How a batter never took the inside of the plate on pitchers like Bob Gibson or Jim Bunning. Why Henry Aaron was one of your heroes and how a kid from Benger, Oklahoma, named Bench was the best catcher ever.

"A visit to the ball park harkens us back to a time when we kept our front doors unlocked and our windows open. If we close our eyes and think hard, we can almost hear the sounds of our street in the summer as we sat on the porch with our parents and listened to the game. For me, the most distinctive sound of my childhood was Waite Hoyt's voice announcing a Frank Robinson home run over the ten or so radios tuned into the game up and down our street."

At a news desk in Los Angeles, John Gustine wrote down the quote in the shorthand he had developed as a writer. *This is great stuff,* he thought to himself. *I've gotta find a place to use this in Sunday's column.*

"...This is why baseball remains America's pastime. Baseball is everything great about who we are as a people.

"And if America needs baseball, then baseball needs men like Kevin O'Toole. Baseball needs men who played for the pure love of the game."

In the Georgia apartment, an alarm on the man's watch buzzed, but it was unnecessary. As he listened to Thompson, he had continued to refresh the screen on the Alberato card every few seconds. He hit the 'place bid' button with four seconds left to go in the auction. "Bang!" he said pointing his index finger at the screen like a pistol as the "You Won" screen popped up confirming he had indeed won the Alberato card.

He laughed a low bass, guttural "Huh, huh, huh, huh" which seemed to emanate from somewhere just below his diaphragm and would have sounded vaguely disturbing to anyone else there to hear it. After clearing his throat, he clicked *C-SPAN* back up onto the screen to hear the end of Thompson's speech.

"... Kevin O'Toole pointed out steroids and other performance enhancing drugs were as big a threat to the integrity of the game today as gambling was following the 1919 Black Sox scandal."

Thompson stopped. He was getting choked up and the pause allowed him to collect himself before he continued. "Kevin O'Toole believed in baseball."

Back in Thompson's office on the seventh floor of Longworth, Thompson's Chief of Staff, Josh Barkman, looked around the room at the staffers who were gathered to watch their boss on television. "Any idea where the hell he's going with this?" he asked.

"I have absolutely no idea," said Chief Counsel Kemen to the rest of the staff who were staring at her. "Hey don't all y'all blame me. None of this was in the prepared text I wrote for him."

"Hang on to your ass, gang," said Josh, looking up at the ceiling. "The Boss is flying solo now."

On the floor, Thompson continued with his extemporaneous comments in memory of the fallen O'Toole.

"He believed and I believe. So what will be Kevin O'Toole's legacy?" Thompson asked his fellow members.

"Well, I am sure Florida will name a bridge after him somewhere. But, to me, we can pass along a legacy that is much stronger and longer lasting than some well built bridge over a canal. Kevin O'Toole's legacy should be protecting the integrity of baseball."

"Told you so," Korey said nodding to Stacy. "He's the one we have to look out for."

"...So today, let's carry on Chairman Kevin O'Toole's love of baseball by standing up for those things he held dear. Fair play in America's game. Let's continue these steroid hearings and, if necessary, re-examine the anti-trust exemption enjoyed by the game..." Thompson paused to gain the composure he had momentarily lost.

"Bingo," said Korey.

"Yes, sir," replied Stacy. "He just said the magic words."

"Let owners and players alike be forewarned. If you think the current steroid and other performance enhancing substance problems are a public relations nightmare, wait until Congress gets a hold of you. It will be far worse. Grand juries, exemptions from antitrust laws and dwindling gates will be the least of your concerns. We won't be governed by the same limitations that govern a trial. We will ask the tough questions a squishy prosecutor is afraid to ask and perjury will be the least of your worries."

The man in Georgia went to his Outlook page and opened up a new folder in which to place Google news alerts. He named the folder simply—Rep. Richard Thompson.

Chapter 6

Ulysses S. Grant was the 18th President of the United States of America. Born and raised in a small town called Point Pleasant, Ohio, just east of Cincinnati, he was Abraham Lincoln's top general in the Civil War. A graduate of the United States Military Academy, he was known as a master of military tactics.

He was also a drunk.

As a young officer, Grant was forced to relinquish his West Point commission and resign from the Army after being caught drinking on duty. The incident haunted him the rest of his life.

He returned to the military when Lincoln called for volunteers following the Confederacy's assault on Fort Sumter. His military career in the Civil War was marked with brilliance. The blockade he executed on Vicksburg has been compared with Napoleon's campaign against Borodino. Yet, there continued to be questions about his drinking habits.

President Abraham Lincoln didn't seem to care. When asked by the Washington press about Grant's imbibing, Lincoln replied, "I wish some of you would tell me the brand of whiskey Grant drinks. I would send a barrel of it to my other generals."

After Lincoln's assassination, Grant kept his military command and in 1868 became the consensus nominee in the Republicans' bid to recapture the Presidency. With the campaign slogan "Let Us Have Peace," he won a huge victory and served two terms in the White House.

As President, Grant continued his drinking.

Grant's wife would not allow alcohol in their living quarters at the White House. So just about every evening during those eight years, Grant could be found in the circular bar of The Willard Hotel. A quaint and intimate little bar, which still stands today, Grant went there with his buddies to drink his favorite liquid — Old Crow bourbon whiskey—and play cards.

An entire cadre of men hung out in the lobby of the Willard Hotel waiting for Grant to leave the bar to relieve himself. As he went, one-by-one, they accompanied him to the men's room, each to discuss his particular issue or expenditure. These men became known as Grant's "lobbyists."

Of course, today, the term lobbyist doesn't mean a person who follows a lawmaker to the bathroom to assert influence. If that were the case, the police officer who arrested Senator Larry Craig at a restroom in the Minneapolis airport would be referred to as a lobbyist. Still, many find the practices of today's lobbyists just as demeaning as bathroom shakedowns.

Everyone hates Congress, but with amazing consistency the voters in each district reelect their personal Congressmen. The same holds true for lobbyists. The only bad lobbyist is the one working against the issue you support.

Energy companies hate environmental lobbyists and vice versa.

Unions hate business lobbyists and vice versa.

Lobbyists for seniors groups want more spending on seniors' programs, which The Club for Growth believes should be eliminated.

Even the White House has its own lobbyists, hired by the President to support his agenda.

The fact of the matter is, whether they have ever met them or not, everyone has a lobbyist for something they believe in.

Good Members of Congress seem to gravitate to those lobbyists who are trustworthy and present an issue to them in an honest fashion, explaining all the variations on the table. Congressmen who get busted hanging with the likes of Jack Abramoff seem to have a predisposition to bad behavior. In Washington, likes attract each other. Change the people you send to Washington and you will change the people who lobby them.

Many observers with a deep knowledge of Capitol Hill argue we don't need more ethics laws governing Members of Congress and lobbyists—what we need are more ethical Congressmen.

Thompson had known lobbyist John Cooper since college. Also a graduate of Eastern Kentucky University, Cooper got a job out of college in the Kentucky State Senate staffing for leadership in the upper chamber. His reputation was quickly established as a young man who knew how to operate the Senate.

Although separated by distance, Cooper and Thompson remained close friends. Both had stood up in each other's wedding. About the same height and stature, Thompson and Cooper could have passed for brothers, except for the fact Cooper never seemed to age. Thompson continually accused him of dying his hair to keep looking younger than his years.

When Thompson was elected to Congress, he knew he could trust Cooper as a lobbyist who would always shoot straight with him. That's also why he was a little surprised when he learned Cooper had decided to represent baseball in connection with the steroid issues.

Thompson arrived at the office following a morning policy committee meeting and was greeted by the short central Kentucky lobbyist already waiting for him in the office reception area.

"Well, well, lyin' Johnny Cooper," laughed Thompson as he greeted his old friend. "Are you still feeding my goddaughter by letting people give you money to come up here and lie for them?"

"Hey, man," said Cooper with a light country accent. "I only represent good, God-fearing Americans. You should know that by now."

"Yeah. Right," replied Thompson. "And I'm going to turn down PAC money in my reelection bid!"

"Man, I sure hope so," laughed Cooper. "Knowing what I know about you, it's tough to ask all my clients to have their PACs chip in for you."

"Don't worry," said Thompson. "I'm just kidding. I'm taking PAC checks. You will be able to back me with other people's money."

"Not a chance," said Cooper. "I have to write a check myself or my wife will kill me. You are the only person she ever insisted we write a check for. I couldn't get out of this one if I tried."

"Good for her," said Thompson as he turned and headed to his office, "I'm glad someone in your family still has walking sense. Now, come on back and tell me why the hell you decided to accept money to represent these people in baseball."

"Good money," Cooper said to Thompson as he closed the door to the private office and sat down on the black leather sofa. "I've turned down a lot of folks who wanted me to lobby you. Baby, I couldn't turn this one down."

"Why?" asked Thompson.

"Too damned much money," Cooper replied. "Chrissie's headed to college next year."

"You got the whole baseball account?" Thompson queried.

"Nope. They are paying me just to lobby you," he replied.

"Paying you big bucks for one Member," said Thompson. "I don't get it."

"Me neither," said Cooper. "I mean, not only one Member, but a minority freshman." Cooper paused. "Hell, you are number 435 out of 435."

"Yeah, I know. I figured that out already," said Thompson. "Have you seen where my office is? The guy from America Samoa has a nicer office than me."

"Well, something has their attention," said Cooper. "They hired me at my top rate and wired me a retainer within hours. They wanted me up here immediately, so I came up last night."

"So what are you lobbying me on?" asked Thompson.

"Well, that's the funny thing," said Cooper. "I got in town last night for today's meeting. They called me right after your speech to tell me about it. I didn't see it but they told me you were pretty strong. I told them you were pretty much of a case. That once you made up your mind on an issue, no one would change you."

"And?"

"And they said they were fine with that," Cooper continued. "They just wanted to start a dialogue with you and the staff. They want me to come up here and talk with your staff about the antitrust exemption and why it's important to baseball."

"Important to baseball..." laughed Thompson.

"I'm still learning about it myself," replied Cooper. "But their big point is football shares revenue and baseball doesn't."

"So?" asked Thompson. "Why does that matter?"

"Stability," said Cooper. "Football keeps itself stable through capping salaries and sharing revenues. Baseball does it by controlling the ownership and movement of teams without antitrust concerns. It adds to the stability of the game."

"Stability?" asked Thompson.

"Yeah," said Cooper. "Stability."

"Do you believe that, John?" asked Thompson.

"Shit, Rick, it doesn't matter what I believe," laughed Cooper. "You know that. I'll give you the facts as I know them and then it only matters what you believe. I told the guys that hired me, I'll educate on this, but I won't advocate. You can make your own call after that."

"I trust you, John, but I don't trust them. You need to know that going into this thing," admonished Thompson. "I don't trust the players and I sure as hell don't trust management."

"Hey, man, calm down. If you want me to drop the representation, I'll do it," said Cooper. "I'm not going to risk our friendship over these guys. It's not worth it."

"Naw," replied Thompson. "I can't ask you to do that."

"If you did," replied Cooper, "I would drop them in a New York minute."

"I know you would. That's why I trust you," said Thompson. "Go ahead, Coop, represent them. I would rather have you taking their money than some stranger. Just remember, John, this Commissioner ain't no Bart Giamatti. He's not necessarily in it for the fans."

Thompson paused before standing up and escorting Cooper to the door.

"All right man. Educate away. I'll walk you around and introduce you to the staff."

Chapter 7

Sam Kenison once described the Rainbow Bar and Grill on the Sunset Strip in Los Angeles as the place where "the possessed go to mingle."

Warren Zevon wrote about it in his classic rock tribute to love induced suicidal depression, *Poor Poor Pitiful Me*:

I met a girl at the Rainbow Bar,
She asked me if I'd beat her,
I took her back to the Hyatt House,
And...I don't want to talk about it.

The Rainbow Bar was the heart and soul of the Sunset Strip long before Kenison and Zevon ever hit the L.A. scene and, as if in tribute, it has outlived them both as well.

Just up the street from Whiskey a Go-Go, whose house band was once The Doors, The Rainbow Bar has been a permanent fixture on the Strip since the 40s. The dark walls and low lighting inside conjure up memories of Judy Garland and her husband, Vincent Minelli (the original Rainbow Bar and Grill owner), cuddled up in one of the maroon leather semi-circular booths. At lunch time on most days, the indoor booths sit empty.

The outdoor bar and café serves a very different purpose. There the fast-moving, beautiful people of West Hollywood want the bright sunshine of L.A. to illuminate their ability to see and be seen on the Strip.

At the bar, on this particular day, an aspiring actor traded stories of sexual conquest with an independent record producer, while they both waited for their lawyers. Behind them two old hippies traded stories of what bands they got high with over the years. Bob Dylan's *Mighty Quinn* played over the sound system.

At a table near the front of the outdoor patio bar, *Los Angeles Journal* sports reporter, John Gustine, sat with freelance journalist,

Joyce Lang, discussing their series of investigative stories on the use of steroids in professional sports.

Gustine and Lang had been covering the raid and on-going FBI investigation of a performance enhancing drug distribution ring that had been run out of a "nutrition" store in Mission Viejo, about an hour south of Los Angeles. The raid on the small non-descript store in a strip center had produced evidence that was well worth presenting to a grand jury. There were rumors the evidence obtained in the raid reached to the highest levels of amateur and professional sports, linking the day's top athletes to the use of designer steroids, human growth hormone and other performance enhancing drugs.

John Gustine was in many ways a typical sports reporter. He had played some ball in high school, but, even then, he enjoyed writing about sports more than he did playing them. A graduate of the well-respected journalism program at Western Kentucky University in Bowling Green, he had won the prestigious Tom Harmon Award given annually to an up and coming sports writer and had turned that into a job at *The Los Angeles Journal*.

Sports was his beat, but his love was baseball. He was a walking Elias Sports Bureau, knowing, with almost infallible accuracy, vague statistics about even marginal athletes. His dark hair, cut in a boyish mop-top cut, didn't fit well in the L.A. scene, but he didn't much care. He personally thought the hairdo made him look like Pete Rose and he was fine with that.

On the other hand, if you saw Joyce Lang on the streets, the last thing you would ever peg her for was someone co-authoring a series of articles having anything to do with sports. Her blond hair atop her perfectly proportioned face, her petite slender build and her red stiletto heels, made her look like one of the aspiring actresses or models attracting stares at Huntington Beach rather than Gustine and the crumpled crew of men and women who hang around the press box at any sports stadium. Joyce Lang was the city's best known investigative reporter—she had earned her reputation two years previously for a story on city hall corruption that caused two council members to resign and sent the deputy-mayor to jail.

She also had a reputation for using any tactic, including her sexuality, to get a story. The word around police headquarters was she was once able to get otherwise classified documents from a police detective by giving blow jobs to both the detective and his partner.

Lang didn't seem to care much about her reputation in the community of Los Angeles journalists. How she got her information didn't bother her, so it shouldn't bother others. She had a future and would not be denied. Simply put, Lang was a climber. She already had Los Angeles, but she wanted an even bigger stage.

So after reading a column by Gustine on the use of steroids in professional baseball, she sought him out and suggested a partnership. Together, they would go after the story that could blow the lid off sports and bring national acclaim to them both.

Gustine's role would be the sports side and his reward would be protecting the game. Lang added the investigative reporter instincts and she had hopes of a Pulitzer at the end.

Lang was to spend her days hanging around the courthouse, where the grand jury was in session, hoping to get a glimpse of who was testifying. Meanwhile, Gustine would focus on the effects of steroids on the field of play. He knew how to speak to jocks and gain their confidence. Collectively, they would try to link together enough confirmed sources for a series of articles for the nationally known *Los Angeles Journal.*

The partnership had worked. Their first effort, on the raid of the "nutrition" store, got them mentioned on two national network news shows as well as *ESPN.* They followed up with three more front page stories, accumulating information and making connections between facts others had been unable to uncover. Lang didn't ask Gustine about his sources and Gustine sure as hell didn't want to know how Lang came up with her facts.

One story got them the PR bonus of being on the front page of the Sunday edition and revealed that based on testimony already given by others, the grand jury was going to subpoena baseball superstar Donny Alberato to testify. While unconfirmed, they reported Alberato would be called as a "target" of the investigation, rather than a supporting witness. The Judge was furious the testimony was leaked and threatened to put the two reporters in jail if they refused to reveal their sources—a statement which both delighted and dismayed Lang and Gustine.

Threats of jail time sells papers and sets up book deals. However, the way the judge and the grand jury were heading, it was beginning to look as if journalists reporting on steroids might face more jail time than the athletes who had actually abused them. Such an outcome didn't exactly seem like American justice to either reporter.

As Lang settled into the table, she looked around at the bar. "I never really figured you as the Rainbow Bar type," she said to Gustine with a laugh.

"I'm not," replied Gustine.

"Then why are we here?" asked Lang.

"Early in my career at *The Journal*," said Gustine, "I did a story about a local L.A. kid who made it up to the bigs with the Cubbies as a starting pitcher. He was making his first start in front of his home town crowd out at the stadium. He wanted me to meet him here for lunch. He was the Rainbow Bar type…a real head banger. He was arrested for possession down the street at The Viper Room on his next road trip through town.

"Anyhow, he wanted to meet me here. The atmosphere was kind of fun and I liked the pizza. So I do a lot of my interviews here now."

"Pizza," muttered Lang in a snide tone. "You sports guys are all alike."

"Besides," added Gustine, "the Rainbow has a great baseball angle. This is where Joe DiMaggio took Marilyn Monroe on their first date. And, don't sell the food here short. The owner, Mario, is an old Italian guy from Chicago. They have the best marinara in town."

"Yeah," said Lang. "It's also where John Belushi had his last bowl of lentil soup before partying himself to death next door at The Roxy."

"Well, it looks like you know your dead icon trivia," said Gustine.

"Let's just get some food," Lang replied.

"Well, it's no worse than some of those greasy diners where you court beat reporters hang out down by the L.A. Courthouse," said Gustine. "That's a pretty harsh section of town. I can't exactly picture you eating a greasy sandwich at a Pioneer Chicken stand."

"I steer clear of those places," said Lang. "The other reporters see you talking to someone and they all try to listen in. I'm surprised some of them haven't gone to walking around with those big parabolic microphones like the television guys use on the sidelines in football games. It's a den of snakes in those places. Nothing is sacred. Why do you think I get the exclusives? I stay away."

That's not how I hear you get your exclusives, Gustine thought to himself as he looked at the low cut top Lang was wearing.

"Speaking of exclusives," queried Gustine, "do you have anything new?"

"Just the same crap everyone else has," replied Lang. "Johnson testified the other day, but they snuck him in through the basement booking entrance. Nobody had a shot at him and, from what I can tell, no one will."

Gustine had been chasing down information about Johnson. "I called one of his old teammates and he said it was well known Johnson was on 'the juice.' Apparently, he told a couple other players he could get them some 'clear' from his nutritionist, if they were interested."

Gustine pulled a notebook from his brief case entitled "Steroid #2" and flipped through it to read what he had written down during his conversations with Johnson's former teammate. He read aloud: "He told us this new clear juice couldn't be detected by the league office, even if we were randomly sampled. He said his nutritionist assured him it was so new it was ahead of any testing procedure and they were learning to mask it faster than the league office could come up with new testing protocols."

"Clever," said Lang. "So they were cooking new versions of this stuff up so quick the league couldn't test for it."

"Well, Johnson is in deeper than he ever thought he would be. The players' union can't protect him from this one. He has to be indicted."

"I don't know," said Lang. "I don't think they are targeting him as part of the ring. He's small potatoes. I think they are using him to build their case against the store and its connection to Donny Alberato." She paused. "It doesn't matter anyway. Everyone else is already trying to cover that angle. Johnson had a lot of teammates over the years and my guess is most of them probably knew he was using and most of them are probably talking about it with any reporter who contacts them. It was never really much of a secret. I mean, look at his head. It's so damn big he looks like one of those big paper mache heads in the Mardi Gras parades in New Orleans."

"You are right. My source had three other calls to return after he spoke to me. Who knows how many he spoke to before me."

Lang paused while looking at the young woman serving drinks to the patrons. "God, is every young girl in this town trying to look like Paris Hilton?" She asked the question rhetorically and shook her head with a combination of disbelief and disgust, before getting back on track. "We need something fresh," she said, turning her attention back to Gustine. "Were you able to come up with anything new on the gym across the street from the store?"

"Well, that's clearly where Johnson was getting his juice. He told everyone Greg Graham was his nutritionist and weight trainer. Hell, he even had it on his web site at one point. Graham's links to Alberato are more blurred. Though I would say there is a better than 50/50 chance Donny was using Johnson to order from Graham."

"Gregory Graham…the trainer to the stars…" muttered Lang. "We need to unblur those links. I bet if we could get Graham to sit down for an interview, we could find out what was on those computers taken in the raid."

"Well, nice thought," said Gustine. "But you obviously didn't hear the news, did you?"

"What news?" asked Lang.

"Graham is dead," said Gustine.

"Dead?" asked Lang. "How? When?"

"The story came into the newsroom at *The Journal* right before I came over here to lunch," said Gustine. "They found him at some sleazy juice gym down in Huntington Beach. Someone put a 50 pound weight in the back of his head."

"Dear God," said Lang grimacing. "Any suspects?"

"That's for you to find out from your police contacts," said Gustine. "To me, it sure sounds like a muscle bound goon in a 'roid rage. For our purposes, it's not all that important who killed him. We just have to scratch him off the list as a potential source— he's sure as hell not gonna tell us anything now." Gustine smiled weakly. The blank expression on Lang's face made it clear to him she didn't find his last comment amusing at all.

Awkwardly, he continued. "Of course, that is assuming he would have talked to us. What I would really love to know is what was in his computer files."

There was an uncomfortable pause.

"Any ideas on how we can get a hold of those files?" asked Gustine, thinking of the stories about the two Los Angeles detectives, but not wanting to make his comments any more personal than necessary.

"I have some friends down at the station," said Lang in a monotone, not wanting to reveal the nature of the relationship. "They were already working on it for me."

"And?"

"And, the FBI has custody of them," said Lang. "For the time being, we're screwed. Those guys are tough to crack. They decide when to leak and to whom. I'll keep at it."

"So do we try to go after his celebrity clients?" asked Gustine. "He trained a lot of stars as well as jocks."

"Well, you are right. In this town Greg Graham was like gold for a while," said Lang. "Everybody wanted a personal trainer and he was the one all the stars and wannabes around town just had to have."

"So do we go down that road? Any stars on the juice?" asked Gustine.

"I don't think so," replied Lang. "Stars just need to look good—they don't really need muscles."

"True," said Gustine. "And who would even care if they did. It's all fake anyway. It's not like the integrity of Hollywood is being damaged if some actor has muscles courtesy of human growth hormones."

Now Lang was smiling. "Who would test for it?" she asked.

"The same dweebs who set the parental ratings for movies?" laughed Gustine, noticing Lang's beauty when she smiled.

"Anyway, that's just another angle every other reporter in town will be trying to cover, especially now he's dead," said Lang after thinking about it for a moment. "I wouldn't even be surprised if those schlocky 'entertainment today' television shows start covering the connection between Graham and lots of his former movie star clients. There is plenty of potential for meaningless innuendo there, now somebody has killed him. It's all too obvious. Listen to me, we need to stay focused on the story we set out to cover. We're starting to bog down. We need something fresh."

Gustine bit his lip thinking. "How about we do something on that dead Congressman down in Florida? The one who died after holding the steroid hearings? What was his name...O'Toole?"

"Yeah. What about him?" asked Lang.

"Well, some other Congressman, a newly elected one from Kentucky, has vowed to take up the cause. Apparently, he was there when O'Toole died and—when he was supposed to be eulogizing O'Toole—he feels some kind of fraternal duty to carry on with it. This guy was so wrapped up in a floor speech last night he got air time on *ESPN's* top 10 list today."

"How do you know about this?" Lang asked.

Gustine leaned forward. "I was watching the speeches on *C-SPAN* last night about the Congressman who died down at spring training. I was hoping somebody would say something mildly quotable about what Congress was going to do on the steroid issue. I wasn't getting much of anything. Then this guy from Kentucky came on and he spends pretty much his entire speech talking about baseball and the integrity of the game and how O'Toole would have wanted Congress to get tough on baseball unless baseball cleans up its act. Here—I got a copy of it from the *Congressional Record* web site this morning."

Lang quickly glanced at the copy of the speech Gustine had handed to her before tossing it aside. "Not exactly Pulitzer material," she replied.

"You can always try the menu at the greasy spoon," said Gustine, in a tone that reflected his annoyance at Lang's obvious disdain for his suggestion. "Anyway, if we focus on a Washington angle, it at least buys us a story or two until we get a break. We have to keep this thing alive."

"I hate politicians," grunted Lang. "What you are describing sounds like a fluff piece."

"So I'll do the interview. I can do a couple of other stories while I'm there. I checked and this new guy is from Northern Kentucky, which is just across the river from Cincinnati. I can write a sports line about the Reds' opening day at Great American Ball Park and kill two birds with one stone."

"I don't know."

"Come with me then," said Gustine. "The Reds have a great opening day parade. The whole city gets into it. It's like a national holiday. I went to college a couple of hours from there. We used to skip class and drive up for it."

"Not a chance," snarled Lang.

"You can dig into the Congressman's background, then," suggested Gustine. "See if he juiced up playing high school sports."

Lang didn't respond. Not even a grin.

"I'll get us front page again," he said with a smile, knowing that would grab Lang's attention. Pulitzers are not awarded to people who write stories that appear on the third page of the Local News section.

"Okay," she said reluctantly. "I just think we have enough skuzzy types in this story without getting some Congressman from Kentucky involved."

Chapter 8

Members of Congress are accustomed to having staff use the Member's own personal office on the Hill for meetings. The three-office suites are so cramped, most of the time they have no other place to go. So when Thompson entered his seventh floor suite he was not surprised to hear from the intern watching the reception area that Josh was meeting with someone in Thompson's private space. What surprised him was the visitor was his long time friend, Michael Griffith.

As gruff as he was bald, Michael Griffith was among the elite of Washington political consultants. He had made a reputation early in his career when, as a staffer for the National Republican Congressional Committee, he would go into a district and win an unwinnable campaign. The success in those early races led him to a job with Peller & Marks, a full service campaign consulting firm, where he was now a partner.

As he continued to win races at his new job, he gained the reputation as a no-holds barred, street brawling campaigner. He would beat an opponent raw, all the while finding the right balance of positive and negative ads to keep the public happy with his own client.

Griffith also had a reputation for treating his own clients just as bad as he did their opponents. If a candidate didn't want to listen to Griffith's advice, he had no qualms about firing the candidate and moving on to another race. People were lining up at his door for political advice, so he refused to waste his time with someone who wouldn't listen.

Such a matter-of-fact attitude, coupled with his uncanny ability to quickly turn a phrase, made him a popular guest on the nightly news shows. If a talking head could announce throughout the day they were going to have Michael Griffith as a guest that evening, ratings would go through the roof.

Griffith had been Thompson's roommate at the Phi Delta Theta fraternity house in college and the pair continued to be roomies when they moved together to Washington after graduation. Thompson was the policy wonk of the pair, while Griffith knew politics better than anyone else in town. Griffith had run Thompson's tumultuous campaign for United States Congress a few months ago by using his famed '*Godfather* Rules of Politics.' By stealing lines from the *Godfather* trilogy of movies, Griffith guided the strategy of the campaign to victory.

"Don't hate your enemy. It affects your judgment," he would tell Thompson when he became angry at the actions of their political opponent. When Josh told Griffith he didn't understand the finance side of politics, Griffith quoted from *Godfather III*: "Finance is a gun. Politics is knowing when to pull the trigger."

Griffith and Thompson met while trading notes in an introductory political science class at Eastern Kentucky University and quickly became friends. Their first year spring break, they were on their way to Key West when they stopped at Holiday Park in Ft. Lauderdale to attend a political rally for Ronald Reagan, who was then running for his second term as president against Walter Mondale. They found themselves standing among a bunch of Cuban-Americans shouting "Reagan Si! Castro No!" The exuberance was contagious. The pair became instant political junkies and seemingly joined at the hip for a lifetime.

The rigors of working in politics for a career had been kinder to Thompson than Griffith. Michael Griffith worked hard, but played harder. Griffith shaved his head to hide his receding hairline, but rarely shaved his beard. The look was intimidating to friend and foe, alike. Thompson couldn't help but be concerned about how the hard-driving lifestyle was slowly taking its toll on his old friend. *How much longer can he keep up the image that fits the look?* Thompson thought to himself.

"How you doin' boy?" asked Griffith as Thompson entered the cramped office.

"Boy?" asked Thompson in a tone of feigned shock. "It's Congressman Boy to you."

"You heard me," said Griffith. "I'll play kiss up and call

you 'Congressman' in public, but don't expect me to cut you any slack behind the door."

"You finally have some new boots," said Thompson, noticing the new white python snake skin boots Griffith was wearing.

"Yeah," said Griffith. "The old ones finally split in two. I'm keeping them though. I'll need to wear them on election night, split skins or not. I've worn them every election night since Bush '88."

"A little superstitious?" asked Josh.

"A little superstitious?" exclaimed Thompson. "That and a little Obsessive Compulsive Disorder. I remember when he first got too fat to wear the jeans he wore on election night in 1988. He nearly refused to come out of his apartment for fear of the cosmic disturbance it would cause in the universe! God knows what would happen if the Republican boots had to be thrown out too!"

"Republican boots?" queried Josh.

"You bet," replied Griffith. "Snake skin. They are made out of endangered species." He paused and, with a sincerity born of their friendship, he asked, "Seriously, how are you doin' in the new job?"

"I'm still getting used to it, Griff," replied Thompson. "People are looking at my lapel pin and treating me like I'm someone. It's awkward. I don't like it."

"Make sure it stays that way," said Griffith. "When it doesn't feel awkward anymore and you start enjoying it, you've become one of them." He paused and looked towards Josh. "How about Junior over here…he still working out? Or do you need me to go through the resumes at the NRCC to find a replacement?"

"Hey, I'm in the room," Josh interjected.

"Punk kids on the Hill," said Griffith in a sarcastic tone. "They think they run the fuckin' town."

"I'm living the dream, man," said Josh. "I get to drive up every morning to the United States Capitol and say to myself, that's where I work.'"

"Just remember what I told you…" said Griffith now totally serious.

"I know. I'm working at a place where I'll have a lot of acquaintances and very few friends," replied Josh dutifully.

"That's right," replied Griffith. "Moreover, if you can't tell the difference between the two, they will eat you alive here."

"Thanks, Dad," laughed Josh.

"No problem, son. By the way, thanks for the one liner last night," said Griffith.

"What one liner?" asked Thompson.

"I was on *CNN* last night," replied Griffith. "The kid gave me a great line. It got them all riled up."

"You are writing for him now," asked Thompson. "Are you working for him or me?"

"Sometimes I wonder," said Josh laughing. "Don't worry, boss, you could never use this one in any of your speeches."

"What the hell did you say *this time*, Griff?" Thompson asked.

"Well, we were talking about past-Presidents and I merely said Carter and Clinton are my favorites," replied Griffith.

"That got them riled up?" asked Thompson. He paused and smiled. "What else did you say?"

"Well, I just pointed out the fact every time Jimmy Carter and Bill Clinton are on television they are complaining about something. And, thanks to that, they are single-handedly turning the Democrats into the party of angry old white guys."

Thompson laughed out loud as Griffith stood up and moved to the window. "You said that on *CNN*? The Clinton News Network! Yeah, Josh, keep writing those lines for him, not me," Thompson instructed.

"Man, the top floor of Longworth…you really are the last whore on the floor, aren't you," said Griffith as he looked out the window behind Thompson's desk. Glancing down, all he could see was the HVAC on the roof of the cafeteria some 6 floors below.

"Even the 'dead and indicted' rooms are the big leagues," said Thompson.

"You bet your sweet ass," laughed Griffith. "At least the suite doesn't smell like dead rats."

Josh looked at the pair, both of whom were chuckling at what was obviously some kind of inside joke. "What do you mean by that?"

"You want to tell him or me?" asked Thompson.

"Oh, you do it," said Griffith. "You had the joy of living with the smell that week."

"All right," said Thompson. "Congressman Jackson had read something about how computers could be linked together through an office network. You've have to remember, this was the late 80s. We were one of the first offices to run computers through a server which linked D.C. to our district offices. To do so the House electrician had to run special power lines to our office through the air conditioning vents. The office was over in Cannon, just above the trash dumpsters and we had a big problem with rats."

"Rats?" asked Josh.

"Rats," Griffith confirmed. "It's an old city and these are old buildings, boy. There are rats all over the place."

"Yuk," said Josh. "Make sure we don't bring that up at the next staff meeting. They have committed to staying through your first reelect, but stories about rats in the building might send them on the Blue Line to K Street. I don't need stories of rats to cause them to get their resumes together."

"Anyhow," said Thompson, "apparently there was a nest of 'em living in the air conditioning vents leading to the bathroom, which we had converted into our server room. One day, mid-August, all the power blows and every computer in the office goes down."

"Hell, half the building went down," interjected Griffith.

"Seems a rat had chewed through the power line and fried itself in the air conditioning vent just above Garrett's desk," said Thompson.

"I came over the day it happened and it smelled like …well...it smelled like what you would expect a fried rat to smell like in mid-August," laughed Griffith.

"So when did you guys come up here?" asked Josh.

"Winter of 1987," said Thompson.

"Second half of Reagan II," interjected Griffith. "Damn, the town was a helluva lot different then, wasn't it?"

"You bet," Thompson said.

"How so?" asked Josh.

"Technology, for one," said Thompson. "Computers were basically word processors and not much else. I could pull up the AP wire, but there was no internet."

"Al Gore hadn't invented it yet," laughed Griffith. "No emails. Blackberries were in pies."

"And Conestoga wagons roamed the streets of D.C.," said Josh.

"Watch it, boy," said Griffith. "I'm not so old I still can't kick your ass."

"Sorry, sir," Josh replied in a mocking tone. "Tell me more about the olden days, Daddy."

"God," said Griffith. "How I long for the days of Reagan. We were in the minority then in Congress, but it was a great time to be a Republican running for office."

"Why?" asked Josh.

"Commies," replied Griffith.

"Commies?"

"You better believe Commies," said Thompson. "Republican consultants loved them in those days. Ruskies elected more Republicans during the Cold War than any suburban grass roots get out the vote effort ever could."

"Russians elected Republicans?" Josh repeated quizzically.

"Damn straight they did," Griffith opined. "Folks were scared shitless of those Cossack bastards. Whenever we had a candidate in trouble, we'd play the Commie card. We could scare voters with the threat of Communism and get people to vote Republican. Only Republicans could be trusted to beat the Commies."

"That's it?" asked Josh. "You simply talked about Communism and people would vote Republican?"

"Sometimes, we didn't even have to talk about it," said Griffith. "Reagan had this great ad about a bear in the woods, where the bear represented communism."

"There is a bear in the woods," quoted Thompson from memory, mimicking a baritone voice-over. "For some people the bear is easy to see. Others don't see it at all. Some people say the bear is tame. Others say it's vicious and dangerous. Since no one can really be sure who is right, isn't it smart to be as strong as the bear? If there is a bear..."

"That got people to vote for us?" asked Josh in a puzzled tone.

"You bet your sweet ass it did," replied Griffith.

"Then the world changed," said Thompson continuing the lesson. "Communism fell. Russia went away. In November of 1989, the Berlin Wall was broken into pebbles by people on both sides of it who demanded freedom. In the next election cycle, we could no longer talk about fear of the Cold War, because our policies had finally won. We won the war, but elections and politics in America changed forever."

"Yup," said Griffith. "And it changed without us knowing it. We never saw it coming in 1992. Only an electorate unfazed by the threat of Communism could elect Bill Clinton president."

"So that's what the Congressman means when he says Ronald Reagan elected Bill Clinton?" asked Josh.

"That's right," said Thompson. "I gave you a copy of *Conscience of a Conservative* by Barry Goldwater when we were on the campaign trail. Go back and re-read it. Anti-communism and the pursuit of liberty is one of the foundations of Goldwater conservatism. When the Wall fell, so did one of the pillars of the movement."

"I read the chapter on Communism," replied Josh. "He had a laundry list of things the United States had to do in order to win over Communism."

"That's right," said Thompson. "Goldwater said we couldn't just struggle against Communism. The goal of the Commies was world domination. Appeasement wasn't an option. We had to have a peace in which freedom and justice prevailed not only over America, but over all Communist governments. We had to defeat it to truly be a free society."

"So that's why you feel so strongly about China and Cuba?" asked Josh rhetorically.

"Damn straight," interjected Griffith. "I cried when the Berlin Wall went down."

"Why, you old softie," said Thompson.

"Call me what you want, man," Griffith replied. "It was like, in one fell swoop, all I was working for in politics made sense to me."

Thompson paused and looked at Griffith.

"I know. I know," said Griffith. "That's when it all went to hell."

"How did it go to hell?" asked Josh.

"That's when the religious right and the neo-cons began to get a hold in the conservative movement. Goldwater's pursuit of liberty was replaced by Falwell and Robertson's pursuit of a new federalism—one that implicitly or explicitly believes the federal government should be making our decisions for us."

"Bitter?" asked Griffith.

"Yeah, I am," said Thompson. "Being a conservative used to mean the federal government should stay out of our lives, until there is a decision so big states couldn't do it on their own."

"And now?" asked Josh.

"Now," replied Thompson, "being a conservative means the federal government should stay out of our lives, until there is a decision too important for individual human beings to decide for themselves."

"So all the pundits who today question the nature of being a true conservative…"

Thompson cut off Josh in mid-sentence "…are not really conservative. You can call them Neo-cons if you want, but they are nothing more than Neo-federalists."

"That's why Goldwater said every good Christian should line up and kick Jerry Falwell in the ass," laughed Griffith.

"It's politically tough being true to the movement," Griffith continued. "Even Goldwater saw the political shortcomings of being a true conservative. He used to say the true conservative should run on a platform which says 'send me to Washington so I can do nothing for you.' Not exactly a great turn-out-the-vote ad, is it?"

"Barry said it," interjected Thompson. "Broken promises are not the answer. Kept promises are."

"I don't get it," said Josh.

"Take education," said Thompson. "Goldwater advocated the Federal Government should not be involved in education. It was reserved by the *Constitution* as a state issue. More importantly, each state can better decide its own education needs."

"Hell, Reagan ran as a true conservative," said Griffith, "Reagan called for the dismantling of the Federal Department of Education."

"Then, along comes the years Republicans control both chambers of Congress and the White House," said Thompson. "And what do we do? We say forget dismantling the Department of Education. Give us more tax dollars and we will do it better. Republicans expanded the Department of Education rather than sticking to their principles and dismantling it."

"Barry Goldwater is spinning in his grave," said Griffith.

"Go over to the Capitol, Josh, and look at all the images of George Washington," Thompson interjected.

"They are all over the place," Josh replied.

"You know which one is my favorite?" asked Thompson.

"No, but I have an idea you are going to tell me," Josh said.

"Good guess," said Thompson. "My favorite is the large painting of General Washington giving back his *federal* military commission following the Revolutionary War. That's a great symbol in the Capitol, but it's apparently overlooked by those in the House of Representatives who are daily calling for increased federal responses to every issue facing this country. Every time we vote, we should look at that picture and remember it was put there to remind us the influence of the Federal government in our lives should be limited."

"Elect me so I can go to Washington to do nothing for you," repeated Griffith. "You know, boy, it just might work some day."

Just then, Thompson's beeper went off. "Three Bells. Three bells, indicating Members have 15 minutes to vote on the *Prewitt Amendment* to *HR 2714*."

Thompson had a big grin on his face as he stood up. "I have to go to work now." He paused. "Walk with me."

"I thought you would never ask," Griffith replied as he walked side-by-side with his good friend out the door of the office.

Chapter 9

The greatest battle in politics is not between Republicans and Democrats, or conservatives and liberals. Varying ends of the political spectrum may sometimes feel great animosity towards the other, but it is nothing like the ill will so often felt between the Congressional staffers located on Capitol Hill and those back in each Member's home district.

Staffers from both offices genuinely believe they perform the tougher tasks for their Boss and their duties are far more important to the success of their Boss than those performed daily by their co-workers at the other venue. Each group perceives the other has an easier job and better working conditions.

District based staffers look at those who work on the Hill as having a glamorous job. Those in D.C. get to work in the shadows of the Capitol dome. They get to go to receptions every night in ornate rooms filled with powerful people, free top-shelf liquor and jumbo shrimp. D.C. staffers get to spend weekends at home with their families, while the local staffers have to travel around the district with their Boss.

The workers who toil on the Hill often have similarly disdainful views of their district office counterparts. District staffers get to work in a regular office building and each staffer gets his or her own office with a desk separated by real walls rather than cork board dividers. Unlike D.C. staffers, who must remain in the office on evenings when Congress is in session, district workers get to head home at 5:00 each evening.

D.C. staffers get power lunches with lobbyists and we get angry phone calls from constituents, district staffers muse.

District staffers watch the clock and head out from their cushy offices exactly at 5:00 while we work until the wee hours and have to share our office with 5-6 other people, D.C. staffers frequently grumble.

There is some truth to both positions.

Today, however, Thompson's district office was abuzz with excitement as some of the glamour of Hill life was taking place in the District itself. Famed *Los Angeles Journal* sports reporter, John Gustine was coming to Kentucky to interview the Boss.

It was 4:30 p.m. when John Gustine buzzed the security alarm for entrance to Richard Thompson's 4th District Congressional field office in Northern Kentucky, so close to Cincinnati, Ohio, Gustine could see the stadium from the parking lot. When the receptionist informed him Congressman Thompson was on the phone, he settled into the government-issued couch to wait his turn in the inner sanctum.

The Congressman was behind the closed door of his spacious private office in the rear of the suite, talking on the telephone with FBI Agent Leo Argo about the investigation into Donny Alberato and the death of Greg Graham. The Fat Man, scribbling notes on a yellow legal pad, sat at the small conference table in far right-hand corner of the office across from Thompson. The Fat Man had placed his tape recorder in front of the speaker phone on Thompson's desk, recording the conversation.

"I don't know about this Leo," said The Fat Man. Argo had just suggested Thompson leak some information in his forthcoming interview with Gustine. "Wiring somebody up to nail a dirty Congressman for the Bureau was one thing, but this is pushing the envelope a bit."

It was clear The Fat Man was sitting next to Richard Thompson not as his friend, but as his lawyer.

"Give me your reasons, Joe," said Argo. "I'll see if I can put some of them to rest."

"There are a million reasons why he should not do this," said The Fat Man. "To start with, Leo, he's a Congressman now. There is this whole separation of powers thing. You are the executive branch and he's on the legislative side."

"We can overcome that," said Argo.

"Probably," said The Fat Man. "Still, it won't make it feel right. It is still a Member leaking information from an Executive Branch investigation. I get your point it is technically part of a homicide investigation relating to the death of Graham, rather than a leak from a Congressional investigation, but that nicety is likely to be lost on the public, the media—and at least half the judges in America. To most of the judges I know, a leak is still a leak."

"It is no big deal," said Argo. "We do it all the time."

"It is a big deal, Leo," replied The Fat Man. "If it gets pinned back to the Congressman, specifically approved by the FBI or not, it looks bad. If the shit hits the fan, can you assure us the Bureau will come out and publicly acknowledge you approved the leak?"

Argo didn't immediately answer the question. After a few seconds, he responded with a tone of resignation, "Look, I need him."

"Why?" asked Thompson.

"Congressman, the Bureau is convinced Alberato has something to do with Graham's death," Argo reiterated. "The problem is our evidence is weak. If we can get him thinking we know something more than we actually know, he may come to us for a deal."

"Or he may come after me to kick my ass," interjected Thompson. "Being a Congressman doesn't get me Secret Service protection or anything. I have a wife and kids to think about."

The Fat Man looked over at Thompson, frowning skeptically. "Despite what happened to you in the past, I don't think it is a realistic concern to think Donny Alberato is going to come looking for Rick with a baseball bat, but there are other big concerns here," said The Fat Man. "Leo, even if we get the legal side worked out, we really don't need the Congressman's name associated with this story."

As a matter of protocol, The Fat Man was normally careful to refer to his close friend by his elected title when the two were in public. Knowing they were being taped on one and probably both ends of the call caused him to be extra careful with his formalities.

"You know, Leo," said Thompson. "Joe's right. I guess it's not I'm afraid of Donny Alberato physically, or in any other way. There is a real chance I'll get slammed by every editorial board in the state… maybe the country. Those that don't call me a liar will blast me for leaking information on an on-going investigation."

"He's right, Leo," said The Fat Man. "Politically, it is a lose-lose situation. There is no compelling reason to do this one."

"You know my affinity for the Bureau," said Thompson. "I would love to help, but I don't see how I can. It just doesn't work for me."

"What if you do it as an anonymous source?" asked Argo. "Doesn't that take care of your political problems and any adverse public relations?"

"Well…" said Thompson thinking for a few seconds "If I could remain anonymous, I would consider it."

"Gustine is apparently a stand-up guy," said Argo. "He's ready to go to jail for not revealing his sources in the steroid grand jury leaks. I think he'll protect you."

"You think he'll agree to those rules?" Thompson asked his counsel.

"You would have to set the ground rules up front," said The Fat Man. "You need an explicit statement from him that whatever you say is on background and not for attribution. If he doesn't agree to the rules, you don't give the information."

"When you tell him that he'll have the exclusive I'm about to give you," said Argo, "he'll agree."

"He'll want to have a second source to confirm," said The Fat Man. "If Gustine isn't going to tell his editors the name of his source, he'll need to tell them he has a second source. Even *The Journal* will make him have a confirmation in order to go to press."

"Agreed," said Argo. "If you consent to do this, I'll have a second source lined up to confirm it to Gustine within the hour."

"Let's be clear on immunity," said The Fat Man. "The Congressman has full immunity for making the leak itself. Right?"

"I wouldn't have asked, if it wasn't already approved by the US Attorney's office," replied Argo. "I have their full authority to offer this deal. He has full immunity. Hell, someone in their office is going to be my second source."

"Hang on a minute, Leo. I need to talk to Joe, privately," said Thompson as he hit the mute button on the speaker phone. "Well, what do you think?"

"I can tell by the look in your eye you've already made up your mind," said The Fat Man. "Your faithful squire Sancho Panza is ready to follow you to whatever windmill you choose to tilt towards."

"Get serious, Joe," said Thompson. "I need you right now."

"Legally, you are covered," said The Fat Man. "We have it on tape. I'm not comfortable with the separation of powers issue, but that's from a purely philosophical standpoint on my part. Members cooperate in Federal investigations all the time. So I suspect there is a basis for it. I would have to research it to be sure."

"Politically?" asked Thompson.

"That's not really my area, Rick. You know that," said The Fat Man. "However, if you can get Gustine to agree to the terms of the interview, I think you are all right. He's willing to go to jail to protect his sources on the grand jury leaks. He's not going to roll over on a Congressman."

Thompson nodded at The Fat Man as he hit the mute button a second time to reopen the line to Argo.

"We agree under the terms specified in this call," said The Fat Man, knowing Argo was also recording the call.

"So what do you have?" asked Thompson.

"I have someone who can identify Albcrato's attorney as being at the scene of Graham's death on the day he was killed," replied Argo.

"No shit," mumbled Thompson.

"I don't get it Leo. If you have an eyewitness, then why the hell do you need the Congressman?" asked The Fat Man. "Why don't you go out and question the attorney. That'll send the same message."

"I can't go that route, Joe," replied Argo. "The eyewitness is all we have. No prints, nothing. If we run straight at him, we think he'll probably just deny it."

"Then why don't you take your eyewitness to the grand jury and leave me out of it?" said Thompson.

"I can't go that way either, Congressman," said Argo. "My witness is some tattooed workout queen so strung out on HGH and testosterone she has the potential to fly into a 'roid rage before the grand jury."

"So video her," said The Fat Man.

"No way," replied Argo. "With the leaks we have been seeing out of that court room, *The Journal* would probably know her name before the evening deadline. She's already so freaked out we have to put her in protective custody…not so much for her protection, but for us to keep an eye on her. I have to get Alberato to flip quickly, or I'm afraid we will lose her. We have to flush him out."

"So you really think this play with the Congressman and Gustine is your only viable option?" asked The Fat Man, instinctively knowing what the answer was going to be.

"It is the best chance I have," said Argo.

"All right," said Thompson. "Tell the Director I put up one helluva fight. If I'm going to do this, he needs to think you are aces because of it."

"I appreciate it, Congressman," replied a truly thankful Argo. "Joe, I'll call you on your cell within the hour with the second source."

"Great," said The Fat Man. "I'll talk to you later."

After Thompson hit the disconnect button on the speaker phone, he crumpled back in his chair, staring blankly at the wall. The Fat Man was waiting for Thompson to speak first. When nothing came, he said he would wait in the lunchroom until the interview with Gustine was complete and left the room.

Thompson sat motionless for a minute or two trying to compose himself enough to sit through the interview he was about to conduct.

Thompson leaned forward and hit the intercom to the receptionist. "MacKenzie, send Mr. Gustine on back."

"He's about to get an interview he never expected," Thompson said out loud to himself.

Chapter 10

Better baseball through chemicals is not anything new to the sport. Steroids may have recently damaged the image of professional baseball, but drug use has been rampant in baseball since World War II. Until very recently, baseball has been pretty consistent in its efforts to ignore the problem of performance enhancing drugs in the sport as much as possible and for as long as possible.

Greenies.

Dexedrine, an over the counter amphetamine (called "greenies" because they are sold in green capsules), entered the training room in the 1940's and were prevalent in baseball by the 50's. Not their use at the time was new or shocking. During World War II, amphetamines were given to soldiers (particularly pilots) to keep them alert. Back on the home front, greenies were used by moms to fight fatigue. Dads used them to fight asthma. When the boys of summer returned from Europe and Japan to their playing fields in America, they brought their new little green friends with them.

The big decision on the baseball field for most of the next 60 years was not "clear" or "cream," but whether to "bean up" or "play naked."

And there were wild stories of those who "beaned up."

Stories of special pots of coffee "for players only" and private bottles of vitamin drinks filled with speed have been circulating around baseball club houses for years. But the door was first blown off amphetamine use in baseball by Jim Bouton when, in 1970, he released his classic tell-all book on the 1969 season entitled *Ball Four*. Bouton revealed speed was readily available on any given game day and was used for everything from a chemical hangover cure, to alleviating general road-trip fatigue.

Baseball Commissioner Bowie Kuhn was outraged at Bouton's book of frat house behavior, but baseball failed to formally respond.

Things grew uglier in mid-1980's when a drug trial involving the Pittsburgh Pirates included allegations Willie "Pops" Stargell regularly distributed amphetamines to fellow team members and Willie Mays kept a bottle of "red juice"—a cocktail of amphetamines and fruit juice—in his locker. Stargell denied the allegation and Mays angrily claimed the "red juice" was cough medicine.

Baseball Commissioner Peter Ueberroth suspended some players, but again baseball failed to offer any other substantive response to amphetamine use.

Over the years, Mike Schmidt, Ralph Kiner, Dale Berra (Yogi's son), Dave Parker, Tony Gwinn, Ken Caminiti and Pete Rose all spoke out one time or another about greenie use in baseball. Despite revelation after revelation about the widespread use of these drugs, baseball still largely continued to turn a deaf ear.

In 2003, baseball even banned an herbal supplement (ephedra) following the death of Todd Belcher from its use, but left amphetamines themselves untouched.

Finally, in 2006, following nearly seven decades of abuse, Major League Baseball decided to ban and test for amphetamines. For quick energy before the game, special bottles of red juice in the locker room were replaced by espresso machines. But, that was far from the end of the story.

Those who have observed baseball's history of sticking its collectively bargained head in the sand on amphetamine abuse should not need to scratch their heads pondering baseball's failure to respond to the use of other performance enhancing drugs. The nature of the problem may be different, but the response is déjà vu.

America loved Mickey Mantle, in part, because of his wild life style. If he needed a little pick me up occasionally, so be it. An earlier generation was willing to smile knowingly about the alleged exploits of their athletes. The players themselves were just happy to get their equilibrium by game time.

Human Growth Hormone, testosterone and other designer steroids, on the other hand, are something more than a chemical hang over cure in the minds of the public.

While the public may not fully understand the effects of steroids and how they work, they understand massive muscle growth in short periods of time. They understand 40-year old players should be on the performance slide downward, not upward. They understand the implications of heads the size of Thanksgiving Day parade balloons and shrinking testicles the size of peanuts. They understand someone is trying to gain an unfair advantage, rather than just trying to counteract the ravages of a rugged lifestyle.

Human Growth Hormone ("HGH") is naturally produced in the body by the pituitary gland, which is located at the base of the brain. Medically, it has several legitimate and beneficial uses. It has been used since the 1950s to stimulate growth in underdeveloped children. Today it is used to treat children with rheumatoid arthritis and to assist adults with carpal tunnel syndrome.

Many older adults see HGH as an honest-to-God fountain of youth, an anti-aging drug. The internet is filled with advertisements for HGH capsules and nose sprays usually showing elderly people at youthful play on beaches and golf courses. Those who market these products claim to be able to "make you look good and feel younger." For the record, most of these are designed to stimulate natural HGH production in the brain and are, for the most part, useless.

HGH also has other uses. In its synthetic form, HGH is the current drug of choice for anyone who wants to build body mass. At age 61, Sylvester Stallone admitted he used HGH to buff up for the filming of *Rambo III*. In baseball, Jose Canseco admitted using human growth hormone (and a laundry list of other chemicals) in his book *Juiced: Wild Times, Rampant 'Roids, Smash Hits and How Baseball Got Big.*

By increasing the body's ability to synthesize protein, HGH allows someone to build new muscle cells and increase the size and number of existing cells. It also strengthens tendons and ligaments and helps the body burn fat.

By law, injections of HGH must be prescribed by a doctor for those have\ing a deficiency in the naturally produced hormone. At $25 per injection, and injections sometimes required as often as three times a day, HGH treatments are not cheap. Prescribed treatments can cost as much as $30,000 a year.

Before concluding HGH is the wonder hormone which many advertise it to be, one must also consider there are serious side effects. Like many of the performance enhancing drugs, HGH can cause aggressive behavior (just ask Jose Canseco's ex-wife, Jessica Canseco, who documented her husband's 'roid rages and spouse abuse in her own tell-all book *Juicy: Confessions of a Former Baseball Wife*). HGH has been identified as a possible cause for diabetes and cancer. HGH can also cause abnormal bone growth and bone density, especially in the skull plates, fingers and toes.

One of the problems with banning HGH in professional sports is there is no known test for its illegal use. Enlarged heads and monthly stops at the shoe store for larger cleats are a good indication of abuse, but the evidence is circumstantial at best.

On the other hand, when a player uses anabolic steroids or testosterone to enhance muscle development, strength and endurance through protein synthesis, the use is generally detectible. The trick for the user is trying to stay one step ahead of the testing protocol.

Like HGH, the body produces testosterone naturally. For most people, the production of testosterone is produced in about a 1:1 ratio along with a substance called epitestosterone. Thus, when sports began testing, they looked not to the level of testosterone in a player's body, but to the ratio of testosterone to epitestosterone. A player can have as much testosterone in his body as he wants, so long as he stays below the 6:1 T:E ratio which is considered to be the *per se* indicative of doping.

Greg Graham had become a leader in the underground world of performance enhancing drugs. The key to his success had been supplying substances to athletes which were either (like HGH) undetectable through testing or were manufactured to stay one step ahead of testing protocols (like certain types of testosterone or other steroids).

In the case of testosterone, Graham simply designed a topical cream containing both testosterone and epitestosterone. The cream did two things. As a topical, the active substances released into the blood stream much more slowly than with a direct injection, resulting in much lower peak concentrations of testosterone. Moreover, the addition of epitestosterone to the topical simply kept the ratio below the 6:1 ratio.

A combined regiment of HGH injections and topical creams had kept Graham's clients growing and, so far as all then current testing protocols could detect, apparently clean.

Donny Alberato had a reputation for spending a lot of hours in the workout room. He lifted continuously throughout the off season at his winter home in Mexico. He was well defined and strong. But, as the years wore on, it seemed his body was taking longer and longer to recover from his daily vigorous sessions of weight lifting.

That was when a fellow player introduced him to Greg Graham. Graham supplemented Alberato's strength training with herbal supplements, injections of undetectable clear liquids and a topical cream. "If you are caught with the white stuff," Graham had warned him, "just tell folks it's an arthritis cream."

Alberato didn't much care what Graham was giving him or whether it was legal. With the regimen of topical lotions, following a workout, his body seemed to recover much more quickly and he could lift daily with muscle popping results. When he reported to spring training following his first winter under Graham's charge, Alberato added a couple of inches to the size of his uniform jersey. Oddly enough, he not only needed a larger jersey, but a larger hat and cleats as well.

And for Donny Alberato, Graham's regimen also produced spectacular statistical results.

The statistics he had added to his resume, after reaching the age of 35, were staggering. Prior to using Graham as a "trainer," the most home runs Alberato had ever hit were 34 at the age of 29. Then at the age of 36, he slammed 53 dingers. Pre-enhancement, Alberato had a lifetime .279 batting average. With the help of Graham, he won two league batting titles.

Alberato didn't particularly care if the fans were talking about his quick bulk up in hushed tones, speculating about steroid abuse. His salary, like his stats, was at an all time high. He had endorsement deals and all the material possessions that come with sport success. That's all that mattered to him. All was right with the world as Donny Alberato knew it.

Then the FBI raided a nutrition store in southern California trying to find and follow the supply chain of illegal steroids used in this country and they confiscated a computer owned by Greg Graham. Suddenly, a steady stream of professional athletes were making their way to the Federal Courthouse in Los Angeles for secret testimony before a specially empanelled grand jury.

Based on what leaked from the courthouse, when Graham was called to testify, he refused to answer any questions, including those he was not eligible to claim 5th Amendment privilege. In particular, Graham would not answer any questions about his relationship with Alberato, a defiant act for which he faced the potential of a year in jail for contempt of court. Unless, of course, he changed his mind and testified about the things that were in his head—not in his computer.

But the contempt order and potential jail time didn't matter much now.

On the same day Alberato's attorney and agent, Adam Murphy, visited Graham, someone had killed him.

The crime scene in the training room of the storefront gym was gruesome.

Police were called to the scene by an anonymous tip to check out the store front in the seedy strip center. As they entered through the unlocked front door with their guns drawn, they could not have expected the scene they found.

Greg Graham was face down in a pool of his own blood. A fifty pound weight, used to crush Graham's skull, had been laid neatly on top of the tattered training table. The weight, as well as the walls around it, was spattered with blood.

Otherwise, the room was sterile.

No vials of HGH. No tubes of balm were on the shelves.

No autographed pictures of Donny Alberato were on the walls.

Chapter 11

Alberato Linked to Trainer's Death

By John Gustine and Joyce Lang

(Los Angeles) A high ranking government official close to the case told *The Los Angeles Journal,* in an exclusive interview, that Los Angeles all-star first-baseman, Donald "Donny" Alberato, is under investigation in connection with the brutal death of his one-time trainer, Gregory Graham.

Graham, who was due to be sentenced in the coming weeks on contempt charges stemming from his refusal to cooperate with a Federal grand jury investigating the use of performance enhancing drugs in professional and amateur athletics, was found brutally murdered last week in a small gym in Orange County. Graham, formally Alberato's personal trainer, was rumored to have provided steroids and human growth hormone to many professional athletes, including Alberato.

According to the source, a friend and close associate of Donny Alberato visited Graham on the day he was killed. The details of that meeting are unknown, as is the time of death of Mr. Graham.

The coroner is expected to give a full report within the next week. The source said Alberato's contact met with Graham near the time he was bludgeoned to death by a fifty pound free weight.

The high ranking government source has requested his identity remain anonymous. *The Journal* has been able confirm the information provided by another high-ranking source close to the investigation.

The Journal has previously reported Alberato was one of the many professional athletes under investigation by the special grand jury meeting in Los Angeles for the past eight months.

When contacted for comment on this story, Donny Alberato referred all comments to his attorney, Adam Murphy. Murphy issued a brief written statement declaring "any comment which accuses Donny Alberato of killing Gregory Graham is absurd. Donny considered Graham a dear friend and his thoughts and prayers are with his family during this very difficult time." Murphy refused further comment.

Bill Pappard, general partner and President of the Los Angeles baseball club, stated the team does not currently have any reason to believe Alberato was involved in the death of Graham. He referred all other questions on discipline to baseball's head office in New York.

Special Assistant to the Commissioner, Colin N. Korey, said baseball would not take any action against Alberato unless or until formal charges were brought against him.

A decision on impaneling a grand jury in the death of Greg Graham has been postponed until the Los Angeles County Coroner issues his report next week.

Joyce Lang spit her toothpaste into the sink and leaned forward to look deep into the mirror. In the reflection, she saw not only her own image, but also the bedroom which adjoined the bathroom. There, she saw a man sleeping in her bed. As troubling as that image should have been to her, it was not. What was troubling was the anger she saw in her own eyes.

The deep fury came not from her relationship with the man. True, if she was going to have a relationship with a married man, she could at least find one who was a better lover. His "shortcomings" caused her sexual angst maybe, but not anger. He served his purpose well. Faked orgasms were a small price to pay for the information he provided.

Using her sexuality for personal profit was nothing new to her. Joyce Lang had been doing so since she was raped by her Journalism professor in college.

In her small town high school, Lang had dreams of becoming a television news anchor. Counselors had told her that her good looks and cheerful personality made her the perfect fit for providing big news on the small screen. She had proudly announced to her family and friends she was going to college as a no one and wouldn't come back until she was a star.

Her first semester did not go well, as her GPA reflected. She was at the top of her class in high school, but in college "A's" suddenly seemed illusive. As she started her second semester, her self-confidence waned. She questioned whether she had the wherewithal to reach her lofty goal of television news stardom.

Things seemed to be looking up when she started having private counseling sessions with her journalism professor who was assigned to guide her through her major. He was also teaching her Introduction to Journalism class. She had not really made many friends during her first semester and this very approachable young associate professor listened to her in a relaxed and friendly way. She had finally met somebody who understood and appreciated her for what she wanted to do with her life. She went to his office regularly and talked with him about everything from the tribulations of being in college to the personal problem of the day.

Lang went to his office late one afternoon in early April for a counseling session. They talked at length and the session lasted well into the early evening. She should have run when he locked his office door and began to rub her shoulders from behind. She didn't and the next 10 minutes or so were a blur. As she trembled under his weight, her naiveté about life was ripped away along with her virginity.

Horrified by the experience, she went through the motions in her other classes, but she never returned to the professor's journalism class for the remainder of the semester. Instead, she sat up nights crying over the experience and she seriously contemplated quitting college all together. She didn't even sit for her final exam.

When she got an "A" in her journalism class, she was puzzled. Puzzled … but in a weird way, empowered as well.

Over the summer, she began to experiment with her own body and her ability to manipulate young men with her sexuality. The back seats of cars became her own psychology lab, as she found men would provide her with just about anything she desired in return for a blow job. The men she went out with never knew they were her personal lab rats, following a maze for sex instead of cheese.

The next fall, she quit spending her time at college in tears. She signed up for another class taught by the same professor who had raped her and she went straight to his office after the first day of class. This time, she was not a naive girl from a small town seeking friendship and understanding. This time, she was the aggressor, mentally and physically. This time she was in complete control.

Thereafter, sex became a tool in her quest for fame and she used it with the precision of a surgeon wielding a scalpel.

What had worked in college, however, sometimes failed her in real life. Lang landed a job at a small California television station and went about building her career with the same sexual aggression she had shown in college. She was fired when a cameraman filed an EEOC sexual harassment complaint against her.

Her reputation as a news slut stuck and she bounced from job to job and station to station until she worked her way out of television entirely. After a while, to make ends meet, she started writing stories on a free-lance basis, selling them to news outlets throughout California. When she submitted a well written and researched story to *The Los Angeles Journal* about city hall corruption, it got front page placement and led to the resignation of two city councilmen and the city's deputy mayor was jailed.

The Journal began using Lang on a free-lance basis as their courthouse beat reporter. It was a far cry from her dreams of being a news anchor, but it gave her a good platform from which to rebuild her resume for television stardom. Over a span of two years, Lang graduated from courthouse stories to investigative reporting. For the next four years, she sold *The Journal* major story after major story, consistently improving her skills and solidifying her reputation as LA's best investigative reporter.

The editors at *The Journal* offered her a full-time position. For fear it would take her out of the game for a television spot in the future, she refused. Still, she continued to sell stories to *The Journal* on a regular basis.

Ever savvy, she had signed an exclusive agreement with *The Journal* to offer her investigative stories to them on a "first refusal" basis. That allowed her to keep the income flowing, but also allowed her to pursue her career as a television anchor. The stories continued to be written, but she had failed in one critical aspect—she was a journalist but not on television.

Lang discovered, to her consternation, even her best investigative pieces were perceived by both local and national news to be too complex for television and lacking in visual pizzazz. The dirty secrets she uncovered were often hard to boil down into 2, 5 or even 10 minute segments and the television stations were usually content to cover prosecutor press conferences and the "perp walks" of dour men in blue suits resulted from her work in 30 seconds of tape and voice-over.

Lang needed something big, visual and with more widespread appeal. She also needed to be able to control the story as it came out, so she could make sure she was the one on camera.

The series of stories on steroid use in professional sports bored her personally, but it was her best shot yet to make it back to television and she was running out of chances.

As she looked in the mirror, she could not remember the last time when she had sex for her own pleasure or for a lasting relationship. So it was easy for her to accept the detective sleeping in her bed. There was no emotion there one way or the other. She felt rage, but her anger arose from Sunday morning's front page headline in *The Los Angeles Journal.*

Gustine had scooped her.

He was the sports writer and she was the investigative reporter. He went to Kentucky to write a puff-piece. He came back with an earth-shattering headline. Sure, she got credit in the byline, but her own input had been limited to one line in the story…and the line confirming the story through a second source, at that.

Gustine, a run of the mill baseball dweeb, had come up with a confirmed source that one of baseball's biggest names was associated with the death of Greg Graham, breaking loose possibly the biggest story of the year. It was a source which he refused to share with Lang.

The little fucker can crow all he wants about journalistic ethics, but the bottom line here is the little creep refused to share his source, Lang thought to herself.

Gustine was spending the weekend getting praise from the editors at *The Journal*. Far more damning from Lang's perspective was that Gustine would be spending the rest of his weekend getting the exposure of interviews on all the 24-hour news networks.

She was spending the weekend getting boned by some greasy detective, while Gustine was getting the television fame she longed for. The detective didn't have the first clue as to who Gustine's source was.

Who the hell else did John Gustine talk to besides the Congressman while he was in Kentucky?

She looked deep into her own eyes in the mirror, as she tried to channel her own anger and frustration into determination.

Still, she was very angry.

On the other side of the United States, Colin N. Korey was meeting with baseball's head of security, M.T. Stacy. They too wanted badly to know the identity of the "high ranking government official," but they had their own reasons for being furious about the front page story.

"I was worried something like this would happen," said Korey. His voice was less modulated than normal, in implicit recognition he and Stacy were the only two people in the entire office suite at 12:15 p.m. on a Sunday afternoon.

"You called it all right, Mr. Korey," replied Stacy. "This is right out of the Justice Department playbook. I just didn't think they would start leaking so soon."

"It's a smart play," said Korey. "It's a smart play."

"How so?" inquired Stacy.

"There is no coroner's report yet," he said. "An early leak means they are trying to flush someone out."

"Who?" asked Stacy.

"That's your job, M.T.," replied Korey. He tossed the print-out of the story Stacy got off the web for him onto his desk. It covered the bad pdf of the same article Pappard had emailed him earlier from Los Angeles showing the story's prominent position on the front page. "There is someone behind this story. That person is the key. Figure out who Gustine has been talking to and we can figure out the government's strategy."

"That should be pretty easy," said Stacy. "Gustine is a sports reporter. He probably told the other guys in the press box where he's been. I'll find out who he has been talking to."

"Pull out all stops on this one, M.T.," said Korey. "Get the payroll on it. If Gustine's source can connect baseball in any way with the death of Greg Graham, it'll be far worse than the steroid hearings in Congress. Gate revenues will plummet; TV revenues will plummet. We will all suffer. We won't be ruined, but all the teams will suffer."

"Big time," interjected Stacy.

"You bet big time," said Korey. "And if the owners suffer, we suffer, M.T. You and me, personally—we will be royally screwed. If we can't control this thing, we're out of here. The owners would love that. At that point, M.T., the only jobs we will be able to get will be at the drive through of some fast food joint."

He looked at the picture of his father on the wall. "Stop at nothing—you hear me, nothing—to get the name of Gustine and Lang's sources. Then, when you've got the names, get the payroll on it."

"Understood," said Stacy.

The odd man with the big nose who spent most of his time on eBay buying baseball cards looked up from his keyboard when the "ding" indicated incoming mail. He clicked on the news alert, which linked his computer screen to an article in *The Los Angeles Journal*. He read the article several times with disturbing intensity.

"No! No! No!" he shouted at the screen, stiffening up in his chair. "It is not supposed to be playing out this way."

He stood up and paced around the room. He ran his fingers nervously through his beard before sitting down again.

"All right, calm down," he instructed himself. "You can make this right."

He clicked on the email containing the article and dragged it into an Outlook folder he had designated for his favorite baseball player, Donny Alberato. As the virtual copy of the article fluttered into the folder, he made a gun with his right index finger and thumb, pointed at the screen and quietly exclaimed, "Bang."

"I can make this right," he muttered to himself.

The ball club had broken spring camp and Donny Alberato was already in Los Angeles when he read the front page story linking him to Graham's death. Murphy warned him at about 5:00 p.m. Saturday it was coming and had issued a statement on his behalf. Still, he didn't imagine the story would look as bad as it did until he read it.

It was a disaster. First, everyone in baseball thinks he's a juicer. Now, he was linked to the horrific death of Greg Graham.

I may have used some supplements from time-to-time. But a lot of guys in the game did the same thing. Call me a cheater and you will have to add me to a pretty long list. But now everybody will think I am a murderer. My career is as good as over. I'll get booed at every park we play in.

He stood still in his kitchen looking out the window. His hand was trembling so badly he was unable to drink his morning coffee, so he slammed it down on the kitchen counter. He tried to take a couple of deep breaths to calm himself down, but that only succeeded in making him feel like he was going to be physically ill.

He started to call his lawyer, Adam Murphy, but stopped.

What if Murphy has gone to the authorities? What if he's the source? Maybe they just called him a high ranking government official to try to throw me off. He could be wired. Trust no one.

"Did you read the story in *The Los Angeles Journal* today?" The Fat Man asked Thompson.

"Not yet," said Thompson in a hushed voice. "I'm trying to keep the peace around here today by being a husband and a father. I don't want to spend any time on the laptop reading news stories. I only took this call because I saw on the caller ID it was you."

"Sorry," said The Fat Man. "You told me to call."

"Yeah. I know," said Thompson. "But, I haven't told Ann about any of this."

"Really?" asked The Fat Man. "I thought you guys talk about everything."

"Normally we do," replied Thompson. "But, not right now. It is pretty tense around here. If I told her I was the source of a national headline story, she would lose it."

"That doesn't sound like Ann," replied The Fat Man. "She's usually a rock."

"Ann's just having trouble adjusting to being a Congressman's wife," whispered Thompson.

"You guys okay?" The Fat Man inquired.

"We're fine," Thompson said. "She's just challenging me to love her right now."

"I'm sorry to hear that," said The Fat Man. "Is there anything I can do?"

"Sure," said Thompson with a nervous laugh. "Tell me what's in the article and then get the hell off the phone."

"In a nutshell, it is pretty much what Argo envisioned. It is real strong. It links Alberato to Graham's murder through his lawyer. Everybody gives bullshit quotes."

"And?" asked Thompson.

"And, if this article doesn't pull someone out of the shadows," said The Fat Man, "nothing will."

The Fat Man was unaware of just how dead on target his statement was.

Chapter 12

The glamour of life on Capitol Hill as a Member of the United States Congress is intoxicating. Members often complain about the all-consuming burdens of the job that dictate and limit their lifestyles, but don't mistake those crocodile tears for real pain.

Sure, they are away from their families for days on end and make much less than they probably could in the private sector. However, a cramped work space and smaller living accommodations doesn't undermine the fact they are Members of the United States Congress. They have staffs who wait on their every whim. They have lobbyists who cater to their egos and constituents who frequently react to them with an almost obsequious deference usually reserved for rock stars, movie stars and other so-called celebrities.

It's a good life.

On the other hand, for the families of Members, life is anything but glamorous. While the Member is in D.C., with a gaggle of lobbyists and staffers laughing at their every joke, each Member's spouse and kids are at home under a microscope as large as the concave structure of the Capitol dome itself. Spouses, especially wives, always have to look the part. Kids, no matter the age, must always be on their best behavior. Marriages must be strong to survive and the children must be carefully mentored and nurtured in order to have a reasonable chance at growing up "normal."

Ann Thompson, wife of Congressman Richard Thompson, was feeling the strain of her husband's new job. Normally a hands-on father, Thompson was now out of the house altogether three to five days and nights each week. Phone calls were nice, but no substitute for daddy's kiss before bed. For Ann personally, phone sex with her husband, while fun and new the first couple of times, was no substitute for the real thing.

Ann discovered the uncomfortable stare of the public almost immediately after her husband's election to Congress. While she was at the local grocery store one day, an older woman approached her in the frozen food section. The woman, without introduction or personal greeting, began lecturing Ann on the benefits of a piece of legislation to which Richard Thompson was opposed. Ann had to listen to the woman's rant and quietly nod while the woman basically called her husband stupid and the values which they held dear insignificant. Ann nodded politely and then boiled with anger for hours following the incident.

Silent acquiescence was not her style. Ann Thompson was a battler. Now, her identity was that of a spouse (and a silent one, at that).

Michael Griffith introduced Ann to Richard Thompson at a reception while she was working on the Hill for a Congresswoman from Florida. Smitten by her, Thompson pursued her until she consented to a date. The rest, as they say, is history.

Romance…marriage…kids…all followed. From the time they first dated, to all who observed the progression of their relationship, they were the perfect couple for politics.

He was the committed policy wonk with the uncanny political ability to own any room he entered. She was the pleasingly attractive and approachable blond with fiery green eyes and an intellect to match her beauty.

Even the most compatible of couples have their struggles and the struggles of Ann and Richard Thompson were as difficult as they could have been for any other relatively young couple on Capitol Hill. Shortly after their marriage, Ann Thompson had to come to grips with the paralyzing fact she was an alcoholic.

For a strong willed person like Ann, it was difficult to understand something had control over her. Early on, Ann and Richard ignored the problem. Sure she drank a lot, but so did everyone else on the Hill. Every night there was a reception with free alcohol and when there wasn't, all you had to do was find a lobbyist with a credit card. It was a lifestyle in which drinking only on the weekends could easily turn into drinking every night.

Comedian Bill Hicks once described his problems with alcohol by labeling himself as simply a weekend drinker. "I would start on Friday and end on Thursday, so I thought I had it under control."

In the first years of their marriage, they realized Ann was facing the same problem, but it was not a joking matter. Though they each silently recognized what was happening, neither dared discuss it with the other. The marriage was young and neither wanted to throw a damper on the life they were living.

Then one night, Ann went on a drinking binge at a D.C. fundraiser for her boss. The alcohol was free, so she drank until she could no longer hold any more liquor, purged in the bathroom and then drank some more. After that, the remainder of the evening was a blur. Ann blacked out and disappeared for several hours. After a panicked search of surrounding bars, Griffith found Ann passed out in a corner of the Grill Room at the Capitol Hill Club.

The next day, after a tearful apology to both her husband and her boss, Ann attended her first Alcoholics Anonymous meeting. "Yeas and Nays" was the name of the group. It was held on Capitol Hill and its members ranged from the powerful to the powerless. She stood up in front of the assembled group and tearfully announced, for the first time, "Hello, my name is Ann and I'm an alcoholic."

That was twenty some years ago and Ann had remained sober ever since.

Even on their annual trips to Key West, the ultimate venue for drinking, Ann hadn't touched a drop. As soon as the plane would hit the ground, Ann would head to the Anchors Aweigh Club on Virginia Avenue to catch the morning women's group meeting. "If you want to remain sober, just attend a morning meeting in Key West," Ann once told her husband. "When someone stands up, looks at their watch and says they have been sober for 4 hours, you will think twice about having a drink."

For two decades, she had survived it all. She had even withstood a special election campaign, where the focus of the nation was on her husband and family. Yet, as hard as the campaign trail had been, it was nothing like the stress of being a Congressman's wife.

Perhaps the biggest problem in being a Congressman's wife was the feeling when things got overwhelming she had nowhere to turn. She couldn't talk to her husband about it. He was in Washington dealing with important issues...issues which she felt were much larger than her own growing depression. Now, because of the ever present public microscope, she felt there was no one in the community she could turn to with her problems.

Ann wanted to talk to her husband over the weekend, but he had seemed consumed with other issues. Whatever was on his mind, he wasn't talking about it. He was even sneaking around the house to take calls from The Fat Man, like she would never figure out something was going on.

When Thompson got on the plane early Tuesday morning to head back to D.C. for the week's legislative session, Ann was alone again.

There was no one in the world to turn to, except an old friend   one she deeply regretted bringing back into her life.

But she did and, as she stood up in front of the group at the AA meeting two days later, it was time to start over.

"Hello, my name is Ann."

"Hi, Ann" replied the crowd.

"I am an alcoholic. It's been two days since my last drink..."

If Ann had realized who had followed her to the meeting, she might have had another drink that very minute.

Chapter 13

The realities of afternoons on Main Street in Huntington Beach in the summer are straight out of a sappy television drama about the left-coast.

Just south of L.A., Huntington Beach is one of the prime spots for sun worship and surfing in southern California. The eight and a half miles of beach is so littered with miscellaneous bodies catching precious rays of sun surfers often have to chart a path just to get from the parking lot to the Pacific Ocean.

Find the pier which juts out into the ocean, look east and you will find Main Street.

On Saturdays and Sundays, Main Street closes down to automobile traffic and becomes a pedestrian walkway to the pier...a Yellow Brick Road for characters just as odd as those who accompanied Dorothy on her trip to Oz. Weekdays are almost as crazy.

John Gustine was barely able to avoid a collision with a bikini clad young woman on a skate board who was carrying a surf board under her arm. He was able to get out of the fray by grabbing a seat on the rail facing the street in the front of Coach's Mediterranean Grill. For the next 45 minutes, he kept a close eye on the Irish pub just across the street, although it was difficult to avoid having his attention diverted from time to time by the parade of beauties and beasts making their way to the pier. Still, as the sounds of an overage Elvis impersonator about fifteen yards away filled his ears, he kept his eyes glued on the entry to the pub.

Gustine had come to Huntington Beach this day at the insistence of an anonymous phone caller. The caller said he had information on Donny Alberato and his relationship with the late Greg Graham. Gustine's voice mail box was riddled with such anonymous messages ever since he and Lang began their series about steroids. Most were dead ends, wannabee reporters who were simply repeating what had already been in a newspaper somewhere else or disseminating wild rumors that defied second source confirmation.

Ten or so women had called to say they were Alberato's road trip mistress and claimed they shot him up with juice while the team was on the road. It wasn't unbelievable he had so many women on the road. However, if you are going to get in line as a road mistress source, you better have more confirming evidence than simply knowing Alberato's box score stats from a three game series in Houston. Most of the women who called Gustine didn't even have the most basic information about Alberato and his habits.

A good reporter knows instinctively which calls are real and which are not.

That's why Gustine agreed to meet with this particular caller today. Something in his gut told him this one was real. Reinforcing that instinct, this guy knew far more than most callers. In the three times he called Gustine in the last 4 hours, he impressed the reporter with his knowledge of the use and abuse of performance enhancing drugs. He seemed to know the industry as well as the muscle bound men walking down Main Street, their massive bull mastiffs trailing them on a thick leather leash as if somehow the big dog would make up for the fact their penises were shrunk by years of steroid abuse.

More importantly, the source mentioned details about the relationship between Graham and Alberato that only Gustine and Lang had discovered, but not yet reported. This guy could become the second source they needed for confirmation and publication on many aspects of the story.

Gustine was supposed to meet the source precisely at 2:00 p.m. It was 1:50 and he watched every person who walked into the bar from his street side seat in front of Coach's. No one who entered the bar had the nefarious look of a steroid junkie.

Gustine made his way across the street to the bar and entered. As his eyes adjusted to the dark bar, he noticed the green walls were adorned with black and white photos of Irish sports heroes. He just sat down at the bar when something caught his eye. At the end of a long hallway leading to the bathrooms, stood a lone figure. His outline was defined, almost entirely, by the sunlight flowing in from the open door behind him leading out into the alley.

When Gustine looked back in the same direction a few seconds later, the figure had not moved. He had the curious sensation this man, whom he could only see in silhouette, was looking right at him, waiting. By intuition, he got up, went down the hallway and walked right to the figure.

"You must be John Gustine," said the man. Up close, his physical appearance was not at all ominous or threatening—he was 30ish and his physique seemed to indicate he had never lifted a weight in his life, let alone used steroids.

"I am," responded Gustine. "And, you are?"

"You have to assure me no one will ever know we have spoken." The man was nervously shifting his weight from left to right as he looked in directions opposite from each rhythmic shift.

"You have my assurance," said Gustine. "I talk to people all the time whose names I don't reveal."

"Well, I need to be one of those people," said the man.

"That's fine," said Gustine.

"No one can ever know my name."

"No one will," assured Gustine. "But, you've got to be straight up with me."

"What do you mean by that?" the man replied.

"I mean you have to trust me," instructed Gustine. "Tell me all you know. Let me decide what is important and what isn't."

"If I do," asked the man, "you will never mention my name?"

"I never have before," said Gustine. "I don't intend to start with you."

"Good."

"Of course, you will also need to help me find ways to confirm what you are about to tell me," said Gustine.

"I don't know," said the man. "I'm going way out on a limb here."

"You've come this far," said Gustine. "You obviously have a purpose in being here."

"I do."

"Good," said Gustine. "That's a start. You want to be here."

"I do," said the man.

"Why?" asked Gustine.

"That stays with me," said the man. "I'll give you the story, but my reasons stay with me."

"Fine," Gustine said. "But you obviously know things about Donny Alberato. Keep your reasons to yourself. I don't care. Just give me the story and a way to confirm it."

"All right," said the man with some reluctance in his voice.

"Well, then, why don't we just sit down at one of the booths and talk about how you know so much about Donny Alberato," said Gustine.

"No," the man replied.

"No?" asked a shocked Gustine. "You don't want to talk now?"

"No. No. No," said the man. "That's not what I meant. I'll talk to you, just not in the bar. There's too damned many weight lifters out there on the street."

"And they will know you?" Gustine asked.

"It doesn't matter," said the man. "I just don't want to do it in there. Let's go out into the alley. We can talk there."

"Fine," said Gustine. He pulled a notebook from his backpack while following the man out the back door of the bar into the alley. Gustine was confused when the man didn't turn around. He stood there a bit dumbfounded as the man just kept walking up the alley. The sour smell of produce rotting in the hot California sun, which was coming from a nearby dumpster, made Gustine wrinkle his nose and squint.

Gustine jumped as, from behind, someone grabbed his forehead and forced his body against Gustine's back. Gustine struggled until an ice pick pierced the back of his brain just above the spine. The attacker behind Gustine folded him over into a lifeless mass. Once Gustine's body had been placed neatly on the ground, the attacker grabbed Gustine's backpack before quickly walking down the alley and melting into the odd crowd of Huntington Beach.

Chapter 14

When Starbucks Coffee first migrated east from Seattle, The Fat Man truly believed its penetration into the social fabric of American society was a sign of the coming apocalypse. Anyone who even so much as mentioned the name "Starbucks" would incur a rant the proportion of which equaled the girth of The Fat Man himself. He railed against the cost and the silly names given to the sizes of its cups. He ranted against the idea there was a tip jar at the checkout for someone who was simply doing the job they were paid to do by serving a cup of coffee. And, you wouldn't even want to get him started on the idea of sprinkling cinnamon in a perfectly good cup of joe.

Then Richard Thompson bought The Fat Man his first venti vanilla latte. His perspective on life was forever changed.

The Fat Man suddenly became immersed in the Starbucks' culture with the same fanatical fervor he undertook when memorizing lines to his favorite movies. He researched the company's business plan, bought SBUX stock and followed its meteoric rise on the NASDAQ. Today, The Fat Man can be found each morning reading a newspaper at a store half-way between his house and his office, surrounded by other middle-aged businessmen and women who start their days off with tasty, over-priced, double shots of hi-test caffeine.

The "Confederacy of Dunces," as the loose collection of people who gather with The Fat Man call themselves, spend a half-hour each morning drinking coffee and chatting about events ranging from the previous night's baseball box score to local and world politics. The Dunces named themselves after the Pulitzer Prize winning book of the same name which was authored by John Kennedy Toole.

The Fat Man's favorite book of all time was *A Confederacy of Dunces*. The title of the book is based on a quote by Jonathan

Swift: "When a true genius appears in the world, you may know him by this sign, that the dunces will be joined in confederacy against him."

The Fat Man loved the New Orleans protagonist in *A Confederacy of Dunces*, Ignatius J. Reilly, because he was a large bodied, self-appointed genius who believed that all around him were idiots. Quite simply, The Fat Man could relate to Ignatius.

The Fat Man was willing to concede to the premise that others in his Northern Kentucky community were perhaps the real smart ones, if, in fact, he were just allowed to organize the revolt against them. This daily small gathering of locals was his personal confederacy of dunces.

His intelligence combined with his unusual way of looking at the world made The Fat Man an odd genius; one who was well respected (and frequently misunderstood) by many in the legal community. Those who had discounted The Fat Man because of his short, portly stature and scruffy pepper beard usually found themselves wondering at the end of a case how they had been bested by such an odd-looking man. They came at him the second time with a new respect of one who had been previously whipped.

When The Fat Man committed to a cause or purpose, he jumped in with a passion and intensity that could not be rivaled. In his younger days, when he was involved in a big case, it was not unusual for him to stay at the office for days on end, going home to clean up and sleep only on the third or fourth night. No young associate at the law firm was truly integrated into the firm's litigation group until he was assigned to assist The Fat Man on a project. It was an initiation by fire—working for several consecutive weeks or months with someone who was smarter than you were and who had twice the energy.

After Richard Thompson came to the firm as a young D.C. hotshot and landed an office next to The Fat Man's, he designed a plan to gain the respect of all the lawyers in the office. Thompson had heard of his new office mate's propensity for all nighters. So as soon as Thompson landed his first high profile case, he enlisted The Fat Man's assistance. By design, in preparing the case for trial, Thompson outlasted The Fat Man in one of his multi-day office marathons. Word spread around the firm like wildfire that Thompson had out "Fat Manned" The Fat Man. It earned him the respect of all the lawyers in the firm, including The Fat Man.

Early on, Thompson had recognized a fact others in the firm had missed. Like many, who are referred to as genius, The Fat Man had some border-line obsessive compulsive tendencies. He didn't do odd things like wash his hands constantly throughout the day or walk around his car five times before getting in. However, once he had set his sights on a task, he was unable to think about anything else until the task was complete. Armed with that understanding, Thompson was the first lawyer at the firm able to figure out a way to harness and direct The Fat Man's obsessive energy to maximum effect. They became the team the firm wanted for the toughest of cases.

Following his introduction to Seattle's favorite coffee, The Fat Man began every day of his life in exactly the same manner— after a shower, he headed straight to Starbucks to meet with the Dunces. Once he had obtained his usual table (third from the door, chair facing east), he would turn the store's flat screen television to *ESPN*. Next, he would fire up his laptop computer. There he could ease into his day by checking his email, while listening to the sports stories from the night before. Above it all, there would be a steady banter of politics and headline issues among the Dunces. It was a multi-tasker's dream.

This particular morning, in between emails, The Fat Man was leading the Dunces in a rather esoteric and theoretical discussion about the impact recent interest rate cuts by the Federal Reserve were likely to have on the local Northern Kentucky economy, when one of the others in the store interrupted him.

"Hey, Joe," said the woman. "Check out *ESPN*. There is another story coming on about steroids." The Fat Man immediately quit talking to look at the television screen. The woman paused and then said to no one in particular, but loud enough for The Fat Man to hear, "Steroids in baseball is the one topic that gets him more fired up than interest rate cuts at the Fed."

The Fat Man cocked his head in her direction, mocked a dirty look and then turned his attention back to *ESPN*. The Fat Man's interest was peaked when a photo of John Gustine was flashed onto the screen, alongside a graphic depicting a bottle of pills and a hypodermic needle superimposed on a pile of sports equipment. "Turn it up," he shouted at the cashier. "Quick, turn it up!"

"And in other baseball news comes a sad story. Tom Harmon Award winning sports reporter John Gustine is dead. While the details of the story are still developing, Gustine was apparently the victim of a brutal robbery/murder yesterday outside a bar in Huntington Beach, California. John Gustine was the sports side of the pair of reporters for *The Los Angeles Journal* who had been publishing a series of stories on steroid use in professional sports. We're now joined live by his writing partner in those stories published by *The Journal*, investigative reporter, Joyce Lang. Joyce, welcome to the broadcast, although we wish it could be under better circumstances."

"Thanks, Zachary," said Joyce Lang. She was wearing an appropriately dark suit, but with a deep red blouse that projected no nonsense strength to the viewers. Her hair and makeup were perfect. "Obviously, we are all very shocked and saddened in the Los Angeles community about this senseless act of violence and the loss of our colleague and dear friend."

"Joyce, the two of you had teamed up on the series of stories about the use of performance enhancing drugs in professional sports," the anchor said. "Tell us what kind of guy he was."

"Well, John loved baseball," replied Lang. "He was really well liked and respected by the players. They all felt he had always been fair with them."

"How did the two of you link up?" asked Nate.

"John was a great sports reporter, but he didn't know much about the investigative side of the business," she said in an ever so slightly condescending tone. "Investigative reporting is a little more difficult than watching a ball game and writing about it. I was freelancing and *The Journal* wanted someone on the investigative side to assist John. That's why *The Journal* put the two of us together, so I could add some depth to his reporting."

"Maybe," said the anchor, "but, wasn't John generally credited recently with getting the break on the story that connected baseball superstar Donny Alberato to the death of his trainer Gregory Graham?"

"He was," said Lang, smiling but shifting an inch or two in her chair. "We are working on the follow up on that story, in order to make sure his efforts won't die with him. I'm taking over the stories solo and will make sure we get to the bottom of every lead John was developing."

"Thanks for being with us, Joyce," said the anchor. "John Gustine was 32 years old. The thoughts and prayers of everyone here at *ESPN* are with the family and friends of John Gustine."

"What a bitch," said the woman who had alerted The Fat Man to the screen.

"Meeoowww," laughed one of the men sitting at a table near her, while raking his right hand in a downward clawing motion.

"Are you kidding me," said the woman. "That woman was far more impressed with the fact she was appearing on *Sports Center* than she was sad about losing her writing partner. Did you see the outfit she was wearing? She's not in mourning. She's in the spot light."

"Aw, come on," said the man. "Give her a break."

"Break, hell," she replied. "That woman is a b-i-t-c-h, with a capital B."

"Too sensitive," said the man. He paused and looked at The Fat Man. "You've been following this steroid story, Joe. What do you think?"

The Fat Man was staring blankly at the television screen. His hands at the keyboard of his laptop computer were visibly shaking as they both turned toward him.

"Jesus," said the woman. "Are you all right, Joe? You look like you've just seen a ghost."

"I think I may have," mumbled The Fat Man as he tentatively pulled his cell phone from his pants pocket. His only decision was who to call first, Thompson or Argo.

Chapter 15

Josh Barkman walked into the private office of Richard Thompson with his personal cell phone in his hand. Thompson had just arrived back in the office from an Oversight Subcommittee meeting minutes before, but he was already on the phone, apparently starting into his list of return calls from the morning.

Josh took a look at his boss leaning back in his chair, looking out the window and listening intently on the phone. He thought to himself how natural Thompson looked in the position. *This guy was meant to be a Congressman*, Josh thought silently to himself. *He looks so damned comfortable in his position. If we only had 435 of him up here…*

Josh stopped in front of the Congressman's desk and got Thompson's attention.

"The Fat Man's on my cell phone for you," he said to the Congressman in a whisper loud enough for Thompson to get the message, as he held the cell phone up in the air.

Thompson held his thumb and forefinger about an inch apart indicating he was going to be on his current call for only a short time longer. Josh quietly relayed the message into the cell phone to The Fat Man. "I let him know you are on the line. It's been a shitty day so far, Mr. Joseph. Apparently, some Kentucky lobbyist is leaking all kinds of crap to a New York tabloid about the Congressman and we're responding to it. It is mostly bullshit. No one will believe it about the Boss, but it sure is a bad way to start the day."

On the land line, Thompson sounded like he was wrapping up. "Again Joyce, my sincerest condolences to you and everyone at *The Journal*. Like I told you, I only met him one time, but I had read his stories over the years. He was a great writer and a good guy. The sports world is going to miss him."

Thompson leaned forward in his chair and picked up a baseball from his chair. He casually tossed it from one hand to the other while listening. "Well, he certainly knew baseball as well as any reporter whose work I ever read. The baseball world has certainly lost one of its champions."

Another pause. Apparently, another question. "We're pushing forward on the steroid issue, Joyce. The integrity of America's pastime is at stake here. It is up to Congress to come up with some answers. We need to make sure when a family goes to a ball game, they are comfortable everyone in the lineup has a level playing field. In answer to the second part of your question, if we find evidence Donny Alberato perjured himself before our committee, I expect we will turn that evidence over to the appropriate authorities. We can't prosecute ourselves, but we can certainly find him in contempt of Congress if he lied."

He rolled his eyes at Josh and paused again for what he hoped was the final question. "I've got a political event in LaGrange, Kentucky, on Saturday. I'm going with my wife to a Republican Women's Club luncheon there. Then on Sunday, I'm headed to the ball park on Sunday to watch the Reds play. In fact, here's a quote for you about John. Baseball fans are prone to say that if you miss the first pitch, you miss the whole game. Well, on Sunday, I'll be thinking of John when the first pitch hits the mitt."

He paused. "Sure, you can use that in the story. Everything I said was meant to be on the record." He paused again, making a strained face at Josh, in mock exasperation at the growing length of the call. "Well, I'm glad you will be continuing the stories now that he's gone. Feel free to call me anytime. If I'm not around ask for Josh Barkman. He's my Chief of Staff. He'll always know how to get a hold of me on short notice...you too...good bye."

"Thanks for giving my name to another reporter," Josh said as he handed the cell phone to Thompson. "At least you didn't give her my personal cell number, like you did for Mr. Bradley."

"What's up, man?" Thompson said into the phone as he smiled up at Josh.

"I've been trying to reach you all morning," said The Fat Man in a frantic tone. "Where the hell have you been?"

"Doing the people's business. Keeping the nation safe for democracy. You know, the usual stuff. I was going to call you in a few minutes. I've been in a hearing all morning and the phone was ringing when I walked in the office a couple of minutes ago."

"Well, I've been calling all morning trying to get you," replied The Fat Man. "When I couldn't get you, I figured I should call Josh."

"What's the problem?" asked Thompson. "Are the Reds trying to trade one of your fantasy team players again?"

"No, man. This is serious. Did you hear about John Gustine?" asked The Fat Man.

"Yeah," said Thompson. "I just got off the phone with Joyce Lang, his partner in writing the steroid stories. What a horrible tragedy."

"Horrible tragedy?" asked The Fat Man incredulously.

"It sounds like it," said Thompson. "Apparently, he was mugged outside a bar in Huntington Beach."

"You've got to be kidding me?" The Fat Man said, nearly shouting his response into the phone.

"Kidding you?" asked Thompson. "Kidding you about what?"

"About what?" The Fat Man asked rhetorically. "Do you believe John Gustine's death was some sort of street crime gone bad?"

"I'm not following you," said Thompson with all sincerity.

"You aren't one bit curious about why this guy ends up dead right after he prints your leak on Donny Alberato being connected to the murder of Greg Graham?" asked The Fat Man.

"Oh, God, Joe, please don't start. I'm having a bad enough week as it is," pleaded Thompson.

"What do you mean by that?" asked The Fat Man. "Don't start."

"You know exactly what I mean," said Thompson. "I can hear the gears in your head turning all the way from here. You are already trying to link together pieces into a grand conspiracy puzzle that just isn't there."

"How do you know that?" The Fat Man asked in a voice that was somewhere between sheepish and peevish.

"Because you believe there is a conspiracy associated with just about every action which transpires on this earth," Thompson replied.

"Not every action," said The Fat Man.

"Why did the Reds trade Tony Perez?" asked Thompson.

"The Reds general manager was told to do it by the Commissioner of Baseball over fear of creating a dynasty in a small market town," The Fat Man replied. "If a small market dominated baseball, television revenues would plummet and baseball would collapse. Perez had to be traded to save revenues in baseball. Why?"

"See," said Thompson. "I rest my case. Every time you find a situation where there is an answer you don't understand or accept, you obsess about it until you put together a grand conspiracy."

"All right, so I may need a little more proof on the Tony Perez trade," replied The Fat Man. "But, I've got a pretty strong gut on this Gustine murder."

"Joe," said Thompson. "You've got a pretty strong gut on everything."

"Hey, that hurts," laughed The Fat Man at the reference to his rotund figure. "I've got feelings too, you know."

"That's not what I meant and you know it," said Thompson.

"I know what you meant," said The Fat Man. "No offense taken. Just please listen to me. I'm worried. There are a lot of people who are on Donny Alberato's 'shit list' who are dead right now."

"So your theory is Donny Alberato had Graham killed to shut him up and now he's had John Gustine killed for writing about it. Is that what you are saying?" asked Thompson.

"Well, somebody sure as hell killed him," The Fat man responded. "I called Argo this morning…"

"You didn't bother Leo with this crap about Gustine, did you, Joe?" Thompson interjected.

"Damn right I did," replied The Fat Man. "I called him before I tried to call you the first time."

"Thanks," said Thompson.

"He's easier to get a hold of," said The Fat Man.

"All right, you got Leo," said Thompson. "What does he think? Was Donny Alberato on the grassy knoll in Dallas the day Kennedy was shot?"

"Very funny," said The Fat Man.

"Or is he a 'black helicopter' pilot in the off-season?" continued Thompson.

"Knock it off, Rick—I'm serious here," The Fat Man interjected. "And Reagan did start the black helicopters back when he was Governor of California."

"I know you are serious, Joe, and that's what bothers me. You are serious, which means you are not going to stop weaving theories on this until you drive both of us nuts." Thompson paused. He didn't want to hurt The Fat Man's feelings, so he went ahead and asked the question again: "So what did Agent Argo have to say about Gustine?"

"Leo says the FBI is treating it as mugging right now. They are letting the Orange County Police Department handle the investigation, but they are having their local office monitor it."

"See, Joey, even Leo and his boys don't see Lee Harvey out there on this one," said Thompson.

"Somehow, I knew you were going to work Oswald into the conversation," said The Fat Man. "I'm just worried you are on Donny Alberato's, or whoever's, list out there somewhere."

"I know you are worried, man," replied Thompson. "That's why I need you around. I need someone watching my back I can trust. Let's not overreact this time. Let's not get all fired up until we need to. All right?"

"All right," replied The Fat Man. Purposefully changing subjects, he asked: "Hey, are we still going to the ball game on Sunday?"

"It's on the schedule," replied Thompson.

"Yeah, I know," said The Fat Man. "I just thought since it was a Sunday game, you might want to stay home with Ann."

"Naw, it's a little tense around the Thompson household right now," Thompson said sheepishly. "I'm not sure Ann won't be happier with me out of the house rather than in it."

"Ann's still not fully adjusted to being the wife of a Congressman, I guess?"

"I'm not sure what it is," Thompson said. "I know something is up. I've not seen her in this kind of a funk since we moved home from D.C.. Forget about Donny Alberato. If anyone wants to have me killed right now, it may well be my wife."

Chapter 16

There are no custom driven black Lincoln Town Cars for staffers when they are asked to leave the Hill to go downtown for a morning meeting or an afternoon panel discussion. Rides downtown in soft leather comfort, with the morning paper folded neatly on the back seat, are reserved for Members.

Public transportation is the stuff of staffer trips. Normally, Josh Barkman would use the Metro subway system. It was quick, clean and convenient. He could jump on the Blue Line at Capitol South and be downtown in a matter of twenty minutes, or so. The newspaper wasn't neatly folded and waiting for him, but the time on the subway would give him a chance to catch up on his daily reading. He would zip through the Kentucky headlines provided to Thompson and him each morning by the staff press secretary. Then, he would catch up on the Federal pages of the *Times* and the *Post*. If it was a good day, he would even have a minute or two extra to read the sports section.

On this day however, due to the calls his boss had been getting all morning, Josh was running late. He had to grab a cab outside the Longworth Building. With the sights and sounds of the city rushing past him, he found it hard to read. It's tough to get into the Washington Nationals' box score when you've got to pay attention to the traffic for the unassuming taxi cab drivers of the nation's capital, for fear they will hit somebody with their cab.

He loved to talk to the cabbies, especially the older ones who had been on the road for decades. One day, he found himself in the cab of an old man who remembered the red light district located where the Air and Space Museum sits today. Franklin Roosevelt was the cabbie's favorite president, because Eleanor had insisted the whore houses be torn down.

Unfortunately for Josh, there was no interesting banter today—just another day in the seat of the greatest democracy in the world. But, for Josh Barkman on this particular day, that was good enough.

When he jumped out of the cab on Connecticut Avenue in front of the historic Mayflower Hotel, he was right on schedule.

The Mayflower is one of the historic, old-line hotels in the heart of downtown D.C.. Its lobby and conference rooms are as ornate as the United States Capitol itself. Ornamental gold leaf cherubs and animals surround the ceilings and portraits of the Founding Fathers adorn the walls. The Mayflower is said to contain more gold trim than any other building in D.C., except the Library of Congress. President Harry Truman lived there while the White House was being refurbished and FDR was said to have written his famous line "we have nothing to fear, but fear itself" in one of its rooms. Federal Bureau of Investigation director, J. Edgar Hoover, had lunch there daily.

When you cross through the gold revolving doors, which take you from the hot D.C. streets to the cool warmth of the marble floors in The Mayflower, you can almost smell the power and money in the air.

Just as The Mayflower is famous for its old city charm, it is infamous for the sex scandals it has borne over the past several decades. President John Kennedy kept his mistress at The Mayflower so she could drop by the White House when Jackie was out of town. Monica Lewinsky stayed at The Mayflower throughout much of the news coverage of her affair with President Bill Clinton. .

As Josh entered the lobby, he remembered he was in the building where former New York Governor Elliott Spitzer was forced to resign over a one-nighter of kinky sex with a $4,800 per night call-girl. He laughed to himself and wondered if sex with a $4,800 hooker was somehow any better than the sex he had with the college intern he picked up in Georgetown last weekend.

As Richard Thompson's stock in D.C. had suddenly risen due to the leadership role he was playing on the steroids issue, so had Josh Barkman's. He was being asked downtown to fill-in on panel discussions for D.C. trade associations and recognized as "someone" by college interns in Georgetown. It was enough to make any twenty-something kid feel much wiser than his years. Luckily, Josh had Thompson and Griffith to keep his head in check.

This morning, Josh was joining three other staffers on a stage backed by red velvet curtains to speak to a meeting of the National Sportswriters and Sportscasters Association on the implications to the sports community of mandatory steroid testing for professional and amateur athletes. The trio around Josh represented the wide breadth of people who work on the Hill.

First to speak was an older woman who was a Capitol Hill lifer. In her thirty years on the Hill, she had made her way through the ranks of staff positions for several Members to become chief counsel to the Judiciary Subcommittee on Oversight. She had planned the Florida subcommittee hearing at spring training and she had been on the field with Richard Thompson when Kevin O'Toole died. She spoke first; the authority of her gray hair (like the staff ID dangling from a link chain around her neck) set the stage for those to follow.

She spoke of the historical influx of performance enhancing drugs into professional and amateur athletics and the efforts of Congress to regulate them. When she spoke of the late Kevin O'Toole and the work he had done in the field, she did so with the reverence reserved for those who have attained greatness. It was clear the woman not only admired O'Toole, but respected him for his convictions. Josh listened to her comments closely, seeking some guidance from a senior staffer on what the remainder of the year might bring in committee.

Her closing comments caught Josh a bit off-guard.

"…but the mission will be carried on by the boss of one of our speakers today. Richard Thompson may not have been as good of a ball player as Kevin O'Toole, but his heart is just as big. He believes in this issue and I suspect the future of this issue lies with him and him alone. I look forward to the comments by Josh Barkman to see how he and his boss intend to shepherd this issue to the floor."

The young personal staffer of a House Judiciary Committee member was next to address the group. Slightly disheveled in his crumpled white button-down shirt, this staffer had prepared for his five minute presentation as if it were his own confirmation hearing for a seat on the United States Supreme Court. The audience quickly got past the fact his pants were about an inch too short for his height, as he went through stacks of papers which set out the statistical basis for his argument that steroids had totally ingrained themselves into baseball.

Constantly pushing his thick rimmed glasses back up the bridge of his nose, the man compared the recent successful seasons of Donny Alberato to the best seasons of Hall of Famers Babe Ruth and Jimmy Foxx. The Bambino's best year offensively was 1921, when he hit 59 home runs and batted .379. Jimmy Foxx had a similar season in 1932 when he hit 58 dingers. The only major difference in their statistics was that Babe had his best year when he was 26. Despite a long career, Jimmy Foxx had his historic season when he was 24. Donny Alberato's numbers were at their peak when he was 34.

The sports writers appreciated the thoroughness of the presentation and scribbled furiously in their pads as the speaker threw stats at them like a high and tight fast ball. Josh even made note of a few of the stats himself.

A young male staffer from the Senate side was next. Josh took notice of his blue striped shirt, leather suspenders and maroon bow tie. He laughed to himself at the jokes made by House staffers at the expense of their Senate counterparts, but this guy fit the stereotype of the Senate staffer from the tip of his well coiffed head to the tip of his Gucci shoes.

It was clear from his demeanor he thought as much of himself as of the Senator for whom he worked and he was speaking at this event to promote himself as much as his boss. He carried himself with the arrogance reserved for those on the Senate side of the Capitol and spoke of his boss (as well as himself) in the third person. He was clearly the most intelligent person on the panel…all you had to do was ask him.

Sportswriters have a way of ignoring the prima donna, on the field and off. They appeared to do so with this particular staffer as most in the audience checked their blackberries for messages from the office and browsed *ESPN* updates as he spoke.

Finally, it was Josh Barkman's turn to address the audience. He had decided to keep his presentation short and tell the audience about a new piece of legislation the Congressman was going to introduce in the coming weeks. He explained Congressman Thompson's belief that baseball and the players' union would never come to an agreement on an acceptable testing protocol for performance enhancing drugs. Thompson, therefore, was going to introduce legislation forcing testing and stiffening penalties for those caught using those drugs.

"Congressman Thompson believes if there is not a tough penalty for the user, the problem will continue. Furthermore, Congressman Thompson will ask the Chairman of the House Judiciary Committee to hold hearings on baseball's antitrust exemption and how antiquated federal policy impacts the attitudes of management towards the issue."

With the calculated addition of the "antitrust exemption" into the discussion, Josh got the attention of more than just the sportswriters in the room. Sitting in the back of the room, M.T. Stacy scribbled a note onto his yellow legal pad.

In 1922, the United States Supreme Court ruled baseball was not interstate commerce and, therefore, exempt from the nation's antitrust laws. Of course, the rationale for the decision is absurd by today's standards (and probably those of 1922, as well). In subsequent decisions, the Supreme Court explicitly left it up to Congress to change its ruling and, with the same lack of diligence which baseball displayed in failing to attack greenie abuse, Congress has ignored the high court's ruling for nearly a century.

Not that the issue hasn't been raised on occasion. With the exemption intact, baseball is able to control the number as well as the ownership of its teams. Baseball, in its infinite wisdom, has only expanded the number of teams on the rare occasions when Congress has threatened to apply antitrust laws to the business of baseball.

Many of today's teams exist because someone in Congress threatened to repeal the antitrust exemption. It is the ultimate stick to be used against baseball.

No one, not even Kevin O'Toole, had threatened removal of the antitrust exemption over the steroid issue.

Josh had their attention. "In fact," he said, "if baseball fails to act by the end of the current season, Congressman Thompson will not only just ask the Congress to strike down the exemption entirely—he has pledged to lead the effort to do so. In preparation for the introduction of legislation, Congressman Thompson will today ask the Congressional Budget Office to investigate and issue a report on the economic advantages an owner of a baseball club receives as a result of the exemption. If baseball fails to act on its own accord, you can expect a call from my boss when the report comes out in the fall."

Josh looked over at the first speaker, the gray haired staffer, as he finished his remarks. The older woman nodded her approval.

As they broke from the panel, the older staffer walked with Josh to the door, chit-chatting about how each was planning on getting back to the Hill. Before they reached the door, M.T. Stacy approached the pair.

"Hi, Barkman," he said. "I'm M.T. Stacy with the Commissioner's office."

Josh returned the pleasantry and stuck out his hand. Stacy didn't make a move to return the gesture and went right to his point.

"Those were some pretty strong words in there," he said. "I hope those words were the bravado of a young staffer and not the true feelings of his boss."

"Excuse me?" said Josh, taken back by both the man's refusal to shake his hand and his quick, rude attack.

"Well you know, boy, baseball is pretty damned popular in your boss's district. You've got a big league club right across the river. Hell, a bunch of players live in your district. I would hate like hell to have to get all those people working against you in the next election."

"Are you threatening the Congressman?" asked Josh.

"I'm not threatening, son," said the stocky man. "I'm just stating facts."

"I don't know who you are," said Josh, "but you are way out of line."

"I'm not out of line," said Stacy. "I know precisely where the line is located. I don't think you do. You and your boss better figure out where the line is and watch your step."

Chapter 17

Dulles International Airport in suburban Northern Virginia is a wonderful aviation facility. About 25 miles from downtown D.C., it was dedicated in 1962 by President John F. Kennedy and named after the former Secretary of State, John Foster Dulles. It boasts two parallel runways and one cross-wind strip. The terminals are first-class.

It is also rarely used by Members of Congress traveling to and from work.

When it was built, the plan was for Dulles to replace the facility now known as Reagan National Airport. Located in Crystal City, Virginia, the sole jet runway for National juts out into the Potomac River. The runway is very short and cannot accommodate larger aircraft. Additionally, night landings are restricted due to the airport's proximity to local neighborhoods.

So why was National never closed in place of Dulles?

The answer is simple: Congress.

Reagan National Airport is located on land on the Virginia side of the Potomac River. However, most of it sits on land which was originally underwater and was filled in to accommodate the short runway. Technically, Reagan National Airport was part of the District of Columbia until a 1945 law declared National Airport to be located in Virginia. Not surprisingly, that same law placed the control and regulation of the airport in the hands of Congress.

From 1962 until the mid eighties, there were multiple attempts to close National Airport. All efforts were thwarted by Congress, whose Members enjoyed the convenience of an airport within eyesight of the Capitol dome. Congressman Gene Snyder, from Thompson's own Fourth District in Kentucky, was the ranking Member of the Subcommittee on Aviation during those attempts.

Democrats and Republicans alike would stand up on the floor of the House and publicly demand the closure of National Airport. Afterwards, they would drop by Snyder's office in the Rayburn Building for the nightly gin rummy game and privately ask the Congressman to use his parliamentary skills to kill the action they had called for only hours earlier.

Eventually, rather than shutting down, National modernized its facilities to get the most out of its short runway. An old hanger was converted into a modern terminal and National was reborn. Convinced the modernization insured the facility so convenient for the use of its own Members would not be closed, Congress relinquished control of National Airport in 1987. It was re-named after President Ronald Reagan in 1998.

For the most part, the modernized facility works well. However, getting 18.5 million people annually through security at an airport located within one aeronautical mile of the Capitol, the White House and the Pentagon can be a challenge. It has some of the longest security lines in the country.

Late Thursday afternoon, as Richard Thompson stood in one of those long lines to catch his flight home, he got a call from Michael Griffith.

"Hey, boy," said Griffith. "You at National yet?"

"Yeah," Thompson replied. "I'm in the security line. It seems to get longer every week."

"Well, then it's wheels up in the Longworth Building," replied Griffith.

"It's funny, Griff," said Thompson. "They really think I don't know what goes on after I leave on Thursday. They seem to forget I was a staffer and know 'wheels up' is the official start of the weekend."

"You ought to skip the flight home one Thursday," laughed Griffith. "Have Josh drop you off at the airport. I'll pick you up and we will circle back to the office about 45 minutes later. That would fuck with their young brains."

"Oh my God," Thompson replied. "I couldn't do that to Josh. Could you imagine his face if we walked in just as they toasted with bourbon that I was gone for the weekend? He would die on the spot."

"Oh, let's do it," Griffith said with devilish encouragement.

"Naw," said Thompson. "He put together a good team. You remember when I was a staffer? The Thursday afternoon 'wheels up' party is an important part of building office morale. Let the kids think they are getting away with something."

"Fine," said Griffith. "Just don't get pissed if I join them one Thursday afternoon. I want to see if I can still run with the young pups."

"You have my permission," Thompson replied. "But don't expect me to pull your ass out of bed when they run you into the ground."

"Hey, I do have one piece of business to discuss," said Griffith. "I'm going into the field with a new survey on Monday before I head off overseas. I want an over sample on this steroid issue."

"Why?" asked Thompson.

"Well, I'm not sure it's going to help us in the re-elect," Griffith replied.

"I don't care," replied Thompson. "It is the right thing to do."

"I know you feel strongly about it," Griffith interjected. "I'm just not sure it doesn't have a down side. There are a lot of issues out there affecting the country right now. The economy is on a slide and unemployment is up. We're fighting a couple of conflicts overseas—and you are all fired up about baseball. I'm afraid we will get some kinda voter backlash over it. I just want to test and see if it's out there, that's all."

Thompson sighed heavily into the phone.

"Hey, man," said Griffith. "Just because you are my friend, don't expect me to treat you special. I would be saying this to any candidate I work for. In the original *Godfather,* what did Tom Hagin ask Michael Corleone at his father's funeral? Do you remember?"

"No," said Thompson. "I don't remember."

"Hagin asked Michael, 'Do you know how they are going to come at you?'" said Griffith. "At the old man's funeral, they were discussing strategy about how the other bosses were going to run at Mike. Well, I've got to do pretty much the same thing for you. I've got to know how they are going to come at you. I just happen to care more because it's you."

"All right," said Thompson. "Put it in the field. Just don't expect me to squish out if you get a bad result."

"I won't, man," said Griffith. "I just need to know what I'm up against next year. Have a good weekend and give Annie my love."

"I will," said Thompson. "Call me when you get back from running that campaign across the pond. Good luck."

Thompson hung up his phone and put his iPod headset over his ears while he dialed up *Pilgrim Chapter 33* by Kris Kristofferson. After a long and trying week, it was probably a bad song for him to listen to, because it always caused him to reflect on his own life.

> *See him wasted on the sidewalk in his jacket and his jeans,*
> *Wearin' yesterday's misfortunes like a smile,*
> *Once he had a future full of money, love and dreams,*
> *Which he spent like they was goin' outa' style,*
> *And he keeps right on achangin' for the better or the worse,*
> *Searchin' for a shrine he's never found,*
> *Never knowin' if believin' is a blessin' or a curse,*
> *Or if the goin' up was worth the comin' down.*

"That's my damn problem," Thompson mumbled out loud to no one in particular. "I can't figure out if believing is a blessing or a curse."

Thompson felt embarrassed when a smartly dressed woman in line in front of him looked back and smiled, indicating he had been talking at least loud enough for her to hear his meanderings.

"Sorry," he pleaded. He could feel his face turning red.

"Not a problem," she replied, looking at his Congressional lapel pin and recognizing its significance. "By the way, from my standpoint, believing is a blessing."

"Thanks," Thompson replied, as he readjusted the headset and continued to listen to the song.

*He has tasted good and evil in your bedrooms and your
    bars,
And he's traded in tomorrow for today,
Runnin' from his devils, lord and reachin' for the stars,
And losin' all he's loved along the way,
But if this world keeps right on turnin' for the better or the
    worse,
And all he ever gets is older and around,
From the rockin' of the cradle to the rollin' of the hearse,
The goin' up was worth the comin' down.*

Thompson thought to himself, *I've done it again*, this time
not sharing his thoughts with others in the line for a security check.
He shook his head as the chorus to the song played in his ears.
*I've put myself in a situation where being a believer has put me
at odds with what's best for myself. I didn't run from my devils
and look what it got me.*

He shuffled a few feet forward as the line slowly moved
toward the security checkpoint. *This is fucking unbelievable,* he
thought.

*My staff is getting threatened by people when they go out in
public. My one best friend thinks I'm on the hit list of a juiced up
All Star baseball player. My other best friend thinks I'm throwing
away my career on a whim and the issues I believe in might get
me beat. I've cooperated in an FBI leak to a now-dead reporter.
And, now, on top of everything else, Ann's pissed off at me for
whatever reason it is today.*

As these thoughts crowded into Thompson's mind, the
expression on his face grew darker and darker.

One nice addition to the hanger-turned-terminal at Reagan
National airport is Delta's Crown Room. It's a comfortable room
with plenty of chairs and tables to accommodate those who travel
enough to use it regularly. The one feature unique to this particular
Crown Room is a full length window stretching across the entire
side of it which overlooks the unsecured side of the terminal
(including the security line Thompson was now in). Thompson

would be there in a few minutes where he would grab a chair facing the window, wait for the boarding call for his flight back to Kentucky and maybe stop feeling sorry for himself.

But for now, a man Thompson would not have recognized stood at the window making notes on his pad as he watched Thompson make his way up the line.

Chapter 18

It was early in the evening when Emily Reed pulled the car into the Thompson's driveway and raised the garage door. She did so with such familiarity anyone observing from the street would have thought she was entering her own house. Anyone who drew that conclusion would not have been far off. Ever since Richard Thompson had chosen Reed to be his District Director, she was at Thompson's house so often she felt like it was becoming her second home.

The interaction of the district staff with the Member is quite different from that of the Washington staff.

As soon as it's "wheels up" for staff in D.C., the Member becomes the responsibility of the staff back home. The direct line of accountability falls to the District Director or the District Field Representative. Not only is that person the face of the Congressman during the week while he or she is in D.C., but the two are seemingly joined at the hip whenever the Member leaves his home.

More than D.C. staff, the district field staff gets to see the Member as he or she actually is. They accompany the Member and the spouse everywhere and get to see them in situations in their normal life at home. They get to see the Member's house in the early hours of a weekend morning, when kids are running around in pajamas and dirty dishes are in the sink. They hear the personal conversations of spouses during the long drives, arguments and all. They see Members and their families at their best as well as their worst.

Familiarity better not breed contempt in these relationships because the district staffers know too damn much.

A few months before, back when Thompson was hiring his top staff in his district office, he got a call from his campaign manager, Michael Griffith, to recite another one of the lessons Griffith had taught the new Congressman from watching *The Godfather* trilogy of movies. "Remember, be like Don Corleone," advised Griffith. "Find yourself a Luca Brazi. Find someone back home who is so loyal they will sleep with the fishes just to protect you."

Emily Reed had turned out to be Richard Thompson's Luca Brazi. She was smart and knew how to handle herself in any situation. Most importantly, her loyalty was as fierce as her long, bright red hair.

This particular day, she had been driving Thompson and his wife to an event at the far western end of the Congressional District in the Thompson family car.

"Thanks, Em," said Thompson as the car pulled into the garage. "You know we appreciate it."

"Yeah, hon," interjected Ann. "Thanks for giving up another Saturday." Ann was doing her best to sound sincere and appreciative. The aggravation she was feeling had nothing to do with Emily Reed.

"Not a problem, Mrs. Thompson," replied Emily. "It's part of the job I signed up for. Glad to do it."

"You know, Ann's an old D.C. staffer herself," said Thompson trying to interject some humor into what had been an otherwise tense day on the trail. "You might convince her some day district staffers are actually of some value."

Ann ignored the comment and walked directly into the house.

"Sorry about today, Emily," said Thompson. "Things are a little tense around here these days."

"Yeah, I gathered that," replied Emily. "I hope I didn't do anything to hurt the situation."

"Naw, kiddo," said Thompson as he walked Emily out to her car on the tree-lined suburban street. "It's got nothing to do with you. We both appreciate what you give up to do this job. I hope you know that."

"Thanks, Boss," Emily said. "I'm doing my best."

"I know," said Thompson. "Unfortunately, you get to see all sides of us, don't you?"

"Ah, it wasn't that bad," replied Emily. "Enjoy the ball game tomorrow and we will get back at it on Monday. You've got a week at home for the District Work Period next week. You and Ann can get some quality nights together and get back on track."

Thompson appreciated the young woman's weak attempt at playing marriage counselor. However, he knew it *had* been that bad of a day for all concerned.

The hour and a half trip west from Northern Kentucky had started out peaceful enough. The trio sipped on coffee, read the daily papers and talked about the state of the party in Oldham County.

At the western edge of the Fourth Congressional District, a town called LaGrange is the county seat of Oldham County, Kentucky. Located just up the Ohio River from Louisville, Oldham County was once a sleepy rural county with tobacco farms and a state penitentiary. Then, thirty some years ago, a Federal judge ordered busing as the judicial answer for school integration in Louisville. Shortly thereafter, Oldham County became the text book county in America for "white flight," as people from Louisville began to develop the suburban tobacco farms into subdivisions filled with high-priced homes and the occasional McMansion.

An outsider passing through the community on the main roads might not be able to see the changes that have happened over the years. Downtown La Grange is still an old-fashioned little gathering place of aged buildings filled with antique shops, small family run restaurants and the county courthouse.

Politically, however, the Republican Party in the county tends to split like LaGrange itself, which is physically divided down the full length of Main Street by railroad tracks.

The influx of outsiders caused a rift that has never healed. At one time during the era when Thompson's predecessor Garrett Jackson held the Congressional seat, there were three separate women's auxiliary clubs for the party. The county party had so many factions that, one year, they had two separate Lincoln Day dinners to honor the founder of the Grand Old Party.

Ann, Emily and Thompson had discussed the history of the divide on the drive down to LaGrange and the apparent truce currently holding the battling groups together, if only for a time.

Unfortunately, the discussion of a family divide in the Republican Party seemed to work its way into Ann and Richard Thompson's personal interaction the moment they arrived at The Garden Party, a restaurant located on Main Street which was owned by one of Thompson's supporters.

The Garden Party was located in a grand old southern style red brick building, with large white pillars outlining the parameters of its front porch. A wrought iron railing encased a deck on the second floor. The building would fit perfectly into the set of any movie which depicted the old South. It was a favorite stop of Richard and Ann Thompson when traveling in the area. They had brunch there before every Kentucky Derby they had ever attended.

But today wasn't the Derby.

It was politics.

Richard Thompson was one of those people who goes through life with a soundtrack constantly running in his head. He was never at a loss for a song to fit any given situation. As Emily pulled the car into a parking space in front of the little café, Thompson began singing the final verse to the Ricky Nelson classic bearing the same name as the restaurant:

> *"If you go to a garden party,*
> *I wish you lots of luck,*
> *But, if memories were all I had,*
> *I'd rather drive a truck."*

Emily, familar with her boss' quirky habit for singing weird songs, started singing the chorus along with him—*"But it's all right now, I learned my lesson well"*—when Ann cut them both off.

"For God's sake," snapped Ann, "do you have to sing a song for every goddamn situation? Can't we just go in, do our thing and get the hell out?"

Emily looked at Thompson for guidance. She was used to seeing the Thompson family in its most private state, but she had never seen the pair in an antagonistic moment. She had never seen this side of Ann Thompson before and she didn't quite know how to react. Frankly, Thompson hadn't seen this side of his wife for years and couldn't provide Emily any cover or advice. He looked at her with raised eyebrows and shrugged his shoulders, but said nothing.

As Thompson exited the car, a smartly dressed woman with perfectly styled blond hair approached him.

"Congressman Thompson?" asked the woman. Before waiting for a response she stuck out her hand in apparent friendship and continued, "Joyce Lang with *The Los Angeles Journal*. We spoke Thursday on the phone."

"Well, yes, we did," said Thompson, more than a bit surprised at her presence in La Grange, Kentucky. "You didn't mention you would be covering me during my weekend schedule."

"I didn't know it at the time myself," she replied as Thompson and Lang walked up the steps of The Garden Party together, following Ann and Emily into the restaurant. "After we spoke, my editors wanted me to come out and cover one of your events. You said on the phone you were speaking here today, so I snooped around and found the details. I flew into Louisville this morning."

"Geez," said Thompson. "If I had known you were coming to Kentucky, I would have planned a different event."

"We don't want a planned event, Congressman," replied Lang. "We want to see you in action in your day-to-day activities."

"Fair enough," said Thompson. "I just don't think you will find this event too interesting."

"Oh, it is amazing what reporters find interesting," said Lang. "I'll find something here."

"I just mean I won't be talking about steroids at this event," said Thompson.

"That's exactly what we want for this story," she replied. "I want to see if your constituents even care about your position on steroids."

"I would guess many of them aren't even aware of it," replied Thompson, hoping to lower expectations for the responses she might receive. "These folks here are more concerned about the economy than baseball."

"You are probably right," said Lang. "Today will draw a great contrast for tomorrow."

"Tomorrow?" asked Thompson.

"I'll also be going to Great American Ball Park for the game tomorrow," said Lang. "You are still going to the game tomorrow, aren't you?"

"Yeah," said Thompson with noticeable reluctance in his voice. "But I would really rather not have to talk steroids there. Tomorrow is my day off. I'm going to the park just to watch a ball game, not to do Congressional work."

"Come on, Congressman," said Lang. "Los Angeles is in town."

"So?" said Thompson.

"So?" replied Lang in chuckling disbelief. "Donny Alberato is going to be playing tomorrow. The two of you haven't been in the same place together since you skewered him on *ESPN* during spring training. This is round two."

"It's not round two. It's just a trip out to a ball game on my day off," said Thompson. "The fact it's L.A. is purely coincidence."

"I find that hard to believe," said Lang.

"Donny Alberato won't even know I'm in the park," Thompson countered.

"Oh, yes he will," Lang quickly responded.

"How?" asked Thompson, already guessing the answer he was about to receive.

"I called his agent to ask for a comment about it," Lang said.

"Please don't turn this into a big deal," begged Thompson politely. "I'm just going to the park to watch a game. I really don't want to do so with a reporter following me the whole day."

"I don't intend to shadow you tomorrow," said Lang. "I'm not a sports person, Congressman. That was John's beat. He understood this fan crap. I don't. So I want to go to the game tomorrow and talk to fans about steroids in baseball. The added fact that you and Alberato get to make eye contact is just a bonus for me."

She paused as they entered the room where the event was being held. "Today I just want to watch you in action and, judging from the looks we're getting from your audience, you had better get to work."

"Well, then let's have at it," said Thompson. There was a distinct lack of enthusiasm in his reply now he understood the angle of Lang's story.

Thompson began working the crowd of women in the room, introducing himself, his wife and Emily simultaneously to each.

"What was that all about?" whispered Ann as they made their way around the room.

"Nothing much," sighed Thompson. "She's just a reporter from *The Los Angeles Journal* in town to do a hatchet job on me."

After mingling for the short reception period, Thompson updated the ladies on what was happening in Washington.

Every Member of Congress has their standard stump speech they do back home to constituent groups. The speech laces the issues of the day with funny stories about how they are adjusting to life in D.C.. The speech is meant to talk current national issues while trying to convince the audience the Member is still "one of them." It's easy for freshmen Members, like Thompson, to pull it off in a crowd. However, as Members increase their seniority on the Hill, it becomes increasingly more difficult for them to convince anyone they are "just one of the folks back home."

As Thompson gave his speech, he looked around the room repeatedly, unable to find his wife. Then, through a reflection in a mirror located in the back of the room, he could see Ann standing alone on the front porch of the restaurant smoking a cigarette, something he hadn't seen her do since her drinking days in D.C..

The observation threw Thompson off his rhythm and he stumbled through the remainder of his speech.

The drive home was pretty quiet. Thompson's apologies to

Emily as she headed to her car did not fully abate the awkwardness, embarrassment and anger Thompson was feeling.

Thompson had never seen his wife act quite this way in front of others before. As he entered the house through the garage, Ann stood waiting in the family room for the question which was bound to start the fight both knew was coming. Both of them knew the kids were at grandma's house, so there wasn't the deterrent of children observing them to keep the inevitable from happening right away.

"What the hell is eating at you?" asked Thompson.

"Not now, Richard," replied Ann in an exasperated tone as she walked away from her husband.

"Yes, now," said Thompson as he followed her into the dining room with a deliberate pace. The pace of the pair was so quick the family dog, a black Labrador, thought it was play time. She picked up her yellow tennis ball and followed closely behind, hoping someone would play ball with her.

"I really don't have the energy for this tonight," said Ann as she took off her earrings and tossed them onto the dining room table.

"And you think I do?" asked Thompson. "It was a long week. I'm physically and mentally exhausted."

"You are in better shape than me," said Ann.

"What the hell is that supposed to mean?" Thompson asked, his voice rising in anger.

"I don't know, Richard," said Ann. "I just know this whole Congressional wife thing is quickly wearing on me."

"Well, you had better get used to it," snapped Thompson. "It's not like we can go backwards now."

"Gee, thanks for the empathy," said Ann. Now she was really starting to get angry.

"Empathy?" Thompson asked. "You've got to be kidding me. You are looking for empathy."

"Yeah," replied Ann, as she took off her shoes and tossed them in the hall closet. "I could use a little dose of it right now."

Thompson fired back. "Instead of wanting empathy, how about providing a little support? Or gratitude...gratitude would be nice?"

"Gratitude?" asked Ann. "Gratitude for what?"

"Look around you, Ann," said Thompson. "Look at all of this. I've provided a pretty good life for you and the kids. I'm working my ass off right now, under pressure you can't even imagine, for us to have a lifestyle we only dreamed about when we got married."

"What the hell is that supposed to mean?" asked Ann. "That I'm driven by materialistic things in life? That I'm not working at this as hard as you? What is happening here is not driven by materialism."

She stormed up the staircase toward their second floor master suite.

"Then what is it being driven by?" Thompson asked. "Because something is happening here and I sure as hell can't figure it out."

"That's the problem, Richard," Ann shouted as she turned on the stairs to look down at him. "You can't figure it out."

"You are not making any sense," said Thompson.

"I just don't know," said Ann, her voice trailing off as she gathered her thoughts.

"Well, you had better figure it out pretty quickly," said Thompson, his temper rising as quickly as Ann's. "You wanted this life just as badly as I did. You wanted to be a Congressional wife. You wanted all the glory of going to breakfast with the First Lady. Now, you are having second thoughts and I'm supposed to back off the accelerator. I don't think so."

"That's not it and you know it," said Ann.

"That's exactly it," Thompson replied, "You don't know the pressure I'm under and furthermore you don't give a damn."

"Oh, give me a fucking break," Ann yelled. "You've got a staff to deal with your pressures. I'm not your staffer, Richard. I'm your wife."

"Yes, you are," said Thompson, "and I could use a little support right now. I've got baseball threatening me through my staffers. I've got an L.A. reporter doing a hatchet job on me that will be national news on Monday. And I've got a whole bunch of shit going down I can't even tell you about and all you can tell me is you need some empathy."

"Yeah, well believe it or not, you are not the only one in this relationship," said Ann. "And the world does not revolve around you and your problems. What about my problems...my pressures, Richard. I don't have a staff to help me with my problems."

"Is that why you were smoking today?" interrupted Thompson.

"Now you are spying on me?" cried Ann.

"No, but the next time you try to steal a smoke, look where the mirrors in the room are located," Thompson said. "From where I was speaking, I could see you chain smoking on the front porch in the mirrors."

"So what?" Ann said as she entered the door to their bedroom.

"So what?" said Thompson. "So you haven't smoked since you were drinking in D.C.."

"Well, guess what Sherlock Holmes?" shouted Ann as she slammed the door to the couple's bedroom. "I'm drinking again, too."

Chapter 19

Donny Alberato sat against the backboard of the king-sized bed in his hotel room in Cincinnati, reading the online clips of the coverage of the week's games on his laptop computer. Players in "The Show" stay only in the best locations and this beautiful well-equipped room was no exception. A flat-screen television was against the wall facing the bed and comfortable leather chairs adorned the room. The mini-bar had been well stocked until Alberato had raided it after the game. Empty little bottles of various liquors were strewn all around the room.

He had a good week on the field, but the clips of his heroics were outweighed by the ongoing coverage of his use and abuse of steroids. There was not a single story about him that did not also include Greg Graham, steroids, human growth hormone or some other performance enhancing drug.

When Alberato tossed the computer aside on the bed in order to get up to see what else was in the mini bar, the front of his complimentary terry cloth robe fell open. He looked in the mirror over the desk and flexed his arms upward. Tilting his head from side-to-side, he admired his body as an art critic would admire a famous painting.

He put his muscular arms down to his side and giggled. He was drunk.

Grabbing another bottle of some anonymous liquor from the mini-bar, he unscrewed the cap and threw the liquid down his throat.

A ringing cell phone disrupted his alcohol induced pity party. He picked up his ringing cell phone to see on the caller ID the call was from his agent/lawyer. "Hey, Murph," Alberato said. His voice was unsteady and he was slurring his words. "What's going on back home?"

"Not much," Murphy replied. "You sound shit faced. Are you celebrating you went 3 for 4 today?"

"I am shit faced," Alberato replied. "Yeah, it's Saturday night after a game where I was star of the game and I'm in my room. I'm getting shit faced all by myself."

"Why?" asked Murphy. "Cincinnati is a small market town, but it can't be that boring."

"It's not boring. I love the restaurants here, but I can't go out anywhere," he slowly slurred. "Everywhere I go people are yelling at me. They are calling me a 'killer' and 'cheater' and yelling insults. I can't even get laid on the road. I've got to worry if every woman I fuck will run to the press and tell them my nuts are shriveled."

"Well, I hate to pile on more shit, but I've got some bad news about tomorrow's game," said Murphy.

"Life can't get too much worse," said Alberato. "What do you have for me now, Mr. Attorney?"

"Remember Richard Thompson?" said Murphy.

"Yeah," said Alberato. "How could I forget him? He's the asshole Congressman who 'dissed' me on *ESPN* in Sarasota this spring."

"Well," said Murphy, "he's going to be at the game tomorrow."

"I've got to play in front of that son of a bitch?" Alberato yelled. "I won't do it. Fuck it. I'll tell the manager I need a day off. Fuck!!!"

The person staying in the next room at the hotel pounded on the wall for Alberato to quiet down.

"Fuck you!" he shouted at the top of his lungs. "Come over here and I'll kick your ass!"

"Calm down, Donny," Murphy said. "You need to just calm down now."

"Well, then, fuck you too," Alberato giggled. "You can sit at home in California and watch me sit my big ass on the bench tomorrow."

"You can't," warned Murphy. "*The Journal* is covering the game with more than the sports guys. That investigative reporter,

Joyce Lang, is in town. If you bench, she will make a bigger deal out of it than what it actually is. Just play your game, get your shower and get back to the bus. The team flies out of Cincinnati tomorrow night to head back to the coast. Monday is a day off. We will play golf."

"Fine," said Alberato, too drunk to recall his suspicions his agent might be wired by the FBI as part of their investigation into the death of Greg Graham.

"Lang says Thompson's simply going to watch the game," said Murphy. "But just in case, look out for him getting anywhere near you on the field before the game. Thompson might be looking for a photo op. We don't need a bad media hit on this."

"Trust me," said Alberato. "If he comes down on the field, I'm headed to the locker room. If I have to shake his hand, I might just punch him in the mouth."

"Do you have a quote you want me to give *The Journal* for tomorrow's game?" Murphy asked.

"Sure," said Alberato before falling onto the bed. "Tell them Richard Thompson can suck my dick."

"I'll take that as a no comment," replied Murphy.

Joyce Lang sat in a bar at a window table overlooking Fountain Square at the corner of Fifth and Vine Streets in downtown Cincinnati typing her notes from the speech by Richard Thompson into her laptop. The bar had a great view of the Tyler Davidson Fountain, a landmark made famous by its appearance in the opening clip to the television show *WKRP in Cincinnati.* The fountain was a massive 43 foot tall statue made of nearly 24 tons of cast bronze. The top of the fountain was capped by a nine foot tall sculpture of a woman, water flowing from the hands of her outstretched arms.

As Lang typed, she paused to look at the statue of the woman atop the fountain and her Christ-like pose. *There is a woman who knows my pain*, she thought to herself.

As she typed she thought about her meeting with Richard Thompson. His speech wasn't that great. He seemed aloof during the delivery and not focused on the topics he was discussing.

I guess I have that effect on the men in my life, she laughed to herself.

Her questioning of those who had attended the Thompson event confirmed what she had thought in the first place. The GOP Women's Club of Oldham County, Kentucky, had little interest in Thompson's work in barring performance enhancing drugs from professional sports. Those who actually knew what the issue represented were barely aware he was involved on the legislative level. He didn't even mention it in his speech.

But they did genuinely seem to like Thompson and his wife, although she was nowhere to be found during her husband's speech.

Lang paused and took a sip from her soy latte. What she found truly interesting was Thompson's reaction to the fact she was covering his attendance at tomorrow's baseball game.

From his reaction, it seemed believable Thompson was headed to the ball park simply to watch the game. If he were wishing for a confrontation with Donny Alberato, he would have relished her presence and the national press would be sure to follow. Instead, he seemed to shun her and the attention.

Richard Thompson was an interesting character for her study. No wonder John Gustine liked him so much based on their first and only meeting. They both had that same type of geek love for the game of baseball and both seemed to live under the foolish assumption that somehow its future rested in their hands.

She mused to herself that maybe, just maybe, Richard Thompson wasn't one of those sleazy political types she despised so much.

Not that it mattered much.

She quickly reminded herself Thompson's personality and motivation were unimportant. What was important was there would be a story at the game tomorrow—and she would be there to cover it for *The Journal*.

Sitting in his plush office in New York City, Colin N. Korey opened a new email from his right-hand man, M.T. Stacy:

Mr. Korey:

I am sitting at my temporary desk at the baseball park. Cincinnati won today. Great game. Donny Alberato went 3-4. It is impossible to determine if his play these days is driven by further drug use. However, on days like today, I am concerned , despite your last meeting with him, he may still be juiced. Greg Graham may have been able to keep him one step ahead of the testing protocol. Perhaps since Graham met his untimely demise, he has found a new source for his drugs. God help us if there is someone else out there as good as Graham was at staying ahead of the tests.

I am not sure why, but the front office here has informed me Congressman Richard Thompson is attending tomorrow's game. I expect he is here to observe Alberato play or to cause some sort of confrontation which will embarrass baseball. Either way, this is not good. I will have the payroll watching him tomorrow to make sure he does not make any attempt to discredit baseball.

MT

Korey called his secretary. "Get me on the morning flight to Cincinnati," he said calmly. "I'm going to the ball game with M.T. tomorrow."

The Fat Man's obsessive-compulsive behaviors got the best of him again. He sat at his computer, running Google search after Google search on John Gustine. He kept reading and re-reading each story, looking for a hint of a boogey man.

Unable to accept the apparent reality his death was the result of random street violence, The Fat Man reasoned Gustine might have put a clue in one of his stories pointing to his killer. He knew there was more to Gustine's death. It had to be out there somewhere. Yet, the stories The Fat Man read appeared to offer no insight into Gustine's death.

He rubbed his eyes and started over with the first story, this time starting his reading with the last paragraph first. Maybe

Gustine had set something up that someone could only catch using that old proof reader's trick.

Ann Thompson lay awake in bed, counting the cracks in the ceiling.

It had been years since she and her husband had been so angry with each other they went to bed without speaking. She couldn't remember the last time it had happened, or the last time they had slept in separate beds because of a fight.

Ann went over and over in her head the sequence of events that led to the fight. It hadn't happened just as a result of the trip to LaGrange (although that was the aggravation which pushed her over the top). No, it had been building ever since her husband's special election to the United States House of Representatives.

She had been on the Hill in her younger days. She knew the pressures and problems. She should have been ready for the public spotlight that had become her life. At this point, however, what was hurting her the most was not her new public persona, but the fact her husband was apparently oblivious to the pressure she was feeling.

She expected the public life of the Thompson family to focus on her husband. But she also expected their private life to continue to be the partnership they had developed over the years.

I wonder how long it will be until he asks me to call him Congressman around the house, she thought, unable to shield, even from herself, the bitterness she was feeling at the moment. *He's even going to the baseball game on Sunday, the day he said he would pledge for our family.*

Richard Thompson lay awake in the guest bedroom down the hall, running through a similar spectrum of emotions. He was frantic his wife was drinking again. He always knew , as an alcoholic, Ann was only one drink away from losing her sobriety. After 20 years, he had just stopped thinking about it as a real possibility. However, now that it happened, he didn't know what emotions to feel first.

He was angry and sad all at the same time. He was livid and defeated all by one drink.

He knew she was blaming him for her falling off the wagon and that wasn't fair. Thompson felt she had shut him out of her life in the same way she had shut him out of their bedroom.

Damnit, it's not my fault she took a drink, he thought. *No one made her do it, least of all me. It's not fair of her to lay that crap on me. I've got enough shit on my brain. She took the drink, not me.*

He tried to take a deep breath to clear his head, but it didn't work.

Hell, maybe she's right. Maybe I am so wrapped up in the role of a being a Congressman I've placed our relationship second to my job. On the other hand, she's got to realize my job requires a focus we have never dealt with before. She's got to understand the pressure I'm feeling goes beyond us and stretches to all those people in the district who voted for me.

He wished he could cancel the trip to the ball game on Sunday so they could talk the whole thing out. But now, with Joyce Lang from *The Journal* covering the game, any thought of cancelling the trip to the ball park tomorrow with The Fat Man was impossible.

At least we have next week in the district, away from D.C.. We can work it out then.

The man from Suwanee, Georgia, sat in the Ft. Mitchell, Kentucky, Days Inn hotel room where he had been living for the last week. His memorabilia for tomorrow's game were neatly laid across the adjoining twin bed, ready to be stuffed into his newly acquired backpack: three Donny Alberato glossy photos with the baseball logo in the corner; four Topps brand limited edition Donny Alberato rookie baseball cards; one major league baseball unsigned and three sharpie pens (two blue and one black).

And a 9mm pistol.

Chapter 20

Richard Thompson and The Fat Man paused at the statue of Joe Nuxhall outside the front gates of Great American Ball Park next to the Ohio River in Cincinnati. The statue was at the end of a narrow patch of grass featuring the pitcher/catcher battery of Nuxhall and Ernie Lombardi. A statue of Ted Kluszewski stands in the batter's box. Just as he played when he was alive, the sleeves of Big Klu's jersey are cut away on his statue, allowing him to swing his huge (non-steroid made) arms with unrestricted abandon.

"It just doesn't feel the same," said The Fat Man as he gently touched the left arm of the bronze statue for good luck. "Nuxy was on the mound when my dad brought me to my first game."

"Yeah?" replied Thompson, as he looked at the bronze likeness of "The Ol' Lefthander" in his classic low follow through.

"Yeah," said The Fat Man. "I was in the third grade and my dad took me over to Crosley Field. Nuxhall beat the Phillies that day 3-2. I kept the ticket stub and had Joe autograph it a couple of years ago at Redsfest."

Joe Nuxhall was the youngest player to play professional baseball in the modern era when, as a ninth grader at the ripe old age of 15, he went 2/3 of an inning against the St. Louis Cardinals. That was near the end of World War II, when most ball players had been drafted into the military. He went on to spend most of his 16 years in the big leagues with the Reds, picking up a lifetime 135 wins. In 1967, he became the Reds' color man in the radio booth and brought the games of The Big Red Machine to a whole new generation of baseball fans.

Joe Nuxhall was a legend in Cincinnati. When he passed away in 2007 at the age of 79, the City of Cincinnati went into mourning for days. All television and radio news coverage focused on the life and times of one of the game's most beloved figures.

"Did you go to the visitation?" Thompson asked The Fat Man.

"I felt like I had to," The Fat Man responded as he shuffled in his pocket for his game ticket and handed it to Zig, their usual ticket man at the main gate. When Zig gave them his usual friendly nod as their greeting to the ball park, they were officially at the game. "It was so big they had to hold it in a high school gym."

"Yeah," said Thompson. "They even covered it in D.C.. We were in session that day and one of the Members from Cincinnati told me about it. I went back to the office and it was on the local network sports cast. "

"Six thousand people showed up. Pete. Johnny. Junior. And a whole lot of fans just like me. I stood in line three and a half hours to pay my respects."

"Baseball sure has changed since Nuxy was a kid on the mound," waxed Thompson. "Do you think fans will stand in line when the steroid users die someday? Nuxy made a 16 year career out of one or two pitches. He worked hard to maintain a career and never forgot the fans. These guys in the steroid report insult me as a fan."

"There are no asterisks in heaven," said The Fat Man.

"Amen," replied Thompson to The Fat Man's simple one-line eulogy.

As the pair made their way past the vendors on the main concourse behind home plate, a young man and his two young children approached the pair.

"Hey, aren't you Congressman Thompson?" the man asked.

"Yes," replied Thompson.

"You are the guy leading the charge in Washington against steroids?" quizzed the man further.

"Yes, yes I am," replied Thompson again. "May I help you?"

"No, I just wanted to introduce my kids to you," said the man.

"Why, thank you," said Thompson proudly as he leaned down to shake the hands of the two children.

"Yup," said the man before he turned and walked away. "I wanted them to meet the horse's ass who is single-handedly dragging baseball down the road to ruin."

Thompson stood silently in place, his arm still outstretched, momentarily stunned.

Seconds later, after the man had left, The Fat Man began laughing uncontrollably. He even snorted once from laughing so hard. Thompson glared back at him.

"And just what the hell did you find so funny about that exchange?" asked Thompson.

"Everything," said The Fat Man as he tried to catch his breath from the laughter. "You were so proud the man recognized you and wanted to introduce you to his kids."

"You think the fact he called me an ass is funny?" asked Thompson.

"Horse's ass," corrected The Fat Man. "And yes, I found it very funny and very useful."

"Useful?" asked Thompson.

"Yeah," said The Fat Man. "Guys like that are going to keep your head in check. Not everybody is going to agree with you in Washington, Rick. You need someone to call you a horse's ass every now and then to deflate your ego and keep you grounded. Just be glad your reporter gal pal wasn't around to hear it."

Thompson mumbled something inaudible under his breath.

"You didn't think everyone was going to love you over this steroids thing, did you?" asked The Fat Man.

"No," said Thompson. "But I thought I would catch crap from players and owners, not fans."

"Hey, most true fans are with you," said The Fat Man.

"That guy sure as hell wasn't," replied the Congressman.

"Well, he's the one who wants to shoot the messenger," The Fat Man said. "There are going to be people out there who would rather see monster homeruns by overgrown goons than a game played with integrity."

"That's just it, Joey," said Thompson. "Baseball has never done anything to police itself. Because they are exempt from antitrust laws, they think they are exempt from all laws."

"You think that guy knows or even cares about antitrust laws and baseball?" replied The Fat Man.

"No," said Thompson quickly. "But that's the point. Baseball has never done anything unless Congress forced them to. Look at expansion. Baseball has only expanded when Congress threatened to remove the exemption. Hold some hearings—get a few more teams. That's the pattern."

"So?" The Fat Man asked with true sincerity.

"So baseball isn't going to clean up the steroid mess unless we turn up the heat," said Thompson. "This is important shit, man and I may be the only guy on the Hill actually paying attention. Government needs to be involved in this issue."

There was an uneasy silence between the pair.

"Let's forget about it," said Thompson. "Let's just go to our seats and watch batting practice."

"I wanted to run upstairs first and talk to Jack," said The Fat Man. "I haven't seen him since Sarasota. I know you haven't. Want to come with me?"

"No, thanks," Thompson said.

"Aw, come on," said The Fat Man. "I didn't mean to piss you off by laughing at you. Come on upstairs."

"Naw," replied Thompson, still feeling a little burned by the comments of his good friend. "I'm going to watch BP."

The Fat Man knew the reason for the coolness he was feeling from Thompson. He had crossed the line between laughing **with** a friend to laughing **at** the Congressman. *I'll just run upstairs for 15 minutes or so. Let him watch batting practice for a while by himself. Once he's had a chance to think about what just happened on the concourse, he'll cool down.*

"All right," said The Fat Man. "I'm gonna go on upstairs to see Jack. I'll be at the seats by the time they throw out the first pitch."

"Miss the first pitch…," said Thompson.

"…miss the whole ball game," The Fat Man said, completing the sentence.

Jack was Jack Renisch, the baseball park's scoreboard technician and an estate planning client of Bradley's law firm.

Whenever The Fat Man had some extra time at the ball park, he would go up to the scoreboard box where Renisch controlled the scoreboard's replays and special effects.

The booth where the team of technicians run the jumbo scoreboard is as complex as the setup inside the television trucks used to produce national sporting events like the Super Bowl—maybe more complex. Nine technicians sit in front of a wall of eighty-four monitors and twenty-two computers, showing everything from fifteen various camera views to the answer to the nightly "score board stumper" which offers trivia questions to the fans in the stands.

The game's producer sits in the middle of it all, giving commands into audio headsets worn by all in the booth. The producer has as much control over the tempo of the game as does a pitcher. The producer even tells the weekend's live organist when to play those little ditties that get the fans clapping their hands in order to encourage a two-out rally.

"Hey, Joey," shouted Renisch as The Fat Man walked through the door to the booth. "Come on in. I'm about to run a new video on the big board. Let me know what you think. Screen one, run *Song Quest* in five, four, three…"

Renisch watched the monitor intently as a video montage of players appeared on the scoreboard each talking about his favorite song. When it was over, Renisch (and everyone else in the booth for that matter) looked at The Fat Man as if he were Roger Ebert ready to critique a first run movie.

"I love it," exclaimed The Fat Man, as all those assembled exchanged high fives.

The Fat Man approached Renisch and shook his hand as he looked over the single aisle of seats where the official scorer and others associated with the stats and scoring sit. From this perspective, he could see Thompson making his way to their seats for the game, a beer in one hand and a super dog in the other. "Enjoy every sandwich," he mumbled to no one in particular. He then turned his attention to Renisch.

"God, you guys have the best seat in the house," said The Fat Man. "Any way I can trade in my season tickets for a season pass up here?"

"You ask that same question every time," replied Renisch. "You know the rules. If you come up here, we will put you to work."

"Really?" replied The Fat Man in mock surprise. "Is that all it takes to get these seats? Whatever you need, I'll do it. I'll run and get your food and drinks from the press box for every game, if I can sit and watch from here."

"What scares me is I think you are serious," said Renisch. "Anyway, there are a couple of baseball's big wigs in from New York for today's game. You can't stay too long."

"Are you afraid they will see me harassing the official scorer?" asked The Fat Man as he gave a gentle slap on the back to the gentleman responsible for judging whether a flubbed ground ball was a 'hit' or an 'error.' "Baseball can put up all the signs they want protecting you from graft and abuse in this box, but you need to know if I were up here, I would be bringing you flowers every day."

"Hey, where's your old law partner? I thought the Congressman was coming with you to the game today," asked Renisch.

"He's here," said The Fat Man. "He wanted to go down and watch BP." The Fat Man thought it best not to bring up the incident that had just happened on the main concourse.

"Just as well," said Renisch. "If he had to walk past all the press on this floor, someone would try to get a comment from him about coming to watch Alberato play ball. There was some babe in the box from *The Los Angeles Journal* stirring up all kinds of shit earlier today."

"Yeah, he ran into her yesterday," said The Fat Man. "He's off duty today. I think he just wants to watch a ballgame. Who's playing and whether or not someone on the field is on the juice is the last thing on his mind."

"Is he at your seats on the first base side?" asked Renisch. "Let me see if I can find him on the camera."

"Just don't put him on the big screen," said The Fat Man. "He wants to stay low profile today."

Renisch spoke into his headset and asked the cameraman controlling Camera Three, on the third base side, to pan the crowd near The Fat Man's seats. "There he is. Camera Three, focus on the guy in the third row in the white polo shirt. Take a look at monitor #8, Joe. He's down at your seats trying to get a view of the field through all of the autograph seekers. The guys from baseball are sitting in the front row of your section."

"Just please don't put him up on the scoreboard," pleaded The Fat Man.

Chapter 21

Thompson had watched as The Fat Man made his way to the elevator that would take him to the scoreboard control room.

God, I love him like a brother, Thompson thought to himself. *He just doesn't get it. This* **is** *important stuff.*

Thompson stood in line for a Guinness and a game dog before he made his way down the steps to the seats he shared with The Fat Man on the first base side just behind the dugout. As the visiting L.A. club took batting practice, he noticed Joyce Lang on the field talking to Donny Alberato, who had positioned himself behind the batting cage. He could only imagine the questions she was asking him, but he was sure Congress and steroids were the topics of those questions.

Thompson made his way to his seats and tried to lose himself in the rhythmic cracks of wood against hide and the chatter of players on the field. The smell of fresh cut grass filled his head and took him to another level of introspection.

It **is** *important. Joe doesn't understand it. Ann doesn't understand it. Griff, well Griff is Griff. But damn it, this is important.*

That guy up there on the concourse can go to hell. I'm doing what's right. The game has to have integrity and it may well just be up to me to see it remains that way. I'm the only one talking about this shit. If I don't do something about it, who will?

Joey just doesn't understand the future of the game may be on my shoulders. He doesn't understand the pressure that's on me to save the game. And, Ann, well, she's just going to have to learn to deal with it. I'm sorry, but she is.

Just then, Thompson's attention was diverted by a young boy, no more than 10 years old. The youngster had an autograph on a baseball from a back up infielder, whose name a committed fan like Thompson didn't even recognize. The boy ran up to his father and joyfully handed him the baseball. Repeatedly jumping up and down, the boy was obviously elated with the treasure he had just received.

Thompson smiled sheepishly and remembered the first autograph he got at the ball park. It was at old Crosley Field where his dad had taken him for his first baseball game. Jim Maloney may not be in baseball's Hall of Fame, but he was a god to Thompson. In fact, Thompson still had the autograph and treasured it as much as an art collector treasures fine art.

As he relived his youth with his own dad by watching the young kid with the baseball celebrate with his father, he remembered the warning about the influence of power which had been given to him by the former White House staffer with whom he had breakfast early in his tenure in D.C..

When you start believing you are important, you are probably not, Thompson thought to himself. *That kid and his dad are going to be the ones who save baseball, not me. They are the reason baseball remains America's pastime. The dad who teaches his kid to take off his ball cap and place it over his heart, blinking back tears when they start to sing the National Anthem, is the important one.*

They will keep the game pure, not government and certainly not me.

What the hell am I doing?

If I believe what I preach about being a Goldwater conservative, I should not even be bringing Congress into this issue. I went on the campaign trail telling voters the federal government should be limited. I told folks the federal government needs to quit getting involved in areas of our lives just because it believes it's needed. I promised I would only expand government where the Constitution allows.

I even quoted Goldwater in my speeches: "Broken promises are not the major causes of our trouble. Kept promises are!"

And what was the first thing I do when I get there? I work to expand government interference into baseball.

Did power grab me that quickly?

As the crack of the bats continued, Thompson drifted deeper and deeper into introspection. A sense of wistfulness mixed with sadness began to envelope him.

There are no right answers, only right questions. And, man-o-man, did I ask the wrong questions this time.

Maybe that guy on the concourse was right. Maybe I am a horse's ass. Except instead of leading baseball down the road to ruin, this steroid investigation by the committee is just one more small step towards leading the country down that same trail.

Let baseball survive, but let one of these fans be its savior—not government.

I'll be lucky if I can be a "savior" as a dad and a fan.

Thompson took another gulp of his beer and sat back in his seat, splaying his arms out across the empty seats on either side of him. As batting practice continued, his ennui started to crystallize into something akin to determination.

Damn. I should be here with my own kid—not The Fat Man.

That's what Ann was trying to get at.

Shit, I need to make this right with her. I've let my own feeling of power get between me and her. Okay, okay, okay. It's the district work period; I'll make it right with her this week.

Then, I've got to figure out how to make this right in D.C..

"Excuse me," said the man who had slowly made his way next to Thompson. "Congressman Thompson," he continued as he pulled a backpack from his shoulder, "Can I trade you a cold Guinness for an autographed baseball?"

"Sure," said Thompson as he grabbed the clean white baseball and the pen which the man had offered him. Thompson held it firmly and wrote his name across the sweet spot of the baseball in blue ink. He handed the signed ball back to the man who had placed the beer in the cup holder in front of Thompson.

"Thanks, Congressman," said the man, with a soft southern accent. "I appreciate what you are doing about steroids in sports. Enjoy the beer."

As the man started to get up, the backpack fell open just enough for Thompson to see it apparently contained numerous baseballs and baseball cards in plastic holders. *This guy must be one of those types who makes money on the side getting autographs and selling them*, Thompson thought to himself. *Still, he's got to be paying attention to the issue if he recognizes who I am.*

The man started to walk away when Thompson, eager to talk to another baseball fan, engaged him. Maybe talking to someone else who shared his concern for the game would boost his spirits by game time.

"So you've been following the issue?" asked Thompson, standing up and stretching.

The man seemed shocked Thompson had asked him a question. He didn't particularly want to talk to the Congressman, but refusing to talk to him would draw attention to himself, as well. So he turned and took a step or two back towards Thompson before responding. "Yes, sir," he said. "I've been following it very closely."

They were both looking out at the field in the general direction of home plate.

"So what did you come here today to see? Do you want to watch Alberato play? Or do you want to watch two ball teams go at it?" asked Thompson.

"Well…," the man began, just as Thompson's cell phone rang.

"Excuse me," Thompson interrupted, as he pulled his phone from his pants pocket. He looked down at the screen and saw it was The Fat Man. He hit the "ignore" button and shoved the phone back into his pocket.

"Looks like you and the Congressman have good seats for the game today," said Renisch as he focused the camera on Thompson in the stands watching the pre-game warm-ups. "I guess he needs the break from all the crap going on in D.C."

"Give the boy a Guinness and a game dog and he's happy," replied The Fat Man.

"He seems to enjoy food," said Renisch.

"The only thing that could make him happier is if the game dog was replaced by an Izzy's Rueben Sandwich," said The Fat Man, referring to one of the classic meals of Cincinnati.

"Well, I can't tell if he's happy," said Renisch. "I can tell you he's got a beer in one hand and some guy just gave him a second one."

"Good," said The Fat Man, remembering the mood Thompson was in when the pair had separated. *Maybe he'll cool down by the first pitch.*

Renisch began instructing the man controlling Camera Three on the third base side to adjust the camera on Thompson while looking repeatedly at the monitor. "Who is that guy?" Renisch asked The Fat Man as he focused in on the man next to Thompson.

"What guy?" asked The Fat Man, moving across the room toward the monitor board.

"That guy," said Renisch as he pointed to the monitor, identifying the odd looking man in a striped button down short sleeved shirt, holding a backpack and handing a baseball to Thompson. "Is he from Northern Kentucky?"

"He doesn't look familiar to me," said The Fat Man. "Why?"

"I don't know," said Renisch. "He just looks like someone I've seen before. I'm not sure where."

"You put so many guys on the big screen," replied The Fat Man. "It's probably just some guy you put up on the Kiss Cam last week."

Renisch's gang in the booth got national attention when they caught a wanted felon on the scoreboard Kiss Cam, which encourages couples to kiss while in full view of those in attendance via a close up on the huge video screen next to the scoreboard. The crowd that day included a probation officer who recognized one of the loving couples on the scoreboard as including a man who had skipped out on his probation. He was promptly arrested.

"Maybe," said Renisch. He continued to stare at the screen as Thompson continued talking to the man. "You just don't forget a guy who looks like that."

"He's just an edit in some clip reel," said The Fat Man.

There was a pause as Renisch ignored The Fat Man's comment while he searched his memory for an image his mind could not retrieve.

"No, that's it," said Renisch in a moment of inspiration.

"What's it?" asked The Fat Man.

"*ESPN*," he said. "He was in the clip I gave to *ESPN* when that Congressman died down at spring training."

"What are you saying?" asked the Fat Man. "That guy was in Florida when Kevin O'Toole died on the field?"

"Yeah," said Renisch. "I'm sure of it. Sara, go over to the AVID non-linear and pull up that clip we gave to *Sports Center*. When you've got it, put it up on monitor number seven."

The clip came up on the screen. Renisch and The Fat Man watched as the clip showed O'Toole at the hearing and on the field at Ed Smith Stadium in Sarasota.

"Hold it," said Renisch. "Right there. Sara, back it up about ten frames and focus in on the guy in the striped shirt handing O'Toole a beer."

The photo was a little fuzzy, but the image of the man was certain. The same guy who had given Chairman O'Toole a beer in Sarasota in the spring a few minutes before O'Toole died was now standing next to Congressman Richard Thompson and handing him a beer. He was even wearing the same ill fitting, striped shirt.

The blood drained from The Fat Man's usually ruddy face. "Holy shit," he said aloud. He immediately dug in his pants pocket for his cell phone and quickly dialed Thompson. "Come on, Rick. Answer the phone. Answer the fucking phone."

The Fat Man watched the monitor as Thompson looked at his ringing phone before hitting the "ignore" button and shoving the phone back in his pocket.

"Call the police and get them down there right now," The Fat Man shouted at Renisch as he bolted from the scoreboard control room. "That guy in the striped shirt killed Kevin O'Toole!"

Chapter 22

As The Fat Man bounded down the open stairwell from the press level boxes to the main concourse, he looked frantically for a police officer. With each step, came a desperate feeling that his friend, the Congressman, was about to sip a beer that would soon be his last. As he hit the final step and rounded the corner to the lower level seats, he finally spotted a female police officer. The call from Renisch to stadium security had not yet made its way into the form of an announcement on the officer's shoulder radio.

"Officer," said The Fat Man in a short-breathed pattern caused by his two story quick descent down the stairs. "You need to come with me. Right now."

"Slow down, mister," said the officer looking at his portly figure. "You are going to have a heart attack. Now, what's wrong?"

"Oh God. You didn't get the call yet, did you?"

"What call, Mister? What's wrong?"

"Please just follow me. Someone's trying to kill somebody. Down on the first base side." The Fat Man grabbed the officer's arm and began pulling her toward the seats.

"Where's the fight?" asked the officer as the pair reached the top of the section where, some twenty rows below, Thompson stood talking to his new friend.

"It's not a fight," said The Fat Man. "See the guy in the white shirt? About 6 rows up. That's Congressman Richard Thompson, from Kentucky."

"Okay," said the officer confused at why the wild man next to her was so wound up.

"The guy next to him—the one with the backpack—is trying to kill him," said The Fat Man.

The officer looked at the two men calmly talking and watching batting practice. "They look pretty friendly to me," she said.

"He's poisoned his beer," The Fat Man said through his repeated gasps for air.

"Look, Mister, if this is a joke…," warned the officer.

"This is no joke," assured The Fat Man. "I swear to God, this is no joke. That guy has already killed one Congressman. And he's going to try and kill the guy in the white shirt."

"By poisoning his beer?" the officer said with obvious skepticism in her voice.

"Yes!" shouted The Fat Man. "By poisoning his beer."

Just then, Thompson finished his first beer with a gulp and threw the cup on the ground in front of him. He reached for the second beer, which the man with the backpack had given to him.

"Oh shit, cover me," shouted The Fat Man as he began running down the concrete stairs with all the speed he could muster.

The officer chuckled to herself and began to turn away when a "Code Thirty-Three—Section 121" was announced on her shoulder radio. Code Thirty Three is a police code for an emergency. The officer announced her presence into her shoulder radio as she turned and saw The Fat Man running down the steps wildly waving his arms and shouting a warning at the man in the white shirt not to drink his beer.

"Badge 457 responding," said the officer as she drew her baton and followed chase after the strange man who had been talking nonsense to her only seconds earlier. "Hold it right there, mister."

But the Fat Man didn't stop and he kept running towards Thompson shouting and waving his hands.

Thompson heard the commotion behind him, lowered the beer from his mouth before he had taken a sip and looked up towards the top of the section where, for some unknown reason, The Fat Man was being chased by a female police officer. "What the hell…" said Thompson, as the police officer caught The Fat Man from behind and shoved him to the concrete in the space between two rows of seats. Officers were converging on the section in double time with batons drawn as Thompson attempted to squeeze past the man to go to his friend's aid.

The man standing next to Thompson had also become aware of the commotion behind them and, unbeknownst to Thompson, had reached into the bottom of his backpack to pull out a 9mm pistol. As Thompson attempted to squeeze in front of him, the man dug the gun into Thompson's ribs.

"Don't even think about it, Congressman," said the man with the backpack. "We're going to calmly walk up that other aisle and get out of here while all the attention is focused on your fat little friend."

Thompson looked down at the gun and then up the aisle. The Fat Man, while struggling against two, then three and four, police officers, was still shouting warnings at Thompson.

"You got the gun. You are the boss," said Thompson as he turned and started across the row of seats toward the next aisle.

M.T. Stacy noted the commotion occurring behind him and he quickly began to make his way along the seats to the opposite aisle.

As Thompson walked slowly up the aisle, his mind raced, trying to figure a way out of his ever worsening situation. When he looked over toward The Fat Man, he heard people begin shouting "wrong guy" at the police while pointing at the scoreboard. In Thompson's immediate line of sight, fans were scattering from the seats around them as they walked up the steps, but at the same time carefully watching something on the scoreboard.

Thompson glanced around at the scoreboard and saw himself on the giant screen being escorted up the aisle by the man with the gun, split screened with a video of The Fat Man lying cuffed on the ground. The words "**WRONG GUY**" were flashing over the image of The Fat Man. The other side of the screen focused on Thompson and the man. A yellow circle was flashing around the gun.

Thompson stopped and nodded his head toward the scoreboard in an effort to divert the man's attention. When the man momentarily glanced around and saw himself with Thompson on the big screen, Thompson turned and grabbed the gun.

People screamed and ran. Against the flow of fans, police ran to the aisle with their guns drawn.

M. T. Stacy, who had pulled a revolver from his ankle holster when the scene was shown on the scoreboard, quit moving toward the pair, went to one knee and took aim.

Thompson and the man struggled for a moment before Thompson pushed the man backwards over a stadium seat, his own body tumbling over the seat with the man at the same time.

Before they hit the concrete with a thud, a shot rang out.

The fans hit the deck.

The approaching police went to their knees, using any nearby seat for a shield while pointing their weapons at the pair lying on the ground.

A moment passed before Thompson stood up and looked down at the blood on his own shirt. He stared at the motionless man on the concrete who was bleeding from a chest wound. Only then did Thompson realize he had the 9mm pistol in his right hand.

Chapter 23

The rhythm by which Ann Thompson kept flipping the edge of her red fingernail across her front teeth defined the tension in the sterile interrogation room. Thompson was explaining to the pair of Cincinnati Police detectives what had happened in the stadium that day for the fourth or fifth time. The room was painted light green, but the dirt and stains on the cement brick walls produced a color which could not be found in the paint section of any local hardware store. A simple metal table sat in the middle of the room with chairs around it. There was a mirror on one wall from which it was obvious someone sitting on the other side could observe any interrogation from a private setting.

Thompson had discarded the bloody white polo shirt and replaced it with a shirt Ann had brought with her in the police escort she had received to the police station. Three uniformed officers, one woman and two men, sat around the table with Thompson and his wife.

"And you two have no idea who this guy was?" asked one of the male detectives.

"None," said Thompson.

"You don't remember meeting him at Ed Smith Stadium in Sarasota this past spring?" one of the other officers asked.

"If I met him in Sarasota this spring, I sure as hell don't remember it," Thompson replied.

"You don't remember him giving a beer to Congressman Kevin O'Toole?" the first officer asked as he casually examined the plastic bag containing the gun police had recovered from the scene.

"No, sir," said Thompson quietly.

"Well, you better be damn glad your boy Renisch up in the scoreboard recognized him," said the second officer. "We're sending the beer he bought you out for testing, but we're pretty sure he slipped something into the beer you were about to drink."

"How do you know that?" interjected Ann.

"When we went through his backpack we found an empty vial labeled Dimethyl Sulfoxide," said a female officer in the room. "The coroner who came to the scene said it's a chemical used to preserve organs during an autopsy. He said it's also used to carry other substances for rapid ingestion into the body. It's so quick if you touch it with your finger, you can taste it. Apparently, it tastes like garlic."

"I don't get it," said Thompson.

"Well, Congressman," said the detective, "the backpack also had two empty packs of over the counter cold medicine with neo-synephrine. The coroner said the DMSO would have been ingested along with the neo-synephrine very quickly into your blood stream, so within minutes you would have gone into ventricular fibrillation. By the time any emergency personnel reached you, you would have no blood pressure. You would have been DOA and it would have looked like a heart attack."

"Jesus, Richard," said Ann.

Just then, another police officer entered the room with a cell phone in one hand. "I've got him right here," the man said into the phone before handing it to Thompson.

FBI Agent Leo Argo was on the phone. Chuckling, he said to Thompson: "Please don't tell me Bradley yelled 'Cover me' before he got bitch slapped by a woman uniform."

"Hi, Leo," said Thompson smiling for the first time since he had left the game. "Yeah, he really did yell 'cover me.'"

"Damn, that's funny. You two okay?" asked Argo.

"The Fat Man's in pretty bad shape," replied Thompson. "He struggled so hard against the three or four cops that took him down, he broke a rib. He's at the hospital right now."

"You are kidding?" asked a surprised Argo.

"No," said Thompson. "Of course, he pulled a hamstring one time while posing for a picture."

Argo chuckled again at the thought of The Fat Man with a pulled hammie, before getting serious. "So how about you, Congressman? Are you all right?"

"I'm okay," replied Thompson.

"You paused," said Argo. "Are you sure you are all right?"

"Someone tried to kill me today, Leo and I shot him," replied Thompson. "He's dead and I killed him."

Ann put her head in her trembling hands in an effort to try and muffle the sounds of her crying.

"I've done it before," said Argo. "Remember? You were there."

"Yeah. I remember," said Thompson.

"Not easy, is it?" asked Argo.

"No, it isn't," said Thompson, while putting his hand on Ann's leg for comfort. "Ann's here and she's just as shook up as I am."

"You just have to remember one very important thing," said Argo.

"What's that?" Thompson asked as he put the phone on speaker so Ann could hear as well.

"It's better Ann is crying right now because you killed some guy. She could be crying because he killed you," said Argo. "He was going to kill you, Congressman, no doubt about it. If you don't kill him, he kills you."

"Thanks, Leo. I'm sure at some point I'll find your words comforting," Thompson paused. "Have you heard what the coroner found in his backpack?"

"Yeah," said Argo "DMSO and neo-synephrine."

"The coroner said the DMSO tastes like garlic," said Thompson. "I remember Kevin O'Toole saying he was belching garlic just before he died."

"I'm having someone review the chemical strip we did on O'Toole as we speak," replied Argo. "We don't normally check for DMSO, because they use it to conduct the autopsy itself. But, I'm guessing when we rerun the strip, O'Toole will have an abnormal amount of it in his system."

"So who the hell was this guy, Leo?" asked Thompson.

"His name was Robert Egarhcs," said Argo. "He's from some little town just outside of Atlanta."

"Why?" asked Thompson "Why did he come after me?"

"I don't know that yet," said Argo. "But I think The Fat Man may be right. He was involved in the murder of John Gustine, too. The backpack he had at the game had markings on it which indicated it belonged to Gustine. We're in the process of figuring out his motive right now. We have the U.S. Attorney in Atlanta getting us a search warrant for his apartment. When I get off the phone with you, I'm heading down to Georgia to see what we find."

"Why are you going down?" asked Thompson.

"Because I don't know if he's just some lone kook, or if there is some larger conspiracy at hand here," said Argo.

"You are kidding me?" Thompson replied, thinking about The Fat Man's warning of some larger conspiracy at hand.

"I'm not too concerned," said Argo. "The limited information given to our profiler thus far points to solo kook. Hey man, this involves a Member, so the Bureau isn't taking any chances. Aren't you guys on District Work Period this week?"

"Yeah. Why?" asked Thompson.

"Because I want you out of the District," replied Argo. "Until I know nothing else is going on here, I want you hidden."

"Come on, Leo," replied Thompson. "Don't you think that would be a little extreme?"

"No, we don't think so, sir," replied Argo. "I'm not going to bullshit you on this one, Congressman. At this time, we cannot determine the threat level against you. Until we can determine that, I want you hidden. You don't have a choice on this one, sir. Until I have some answers, I want you somewhere safe."

"Well, after all of this, I guess Ann and I could use some time away alone," replied Thompson, reaching down to squeeze Ann's leg while he spoke. "A friend of mine has a boat on Kentucky Lake. It would be a perfect place to be alone."

"Don't get excited about the alone part," said Argo. "Until we figure out what's going on, I'm putting a detail on you."

As Thompson and his wife left the interrogation room, Emily Reed met them in the lobby of the police station. She came running up to both of them, unsure of how she should react. As police officers mulled around her in their daily activity, she paused. Emily looked at both of them separately and, then, with tears in her eyes, hugged them both.

"Are you guys all right?" asked Emily.

"We have had better days," replied a weary Thompson.

"I guess," Emily said while wiping her eyes.

"Anyhow, thanks for coming over to get us," said Thompson. "I didn't leave the house this morning expecting to get stuck downtown without a car."

"Yeah, thanks, Emily," said Ann, her voice still shaking from the experience. She wanted to apologize for her conduct the day before, but she was too mentally exhausted to bring it up. She looked at Emily and smiled. "Thanks."

"Not a problem, guys," said Emily, pointing as they got to the door. "Now, we just have to get you to the car through all of that."

Down at the bottom of the steps leading from the police station sat Thompson's car. Unfortunately, in between the door and the car stood more press than Ann Thompson had ever seen in her life. Bright television lights on tall stands lit the way. News trucks were parked on either side of the street.

Police were waiting on the steps to get them safely to their car.

"There he is," shouted one reporter as Emily, Ann and Thompson exited the doors and started down the steps.

A frenzy of reporters, cameramen and photographers suddenly surrounded the trio. People were shoving microphones and tape recorders in their faces. Questions were shouted from all directions.

"Congressman, who was the shooter?"

"Did you know him?"

"Does your wife know him?"

"Have you ever shot a gun before?"

Emily broke free and ran to the driver's side of the car, unlocked the doors, jumped in and fired up the engine. Thompson held Ann tightly against him as they made their way to the rear passenger door. When an officer opened the back door, the push of the crowd against the car nearly thrust Ann into the backseat on her face.

As Thompson tried to enter the car himself, he noticed *L.A. Journal* reporter Joyce Lang was one of the reporters pushing against the crowd for a quote.

"Congressman, can you give me anything?" Lang asked pleadingly.

Feeling like he owed her something in light of the fact the attacker had apparently murdered her writing partner, John Gustine, Thompson leaned towards her and whispered in her ear. "The Feds are getting me out of town for a couple of days. I'm not talking to anyone until I come back. When I get back, you will be my first call."

Thompson pulled back from Lang, got into the car and closed the door. The police pushed people back enough to allow Emily to pull away, the cameramen taking pictures of Ann and Thompson hugging in the backseat as they made their escape.

As the car pulled away, inside the building M.T. Stacy appeared from the room where the viewing side of the two-way mirror was located. He slipped two officers five $100 bills each.

"Thanks, boys," said Stacy. "Let me know if you want to come to New York to see a ball game sometime."

Chapter 24

Early the next morning, Leo Argo ducked his head underneath the yellow "crime scene" tape that blocked the door to the Georgia apartment where the man who had been shot at the baseball game lived. Years ago, Argo had been a member of the Bureau's special unit that profiled serial killers. He wanted to see the man's apartment for himself, to see if he thought it fit the profile.

The white "FBI" logo across the back of Argo's black t-shirt made him stand out. As he entered the apartment, he ignored the questions yelled at him by the throng of reporters barricaded off about twenty yards beyond the apartment.

A Gwinnett County Deputy Sheriff met him at the door. "You must be Mr. Argo from the FBI," said the young man whom Argo guessed to be no more than a few years out of the police academy.

Argo looked down at the man's badge and name tag. "Deputy Quinn. It's a pleasure to meet you." He stuck out his hand.

As the young deputy enthusiastically returned the hand shake, he couldn't help but tell the FBI Agent about all the excitement the case had caused in the small community. "Wildest damn thing to ever happen around here, I'll tell you. We have television trucks from all over the south pulling into the parking lot over there. My wife just called me on my cell phone to tell me she saw me on *Fox & Friends* this morning."

"Yeah," said Argo, amused at the young officer's excitement. "These things tend to draw a crowd."

"She called the station to see if they could get a copy of it on a DVD for her," he said.

"It'll get worse before it gets better," Argo replied. "Where is everybody?"

"Well, your folks left about an hour ago to get some breakfast," said Deputy Quinn. "They said when you got over here, I was to tell you they would be back at about 0-900. I didn't touch anything after they left."

"Thanks, son," said Argo. "Now go outside and look mean while you stand guard at the door. Trust me. It'll get you on the national news tonight."

"Yes, sir," he replied. "My wife will love that."

When the door closed, Argo stood alone in the apartment and surveyed the surroundings. He pulled a pair of rubber gloves from the crime lab box which was still sitting in the middle of the living room. He put them on as he looked around the living room.

The first step in identifying whether an attacker is serial in nature is to determine whether they are organized or not. Once that characteristic is determined, there are certain personality traits that then fit the profile of a serial killer.

Everything is neat and in place, Argo thought to himself. He began to walk around the apartment, opening doors and peering inside rooms as he went.

When Argo came to a room he assumed was a bedroom, he was surprised to find it filled on every wall with file cabinets. He looked at the labeling on one drawer and it simply read: "Topps— 1993." He opened the drawer to find it filled with Donny Alberato baseball cards, apparently from the 1993 season, neatly organized and stacked. Other drawers in other cabinets contained cards from different seasons and various manufacturers.

"Hey, Leo," came a voice from the living room. "You in here?"

Argo emerged from the file room. "Yeah, I'm here," he replied.

"Wow," the female African-American agent jokingly said to the other agent, her male counterpart. "They sent in the big brass on this one."

"Someone had to fly in from D.C. to make sure you two didn't screw things up," Argo replied.

"Thanks," said the male agent. "If we're not good enough, we can always ask the Deputy to come in and do your crime scene investigation for you."

"No. No," Argo laughed. "I'm good with you guys. He's too busy getting his picture on television." Argo paused. "Seriously, gang, what are we looking at here?"

"Well, we think he's probably a serial obsessed with Donny Alberato," the female agent said. "We haven't counted them yet, but all those file cabinets in that other room are filled with Donny Alberato baseball cards. A lot of them are sealed in acrylic holders and professionally graded as being in mint condition and there are a whole bunch more plastic sleeves that appear to be limited editions."

The other agent picked a three ring binder off the computer desk in the living room. "Check this out, Leo," he said handing it over. "This guy created a computer program that tracks the value of each individual card and their projected value over a lifetime. Each one is inventoried and valued on its condition and the print run. He's showing current values on many of the older cards at between $1,000 and $3,000 each. And then he's got more columns that show how the values of each card would change depending on when Alberato gets elected to the Hall of Fame. "

"And did he determine the value of the collection if Alberato gets banned from baseball for steroid use?" asked Argo.

"He sure did," replied the male agent. "Apparently most of those expensive cards could end up being worth $5 or $10 a piece. If Alberato goes down the crapper, this collection of cards goes with him. It looks like the guy couldn't handle it and began knocking off anyone who was a threat to Alberato."

"So you think he's a solo serial?" Argo asked.

"He's organized," said the female agent. "That's for sure."

"Then explain the opaque plastic over the windows," said Argo.

"I'm not following you," she said.

"If a serial killer is organized," said Argo, "it's someone who likes to have control over their victim. They plan out every minute detail of their crime and leave little forensic evidence."

"I'm with you so far," said the female agent.

"They usually have advanced social skills. They use their social skills to gain control over their victims. Ted Bundy was an organized serial killer. This guy kept plastic on his windows so no one could see in. That doesn't sound like a guy with superior social skills to me."

Argo paused and looked at the Elvis tapestry on the wall of the living room.

"Me and Elvis have a gut feeling there is something more here than a serial killer who loves Donny Alberato."

Chapter 25

The District Work Period for Members of Congress is their time to go home from D.C. and spend time with the voters of their respective districts. Due to the long travel time from the east coast, these weeks may be the only time Members from the west get home during the legislative session. And Members from Alaska and Hawaii spend a large portion of these weeks simply traveling to and from D.C., changing planes multiple times just to get home.

Richard Thompson felt himself lucky to be from a District which was only a one hour direct flight from the nation's capital. It allowed him to come home each and every weekend.

But whether you are from Hawaii's First District or Kentucky's Fourth, the District Work Period was an important time to travel the roads of your district to meet with local officials and constituents about what is happening back home.

The shooting at the ball park made national news. The press discovered the dead assassin was a baseball memorabilia collector who specialized in collecting autographs of baseball superstar Donny Alberato. Using a variety of eBay identities, he apparently spent over $200,000 trying to corner the market on Alberato's rarest cards in an attempt to double or triple his money if Alberato made the Hall of Fame. The analysts at various media markets were speculating the Congressional inquiries into steroid use in baseball had already devalued his collection of Alberato memorabilia and he was looking to end the inquiries by ending the lives of those pressing the issue. One network punningly nicknamed him the "Sniper Bidder" after one of the names he used to place bids on eBay. The name stuck and other networks were following suit.

After repeatedly watching the news clips of their Congressman's struggle with an apparent assassin, the folks of

KY-4 were not surprised when Richard Thompson cancelled his entire schedule for the week—his actual whereabouts known only to a few key staff, the FBI and local law enforcement officials.

Those who knew Richard Thompson, however, knew he probably escaped somewhere on or near water. They were right. As he had suggested on the phone to FBI Agent Leo Argo, Thompson and his wife decided to hide out at Kentucky Lake in the western portion of the state.

A Goldwater Republican at heart, even Congressman Richard Thompson himself had to concede the "New Deal" Democrats got it right when they created Kentucky Lake.

In 1937, a horrendous flood caused massive damage across the south and midwest. There were pictures of people taking row boats up the streets of major urban areas along the Ohio and Mississippi Rivers. The devastation along the Tennessee River was just as bad. Cities along the river were hit hard by its rising waters as families fled for the dry safety of higher ground.

For those who lived along the 115 miles of the Tennessee River starting at Calvert City, Kentucky, it would be the final flood they would ever see.

The Tennessee Valley Authority began buying up property and, in fact, entire towns, along the Tennessee River to the juncture of the Mississippi and Ohio Rivers.

Finally in 1944, enough land was bought and the river was dammed to create Kentucky Lake. The lake rose some 50 feet above the original water level of the Tennessee River and, along with the damming of the adjacent Cumberland River to create Lake Barkley in the 1960's, became 160,000 acres of recreational lake with 2,400 miles of shore line.

Thompson had learned to sail on Kentucky Lake long before he had been elected to Congress when a friend had taken him out on his 43 foot sea-worthy sail boat, the Laurie Ann. From the first lesson, Thompson was hooked on the big boat. He went repeatedly to the boat, with his friend and on his own, to sail the lake. It gave him peace and solace to be on the water.

Thus, as the ordeal of the man who had become known in the press as the Sniper Bidder seemed to come to a close, it was only natural the couple would make their way to Kentucky Lake for a much needed break.

As the water plane landed on the northernmost portion of the lake, a black Ford Excursion made its way to the dock. Two agents exited the car and met the sea plane as it pulled up to the dock. Ann and Richard Thompson exited the plane with small bags of travel luggage in hand. They didn't bring much, but living on a boat for a couple of days, they didn't need much.

"Good evening Congressman…Mrs. Thompson," said the man. "My name is Scott Gamby. This is Janice Egger. We're your FBI detail until you are cleared to go home."

"Thanks," said Thompson. "We appreciate what you are doing here for us."

"Are you kidding me," laughingly replied Egger. "I get to leave D.C. and live on this lake for a couple of days."

"Yes, sir," added Gamby in his heavy Long Island accent. "We should be thanking you."

"You are kind," said Ann. "At least there won't be any television cameras here. I had enough of the media yesterday trying to leave the police station."

"We watched it on television before we flew in," said Egger. "It looked pretty hairy."

"It was," said Ann. "They were camped out on our front lawn this morning to get shots of us as we left. Thank God we had already sent our kids to Rick's mom's house."

"Well, we're the only people who know you are here," said Gamby. "And we have strict orders from Agent Argo to keep our distance. He's threatened us within an inch of our lives if we screw up this detail."

"One of us will be following you at all times," said Eggers. "The other one of us will be up in one of the resort cabins we have set up as a command center."

"If you go out on the Laurie Ann," added Gamby, "I'll be following you in a fishing boat."

"Get used to the boat though. We don't want you going into town," instructed Eggers.

"You've been on television too much in the last twenty-four hours," said Gamby. "If you went into town for anything, someone would surely recognize you."

"If you need something," said Eggers, "we will go to town and get it for you."

Thompson looked at his wife and chuckled, "Well, you wanted to be alone."

Chapter 26

Solitude in the time of personal conflict can give a person insight to their soul. It opens a door allowing emotions to escape from hidden rooms of the brain that can consume a moment like a well-crafted piano symphony. Solitude gives clarity. It can be the foundation of creative brilliance.

On the other hand, welcome or not, it can also create a moment in time when all sorts of theretofore hidden demons come to the surface. You can plan the solitude. Unfortunately, you can't plan the result. There is a thin line between the creative brilliance which drive men and women to reach beyond their capabilities and the inner demons which drive them to suicide. In the latter cases, introspection is highly overrated.

Ernest Hemingway. Hunter S. Thompson.

Both reached too deep just once too often.

For Richard Thompson, he tried to carefully plan his moments of solitude. He liked those moments to be the perfect culmination of time and being...letting his mind be inspired by the sights, sounds and even the smells around him.

Quietly looking down the Mall in Washington, D.C., from the window of the Speakers Lobby had inspired his Pete Rose-like headlong dive into the issue of steroid abuse in professional sports. He might have changed his mind on government's role in the controversy, but his involvement to this point had exposed a madman from Georgia before he had the opportunity to kill more than he already had.

As the morning sun beat down on the water, Richard Thompson uncoiled the mooring lines which were holding the boat against the berth. He was hoping the clarity he was searching for on this day would work to heal the personal wounds that somehow crept between him and his wife. One-by-one he uncleated the lines of the big boat and heaved them onto the deck with one hand, while keeping a firm grip on the life lines on the starboard side with the other hand. As he took the line off the final mooring cleat, he gave the boat a strong push away from the dock and jumped onto the push pit.

He quickly scrambled to the cockpit and grabbed the helm. The 43 horse-power diesel engine had been warming up for several minutes, so when Thompson engaged the forward drive the big boat pushed away from the dock and moved out into the center of the lake effortlessly.

The western breeze caused a moderate chop on the big lake. With the sun ducking in and out of the cloud cover, it was going to be a great day for sailing.

"Grab the helm, babe," Thompson said to Ann. "Point the bow of the boat head-to-wind."

"What?" asked Ann, as if her husband were speaking some foreign language.

"Point us right at that white house on the far shore," Thompson said to Ann, pointing the boat directly into the wind so he could begin to hoist the mainsail.

Thompson worked quickly, cranking the winch which would bring the mainsail to full mast. He jumped back quickly taking up the slack before clearing, coiling and stowing the halyard. Moving with due deliberation to the bow, Thompson hoisted the headsail by releasing the furling line and pulling on the jib halyard. The strong wind caused the limp sails to loudly flap and the rigging to clang against the boom.

"Now, turn the wheel and point the boat directly at the lighthouse," he yelled at Ann, directing the full force of the 14 knot true wind into the mainsail. As she turned the helm, the boat bared away and tipped aggressively to the port side as the wind filled the sails and thrust it through the water. Even though she was quickly approaching middle-age (if not in fact already there) Ann had maintained her athletic frame and mindset. As the boat tipped hard, she instinctively compensated her stance to keep her shoulders parallel to the water while pulling the helm in the opposite direction to perfectly catch and hold the full force of the wind in the sail, keeping the boat on a close haul down the lake.

With the feel of the full and complete control of the 10 ton boat in her hands, Ann smiled.

"It's a rush, isn't it babe," said Thompson as he came up behind Ann, grabbing the helm around Ann's biceps at the same time. He pressed his groin ever so lightly against her backside and put his nose in her hair to capture her for the moment in all his senses.

Ann didn't freeze at his grip, but the contact was cool nonetheless. She moved away by gently ducking under his starboard side arm. She avoided turning around to see the look on his face. Grabbing a life line, she slowly made her way to the bow of the boat and took her favorite spot, her lovely legs wrapped around the pulpit, dangling towards the water.

Thompson sighed at the sight of her moving to the bow and knew the distance between them was far greater than the simple measurements of the boat itself.

Ann tilted her head back and looked at the contrast of the white clouds against the blue sky. It seemed the wind was carrying the clouds above at a pace far faster than the regal clipper.

But far slower than the pace of a Congressman's wife, she mused to herself.

In fact, the skyward race between the clouds and the boat reflected the changing life of Ann Thompson. With the wind blowing crisply through her hair, she looked down at the bow cutting through the water. Such a view made the boat seem like it was traveling at a rate far faster than it actually was. Conversely, Ann felt like she was moving much slower than the world around her perceived.

It's all a matter of perspective, she thought to herself.

In the middle of the lake with no other boats in sight (except the motor boat containing an FBI agent trailing them about three quarters of a mile behind), Ann began undoing the buttons on her blouse and slipped the cotton material off her shoulders. In her younger days, she would not have hesitated at going farther and exposing her breasts to the fresh air by removing her bra as well. Now, sadly, her current position in life seemed to prohibit such bold independent action.

"Fuck it," she mumbled to herself as she took her bra off in a defiant move against the constraints of being the wife of a United States Congressman. "God's thermometers," she said as she pulled at her nipples hardening in the breeze.

Is there time in Rick's life for me? Ann thought to herself.

Maybe Griff was right. Every man has but one destiny. I'm sure Richard has found his.

I can't keep him from his destiny, but am I doing so at the surrender of my own?

As the boat cut like a knife through the moderate chops in the lake, Thompson looked at the naked back of the only woman he had every truly loved. He didn't actually need to see her breasts from the front to become aroused by them. He knew her body from the passion that fired their entire relationship…a passion which was suddenly, for the very first time in their life, extinguished.

He stood at the helm and looked at Ann from behind…the mast and boom separating them like the void currently existing in their lives. The wind was making a loud gusting sound on one side of the sail and was eerily silent on the other. His solitude suddenly took a dark turn as he began humming to himself that internal soundtrack he had been living with his entire life:

She's so many women,
That he can't find the one who was his friend,
So, he hanging on to half her heart
But, he can't have the restless part
So, he tells her to hasten down the wind.

He sipped at a bottle of beer, hoping the alcohol would consume his melancholy. Yet, thoughtful deliberate desperation set in with the chop of each wave.

He wanted to release the helm, leave the cockpit and go to her. As he looked at Ann leaning back on her elbows and exposing her naked breasts to the sun, his mind raced with thoughts of making love with her right there on the deck. He envisioned kneeling next to her and pinning her shoulders back while deeply kissing her. His mouth would run from her luscious lips, to her neck, to her breasts. He would pull her clothes from her as if they somehow confined all the sexual frustration both had felt over the past months. Their lovemaking would be free, wild and passionate and he would bring her to a climax unparalleled in their long relationship.

As he continued to sing Zevon in his head, he could not decide what was keeping him from actually leaving the helm to fulfill his fantasy—fear of losing control of the boat or fear of losing control of his life.

As comforting as the solitude of the lake had been on past trips, this time it was only isolating his loneliness and frustration.

The rhythm of the rigging clanking against the boom reminded him every song has a crescendo. Now was not the time for this song to come to a peak.

On the other end of the boat, Ann tried to fight similarly strong feelings. Intimacy itself implies a sense of closeness and it was closeness which Ann felt lacking in her relationship with Richard. The public eye had burned through the intimacy like a pointed laser. Part of the problem was Ann didn't know who to blame for the situation.

Ann had worked for a Member on Capitol Hill. The rigors of public life were not a new concept to her. She had signed off on Richard's candidacy fully aware of what was involved. Still, she was resentful of what their public persona was doing to their private life and the resentment was breeding guilt. Richard was doing what he wanted and she was resentful.

She resented his time away from her and the kids. She resented being under the public microscope and not being able to just be herself. But, most of all, she resented being left behind.

The hurt gets worse and the heart gets harder, she hummed to herself. *Shit, now he's got me singing Zevon tunes in my head.*

As Richard tied the final line to the mooring cleat securing the Laurie Anne back to the dock, he looked up and waved at the FBI agent sitting in the Ford Explorer in the parking lot. The agent flashed his lights in friendly response. The sun was slowly setting off the bow.

"The power's connected, babe," Thompson shouted at his wife inside the cabin. "You can turn on the lights."

Ann appeared from the cabin with a glass of Camus in one hand and a cigar in the other. She handed both to her husband as they settled into the bench seats on the cockpit of the boat. Thompson lit his cigar and took a deep puff. He exhaled and took a slow sip of the wine, taking in the aroma of the cigar and the wine at the exact same time. As Ann lit up a cigarette, Thompson sensed the song was about to come to a crescendo.

"Don't get on me about the cigarettes," Ann warned as she took a deep puff.

"I don't like it," he replied, "but I won't."

"It may be the one thing keeping me from drinking, right now," Ann said.

"I know—it's been a rough couple of weeks," Thompson replied.

Rough couple of weeks, she thought to herself. *My husband has just been on the national news for shooting a psychopath who was trying to kill him and he thinks it's been a rough couple of weeks.*

"I'll quit. I just have to get past what's happened," she said as she exhaled the smoke.

There was an awkward silence. Neither really knew what to say next. For fear of total silence for the remainder of the evening, Ann went ahead and got it out on the table.

"Ever thought about your destiny?" asked Ann.

"You are spending too much time around Griff," mumbled Thompson as he swirled the wine around in his goblet.

"No, really," Ann said. "Have you ever thought about the destiny of Richard Thompson?"

"Please don't talk about me in the third person," Thompson said. "I really hate that. I'm sitting right here."

"But that's just it," she said. "People who are somebody are spoken about in the third person."

"I'm not somebody," Thompson replied. "It's just me, remember? I'm your husband."

"You are somebody now," Ann interjected.

"Stop it," said Thompson.

"No, Richard," she said. "This isn't a joke. You are one of the 435 people who serve in the United States Congress. You remember how you looked up to Garrett?"

"Yeah," he replied. "So what?"

"So what?" she echoed with exasperation.

Their eyes met and he was stunned by the quizzical look on her face.

"You are him now," said Ann. "You are Garrett."

"Honey, I'll never be Garrett," said Thompson laughing.

"Maybe you don't think so," said Ann, "but have you ever looked at your staff when you walk by them?"

"No," said Thompson. "I'm not at that level of egotism yet. Give me a year or two and maybe I'll notice."

"Well, you better start looking now," said Ann. "Those kids look up to you. They believe in you. Josh follows you around like every word you utter is straight from the lips of God himself."

"Really?" quizzed Thompson.

"Really!" assured Ann.

"Kind of like I used to do with Garrett," said Thompson.

"Kind of like you used to do with Garrett," repeated Ann softly.

"But, I'm no Garrett," said Thompson.

"Damn it, Garrett is dead," barked Ann.

"Yeah, I know that, hon," he replied somewhat sarcastically.

"You have to deal with the fact Garrett is history and you hold the seat," Ann instructed. "You can use it for whatever purpose you want. You can make a difference in people's lives or you can become one of the bastards we despised when we were on the Hill."

"Okay, I've lost you there," said Thompson. "This started off with a discussion about my destiny."

"That's just it," said Ann. "Either way you turn, you are living your destiny. You are going to decide it. I have no say in it."

"So that's what this is about," said Thompson. "You think I've found my destiny and it's without you."

"Well… yeah," said Ann.

"Come on, babe," said Thompson, as if somehow he could brush her off that easily.

"No, Richard. Don't 'come on babe' me," she replied stiffly. "This is real. You go off to Washington each week and you determine what happens. You determine what kind of guy you are going to become. You go to the Club. You go to the White House. You are in the middle of it all and you are determining your own course."

Her eyes began to fill with tears and she looked away.

"I stay at home worried something me or the kids do or say will ruin all of that for you. You are fulfilling your destiny and the only thing I can do is screw it up."

There was a long silence as Thompson took in her words.

Thompson finally got it.

He got up from his seat and walked over to where his wife was sitting. He sat down and snuggled in closer to her.

"I'm going to tell you something I've never told you before," said Thompson in a soft, comforting tone. He chuckled. "Hell, I've never told anyone this before."

"Not even Griff or The Fat Man?" asked Ann.

"Not even Griff or The Fat Man," he replied reassuringly. "There was a time when I envisioned myself riding across the Continental Divide on horse back."

Ann laughed.

"Don't laugh," he said. "I thought my destiny was lazily winding up a trail on the back of a horse, wearing a wool lined denim vest and a wide brimmed cowboy hat."

Ann laughed again. "Stop it, Richard."

"Stop what?"

"Stop trying to make me laugh when I'm trying to be serious," Ann said.

"I am being serious," said Thompson.

"Pretending to be John Wayne in *True Grit* as a kid has nothing to do with this whole discussion," said Ann.

"This was no childhood dream," replied Thompson, totally serious. "I had this in mind when I moved to D.C.. My goal was to go to law school and make just enough money in D.C. to buy some land in a small town out west. I would set up a solo practice law office and take in just enough work to pay the bills. I would spend the rest of my time riding a horse to some remote river or stream to catch trout."

"You never said anything to me about this," said Ann.

"Hell, babe," said Thompson, "I just told you, I've never talked about this to anyone. I'm a successful lawyer and a Member of the United States Congress. I really can't just go around telling people I wanted to be a cowboy."

"So why'd you give up on the dream?" asked Ann.

"Well, I met this girl…"

Ann looked away.

"She was beautiful." He gently touched the back of his fingers against her cheek, running his hand downward to her neck. "Her skin was so soft. And her eyes…well they could look right through you."

Tears came to Ann's eyes.

"On our first date, we made love. As I feel asleep that evening with that girl in my arms, I knew my destiny had changed forever." He gently grabbed her chin and moved it towards his so their eyes locked. "That night, Ann Thompson, you became my destiny. Griff is right. Every man has only one destiny and you are mine. I don't need to see my commercial on television or my name on a sign in somebody's front yard. None of that stuff matters without you. You are my destiny."

Ann laid her head on her husband's shoulder and began to weep. For a while, Thompson just held her as he watched the last bit of daylight begin to fade into the horizon.

"I've missed you so much," whispered Ann, breaking the silence. "I felt so damn alone I was drowning in self-pity and resentment. After I woke up from my binge, I was so ashamed I had blown my sobriety; I didn't know what to do. I was afraid my drinking would hurt your career. I didn't know where to turn. I was scared and I couldn't talk to you about it.

"So I got angry," she continued. "I'm not sure what I was angry at, but I knew it was you and this new life as a

Congressman's wife. I was so angry at you when you went to the baseball game on Sunday, I had trouble controlling myself.

"It was like I couldn't get your attention. Griff had it. Josh had it. You were sneaking phone calls to Joe. Everybody around you had your attention, except me.

"I went to an AA meeting and started my sobriety over, but I didn't know how to start over with you. Then, I saw you at the police station with blood on your shirt..." Ann's voice trailed off and she laid her head back on her husband's shoulder.

The pair sat silent for several seconds.

The he leaned forward and kissed her on the lips.

"You have my attention now," he instructed. "And I'm sorry."

"Me, too," said Ann.

Thompson took a sip from his wine glass. "To new beginnings," he said.

"New beginnings," she replied.

Thompson kissed Ann again. The kiss was light at first. Then there was another. Slowly, Ann returned the next kiss. That one didn't stop. The kiss continued with a sensual passion as strong as that first night they made love.

"It's getting dark," whispered Ann as she ran her hand along the inside of Thompson's thigh. "Don't you think it's time we go down below for the evening?"

"Are you sure?" asked Thompson.

Ann rose up and took Thompson by the hand.

"Unless you want me to make love to you in front of the FBI agent up there in the parking lot," said Ann, "you will follow me right now."

Chapter 27

The Laurie Ann was a magnificent vessel. At 43 feet, she was equipped for off-shore cruising with the latest satellite and Loran navigation equipment. She carried a 6,616 pound winged shoal keel for ballast with overall displacement of over 19,400 pounds. The living quarters had all the comforts of a plush vacation condo. The staterooms were located fore and aft. In between were living quarters with a full galley, couches, navigation station and satellite flat screen television. Even the two heads were plusher than those on any boat in the marina, each containing a full shower.

A full 10 feet taller than any other in the marina, the 62 foot main mast of the Laurie Ann stuck out among the hundred or so sail boats docked there. It was easy for either of the FBI agents to sit in the black Ford Explorer in the marina parking lot and keep an eye on boat with the tall mast.

Only days ago, the couple aboard the vessel had been one of the top priorities for Agency protection. However, now that the FBI had swept the home of the crazed Georgia eBayer, the need for ongoing protection had become debatable. With all evidence tending to reinforce the media speculation the gunman had apparently killed only to protect the extensive investment he had in his baseball card collection, the detail guarding Congressman Richard Thompson was fairly low key.

Thompson himself had requested the detail be called off following the search of the Georgia man's home, but Leo Argo had insisted the detail continue until Thompson returned to Washington. Reluctantly, Thompson consented to the ongoing FBI security.

Gamby and Eggers met the couple at the dock on the first night when they had arrived by sea plane. The agents had found them to be a pleasant couple, but the Congressman had clearly indicated they were at the lake for some private time. Gamby reminded the Congressman the two agents were there at the personal direction of the Director, but assured the Congressman they would keep their distance.

When the couple first sailed the lake, Eggers stayed far behind, trailing in a rented bass boat…far enough away not to interfere, but close enough to intercede in case of trouble. Even from her safe distance, with surveillance binoculars, she got an eyeful of Ann sunbathing with her top off.

Eggers had told Gamby of the "topless" adventure on the lake. So when the couple kissed passionately on the deck of the now-moored boat and disappeared to the confines of the cabin, Gamby was pretty sure what was about to take place within. That would make the next few hours of his shift pretty dull, he thought to himself. He played around on the radio searching for a talk show to keep him from falling asleep on the job until Eggers could come to take her shift in the Ford at midnight.

Once inside the cabin of the sailboat, Ann Thompson wrapped herself around her husband as her mouth grew hungrier in a passion she had not felt in months. Thompson tried to undo the buttons on her blouse, but Ann grabbed his hands and intertwined his fingers in hers as she forced him backwards against the wall.

Thompson was quite content with letting his wife be the aggressor at this moment in their lives. He pulled off his own shirt as Ann dropped to her knees to undo her husband's belt buckle—their movements in a smooth sexual sequence like some erotic ballet.

Once both were naked, Ann shoved Richard backwards across the galley table and climbed across his chest.

While the naked bodies of Ann and Richard Thompson writhed in sexual bliss across the galley table of the big boat, a lone figure creeped along side the rear quarter panel of the car where Gamby was listening to the Reds' baseball game. As Gamby poured a cup of coffee from his metal thermos the flash from the silenced gun engulfed the entire car. Gamby jerked forward and then slumped sideways.

In the command center, Eggers was awakened by a call from Leo Argo. "Hey, Leo," said Eggers sleepily. "What's up?"

"We have a problem," said Argo.

"How big?" asked Eggers.

"Huge," Argo said. "I just received the ballistics report. The gun recovered by Cincinnati police at the ball park…"

"Yeah," said Eggers.

"…was not the gun used to kill the Sniper Bidder."

Chapter 28

Ann Thompson was riding Richard to climax when the hatch to the cabin was gently opened. The light in the cabin was dim, but M.T. Stacy could clearly see the pair while they moaned and grunted their way to a mutual sexual climax.

Perfect, he thought to himself. *This could not have happened any better.*

As Thompson loudly announced his climax to his wife, Stacy jumped from the deck of the boat to the floor of the cabin, with a gun in his right hand and a small brief case in his left. His landing on the floor announced his unanticipated arrival with a loud thump.

Ann let out a loud scream as she jumped off her husband and the table simultaneously, looking frantically for something to cover her naked body.

Thompson shot up to his feet and instinctively started toward the intruder until he saw the gun. "Holy shit," he gasped as the desperation of their situation started to sink into the post-orgasmic dizziness of his consciousness.

He paused in mid-step, breathing heavily in part from sexual exertion and in part from the danger-driven adrenalin rush that was now engulfing him. "Just what the fuck is this all about?" he shouted.

"Back away Congressman," Stacy commanded. "You can yell all you want. Your FBI friend isn't going to hear you."

"Jesus, what did you do to him?" cried Ann, still trying to cover herself.

"The same thing I'm going to do to you," said Stacy. "By the way, leave the clothes off."

Stacy placed the briefcase on the floor and used the gun to motion Ann to sit on the couch.

"Richard, what the hell is happening?" said Ann, her voice quivering as she sat down and clutched a pillow in front of her. "Who is this crazy son of a bitch?"

"I have no earthly idea," said Thompson as he tried to think about his next move.

"Allow me to introduce myself," said the intruder. "I'm M.T. Stacy."

"The head of security for baseball?" Thompson asked incredulously. "You are the one who threatened Josh over my involvement in the steroid issue."

"Oh, you know of me then," said Stacy. He seemed sincerely pleased.

"Unfortunately, I do," Thompson replied.

"What the hell is going on here, Richard?" asked Ann, gritting her teeth against the fear threatening to overwhelm her body.

"I suspect he knows our friend from Georgia—and a lot about the deaths of Kevin O'Toole, Greg Graham and John Gustine for that matter," said Thompson.

"You are the perceptive one," said Stacy. "But sorry, I didn't kill your dear colleague Kevin O'Toole or John or Graham. Okay, I killed Gustine. "Georgia boy" got him to the bar, but I stuck him with the ice pick."

"Right," said Thompson, "And I'm supposed to believe you?"

"You should," replied Stacy. "It's true. But then again, quite honestly, I don't care if you believe me or not. After tonight, you are not going to be able to tell anybody anything."

"He's crazy," Ann whispered, half to herself and half to her husband.

"Maybe," said Stacy. "To the world, all of them were killed by your eBay buddy from Georgia. For once, the cable news networks had it right, at least in part. He really was so worried reports about steroid abuse would devalue his collection of Alberato cards that he kept calling my office, wanting to know what people who truly love baseball could do to stop the game from being undermined. So when O'Toole started in on our owners, we put him on the payroll."

"He was an employee of baseball?" asked Thompson.

"Well, not officially," laughed Stacy. "I call him 'the payroll,' because I paid him some cash, enough to ease the pain of the value his collection already lost. And I gave him some really rare memorabilia items related to Alberato. But what he wanted most was encouragement. He really believed O'Toole was the devil incarnate, destroying the national pastime just to get a few headlines for himself. In me, he finally found someone with authority who agreed with him. He wanted to kill O'Toole anyway—we just had to tell him that anybody who did would be doing something good for America."

"You partnered up with a psychopath?" asked Thompson. "One who killed for memorabilia?"

"Sure," replied Stacy. "Why not? Though, if he were here, he could make a pretty good argument he was simply doing what he needed to do for the good of the game. The financial side was important, but secondary. "

"So did you give him some extra memorabilia or something when he killed Gustine?" asked Thompson in bewilderment.

"Didn't have to," he said. "I only had to let him know Gustine was going to sink his whole collection. That scared the shit out of him."

"Why did you kill John?" asked Thompson. "He was just doing his job."

"I didn't really want to, but I needed John's notes," said Stacy. "Baseball's future was in his backpack."

"So you killed him in an alley and made it look like a robbery," said Thompson.

"Absolutely," he said quietly, slowly emphasizing each syllable. "Wasn't that great?"

"So I guess you used him to kill Graham, as well," asked Thompson.

"No, he did that one on his own," said Stacy. "He was afraid Graham would spill the beans on Alberato to the grand jury. So he put a weight through his skull."

"And, I suspect you had him come after me at the ball game," said Thompson.

"You bet," replied Stacy. "It worked so well in Florida, why not try it again?"

"Why?" asked Thompson.

"Once I had Gustine's notes, everything about you fell into place. You showed up on our radar screen after your stirring little floor speech. When I killed Gustine, I discovered you were the government leak linking Alberato to Graham's death. Honestly, I never saw that one coming. If you were willing to do that, you must be some kind of zealot. You had to go," he replied. "Not that it would matter. No one cares much about dead Congressmen."

"And I spoiled your fun when I killed him," said Thompson.

"You didn't kill him," said Stacy smiling.

"What do you mean?" Thompson asked.

"I did. I killed him," said Stacy.

"He was supposed to give you the beer and get the hell out of there," Stacy continued. "When you didn't drink it, he went freestyle. As you guys struggled, I shot him. If he was captured alive, he would have told the police everything. So I shot him. I had to. I used this gun right here."

"You are insane," said Thompson. "All of this over steroids."

"Unfortunately," said Stacy, "when they do the autopsy of Eddie, they are going to figure out the gun at the scene doesn't match the bullet inside him. I came here so I could tie up all the loose ends."

"Loose ends?" asked Thompson.

"Loose ends," repeated Stacy. "I have the gun."

"So what's your plan," asked Thompson, stalling for time.

"Well, I think I'm going to leak my next murder to that female reporter...Joyce Lang," said Stacy excitedly. "Come on, guys. Ask me about the exclusive that will make Joyce Lang famous."

"I guess I have to bite at this point," said Thompson. "What's your exclusive?"

"It's the story of a hypocritical Congressman from Kentucky," said Stacy.

"Me, I'm guessing," said Thompson.

"Oh, you are very perceptive," replied Stacy sarcastically.

"I almost feel sorry you will be the story line."

"And, exactly what is the story line?" inquired Thompson.

"Oh, it's Pulitzer Prize winning stuff," said Stacy.

"I bet," Thompson muttered.

"Congressman Richard Thompson battles against steroids in the halls of Congress while all the time hiding a desperate secret," said Stacy using a mocking tone.

"What's the secret?" asked Thompson.

"All the time, Richard Thompson is a steroid user himself," he laughed at his own inventiveness. "Isn't that a great story? Now that he's away from home so much, the policy wonk wants an impressive body to impress the ladies on Capitol Hill. Also, it makes him look better in political ads so they won't have to photoshop his head onto someone else's body in next year's campaign flyers."

"Why would anyone believe any of that?" Thompson asked.

"Come on," Stacy replied. "The press will eat it up. There is nothing the public likes better than hypocrisy unmasked. And, when it's a politician like you who has been so outspoken on an issue, that's the mother lode. You will go down with some of the great political scandals of all time. Hell, you will be bigger than Elliott Spitzer."

Stacy kept the gun leveled at Thompson, while he reached down to pick up the briefcase. He began to pull out multiple items, announcing his intention as he produced each one. First, he held up a vial containing a clear liquid.

"HGH," said Thompson.

"OOOOHHHH, good guess. Human Growth Hormone," he said while pulling out a syringe. He placed the vial and the syringe on the bar which separated them before taking one step back. "Now, chickee, fill up the syringe and shoot him up."

"I will not," said Ann defiantly.

"You don't have a choice here, bitch," said Stacy, his voice becoming suddenly angry.

"Do what he says, babe," said Thompson as he handed the needle and vial to Ann. Ann's hand was shaking so badly she could not get the needle into the rubber skin covering the opening to the vial. She looked to her husband, fear and helplessness in her eyes. He took the syringe from her hands and filled it with the HGH. Looking directly at Stacy, he knocked the air bubbles to the top by tapping on the side of the syringe and then pushed the stopper until the liquid squirted from the end of the needle.

Still naked, he pinched a portion of skin on his hip and injected the needle. Gritting his teeth, he pushed on the stopper until the HGH flowed into his body.

"Oh, my God, Richard..." Ann softly cried under her breath.

"All right, so now, as far as the public is concerned, I'm a steroid user," said Thompson in a matter-of-fact tone. "What's the next sub-headline in the story?"

"'Roid rage," he replied.

"'Roid rage? What the hell is he talking about Richard?" asked Ann.

"Steroid users are often prone to uncontrolled acts of rage," explained Thompson.

"You really know your stuff," said Stacy. "I'm impressed."

"So what will you leak as my alleged act of 'roid rage?" asked Thompson.

"This is the great part of the story," said Stacy proudly. "Well, you beat and raped your very own alcoholic wife before you shot her." He looked at Ann. "That's right—I know you are a drunk. I followed you to an AA meeting one day."

"Richard..." was all Ann could say.

"It gets even better," Stacy continued. "You shot the FBI agent in the car just for good measure. Then, you turn the gun on yourself. All the time, you are using the same gun which you really used to kill the Sniper Bidder. It was the one you snuck out of the ball park. Double standard, you know. You are a Congressman, so nobody dared to frisk you."

Ann tried to hide her fear, but her inability to control her shallow gasps for air gave away her terror.

Stacy continued.

"I'm so damned creative. I just made the rape stuff up right now," he almost giggled. "What are the chances I would catch you two doing it. God, I'm so fuckin' lucky. You even already have your semen inside her."

Stacy's ice-cold attitude and his evident pleasure in everything that was happening sent shivers through both Ann and Richard Thompson.

"Now," Stacy said. "I just need you to rough her up a bit before I shoot you."

"What?" Thompson replied in earnest shock.

"Smack her around a bit," instructed Stacy. "I need a couple of good bruises on her for the coroner to see."

"You are nuts," said Ann.

"Shut up, bitch!" shouted Stacy, again flaring his anger at her. "Start with the face. A big ol' black eye would look good on the crime scene photos."

"Not going to happen," said Thompson.

"If you don't, I will," said Stacy. "I'll shoot your ass first and then pistol whip your pretty little wife before I shoot her."

"No way," said Thompson.

"I swear to God, I'll beat her to a pulp," Stacy said. "It will be a lot easier and less painful if you do it."

Thompson looked directly at Stacy, staring into his cold eyes for what seemed like a lifetime before turning to his wife.

"Stand up, babe," he said to Ann softly.

"Oh, Richard, please don't," Ann sobbed.

With his back to Stacy, he looked at Ann and mouthed *trust me*. He raised his open hand to Ann and stopped.

"Do it," Stacy commanded.

"I can't," replied Thompson, his voice rising. "I can't hit her!"

"Do it or I'll kill you both right now!" Stacy shouted.

"No!" Thompson shouted in reply.

"Hit that fucking bitch right now!" Stacy said, his voice quivering with anger and resolution.

Thompson raised his hand and slapped Ann squarely across the cheek. The swing surprised Ann and she fell like a limp rag. Thompson followed her immediately to the floor, spreading eagle over her body, his chest covering her face.

Two gunshots echoed loudly in the ship's cabin and blood began to fill the cabin floor.

"Oh, my God, Richard!" screamed Ann, struggling to get out from underneath her husband. "Are you all right? Are you shot? Talk to me!"

Thompson lay prone over top of Ann, grabbing her arms while pinning her body to the floor.

"Richard, say something," screamed Ann.

"Goddamnit, quit moving," he grunted through his teeth as she continued to struggle against his strong grip.

"It's okay," said a female voice from over near the hatch. "You can get up now."

"Is he dead?" asked Thompson. From his position on the floor, he looked around to see Agent Janice Eggers slowly making her way down the ladder from the deck to the cabin. "I saw you over his shoulder. He said he shot Gamby."

"He did," said the woman as he kicked the gun away from Stacy. "His bullet hit Gamby's metal thermos. It deflected the bullet into his side. He's hit but he'll make it."

Ann continued to quiver violently, tears and screams emitting from her muscular frame. Holding her hands to the floor, Thompson moved his body so their eyes met.

"Ann," said Thompson. "Look at me. Calm down. Look at me."

She stopped struggling and looked at Thompson as she attempted to catch her breath.

"Stacy's dead," he said. "Eggers shot him. Look at me. He's dead."

"And you are sure he's dead?" asked Ann, still shaking under Thompson's frame.

"You bet," said Eggers, looking more closely at the body. "Both bullets hit him. You need to get up. I called this in and the place is going to be crawling with police in a minute or so. They don't need to see a Congressman and his wife naked."

"You all right, babe?" Thompson asked Ann.

"Okay, Richard," said Ann, her breath becoming more regulated with each passing moment. "I'm okay. Oh, God, I'm okay. Are you all right?"

Thompson looked into Ann's eyes before he kissed her gently on the lips. "I love you," he whispered to her.

"I love you, too," Ann replied through tears. "But you had better get up. I need to get dressed before those sirens get here."

"Yeah, I need you to help me figure out where the bullets ended up," said Eggers. "If any ricocheted down, we may be sinking. Don't worry if I see you naked. I've seen one before."

"Come on, Richard, get up," repeated Ann. As she rolled Thompson's frame off her body, he let out a loud scream, before quickly rolling back over to his stomach.

"I can't move," said Thompson. "And I think I know where at least one of those two bullets ended up."

With a pair of black sunglasses covering the growing shiner on her left eye, Ann watched the medical helicopter, which would carry both the wounded Congressman and FBI Agent Scott Gamby to Paducah General Hospital for treatment. It circled first before landing in the parking lot of the marina. Thompson, having been treated by a paramedic, lay on a stretcher on his stomach. The coroner was removing the body bag containing the remains of M.T. Stacy.

Ann was on a cell phone to Michael Griffith.

"So other than being shot in the ass, he's fine?" asked Griffith.

"Yeah. I don't know what hurts worse right now, his ass or his ego," replied Ann before pausing. "He saved my life, Griff. If it wasn't for him, that bullet would have hit me in the chest."

"He loves you, kiddo," said Griffith. "I'll call Josh and we will get a private plane into Paducah tonight. This will be a big story and you will need us there to handle the media."

"Thanks, Griff," said Ann. "He needs you right now."

"Not a problem," said Griffith. "I'm supposed to leave tomorrow for an overseas campaign, but I'll tell them I'll be a few days late."

"Hey, Griff, one other thing," said Ann.

"What's that?" replied Griffith.

"You were right."

"Of course I was. About what?"

"Everyone has one destiny."

"Yeah?"

"Yeah. And mine has a helicopter to catch."

Epilogue

Upon the birth of America as a nation, the Marquis de Lafayette said: "Humanity has won its battle. Liberty now has a country."

The United States Capitol stands against the blue sky of the District of Columbia as a modern-day temple to the legislative process envisioned by the Founding Fathers, its symbols making it the American equivalent of the Roman Parthenon.

The center of it all is the United States House of Representatives. The "peoples' chamber," as it was envisioned by the Founders, was a place where public opinion could make its way into government process.

Each and every item on the floor has a symbolic importance to representative government. One could conduct an entire college course on the symbolism of the floor. To sit on the floor, where some of the greatest debates in the world have occurred, is to understand those symbols are as strong as the Republic itself.

The most powerful symbols on the House floor are the fasces.

The fasces are Roman symbols of authority…wooden rods, which on their own could be snapped, but when joined together as one become indestructible. On either side of the Speaker's chair there are two gold fasciae, each with a warrior's ax attached to its end.

The most important fasciae in the House is the Mace. It is the oldest and strongest symbol of authority in the United States House of Representatives.

The Mace consists of thirteen ebony rods bound together by thin silver ribbon and topped by a silver globe. An eagle sits atop the globe signifying the manifest destiny of America. The Mace is the ultimate symbol of power in the House.

As each day's session of the House of Representatives begins, the Sergeant at Arms takes the Mace from its protective case in his office and leads the Speaker onto the floor. Once it is placed in a green marble holder to the Speaker's right, the session can begin. The actual position indicates the nature of the session being conducted on the floor.

During the session, if any Member should become so unruly that he or she no longer represents the decorum which should be afforded others on the floor, the Speaker may demand the Mace be presented to that Member. Thereupon, the Sergeant at Arms would remove the Mace from its holder and merely stand it next to the offending member.

The Member would be shamed into stopping his or her unruly behavior.

While the Mace is rarely presented today, it was a common occurrence during the days leading up to the Civil War. The Mace was often presented on the floor in an effort to break up fist fights over the issue of slavery.

There are only a few recent references to the Mace actually being presented to a Member in *The Congressional Record.* Today a Member so shamed merely has to revise his or her remarks to have the presentation stricken from *The Record.*

At the end of the day, when the Mace is removed from the Floor, the House stands adjourned.

Thompson sat in a room on the ground level of the Capitol known as the Board of Education Room. At the foot of the stairs which leads to the Speaker's Lobby, the room has great historical significance. Its name comes from Speaker "Uncle Joe" Cannon, who would take young Members who did not want to go along with his direction to the room "for a little education."

Vice President Harry Truman was in that room having a drink with Cannon when Eleanor Roosevelt called him to return to the White House immediately. Franklin Roosevelt was dead and unbeknownst to Truman at the time, he was the new President of the United States.

It has remained a place where Members gather for fellowship.

Thompson sat in a chair in the corner, with a cushion under his wounded buttocks.

"Mr. Speaker, I present to you the truest pain in the ass on the Floor," laughed Dale Young, a Republican Member from Iowa.

"Shot-in-the-ass-Thompson," laughed Jared Deuser, a colleague from Kentucky.

"All right guys," said Thompson. "Get it all out of your system now. I don't want to be hearing about this all session."

"Oh, I think it's too late for that," said Congresswoman Shelly Stephenson, yet another member who had just walked into the room. "We will be talking about this one for years to come."

"Great," said Thompson in true exasperation. "Maybe, I can send Griffith into your districts to work against you."

"I don't think so," replied Young. "Did you see the grin on his face at the press conference in Kentucky when he had to explain the trajectory of the bullet."

"He looked like he was going to explode in laughter at any minute," interjected Deuser.

"Thanks, guys," said Thompson. "I'm happy my near death experience has brought you such joy and happiness."

"Where is Griffith these days?" asked Young. "I haven't seen him on any of the news shows since you were shot."

"He went overseas to work on a Presidential race somewhere," said Thompson. "The President in some damn third-world country is trying to hold off a political insurgency by a leftist rebel opposition party. The incumbents hired Griffith to run the President's campaign."

"I swear to God," said Young. "I don't know why he does those foreign races. Those countries scare the bejesus out of me."

"There is good money in those races," said Deuser. "They pay as much as a United States presidential, maybe more."

"Still, I don't think I would want to be involved," said Young.

"I don't know what would be worse for your health," said Stephenson, "consulting for the winner or the loser."

"Griffith always says it's best to get out of town before they count the votes," laughed Thompson.

Just then the beepers of each Member in the room went off. They all went quiet and listened for the anticipated announcement the daily session would begin in 15 minutes. Instead, an announcement came over the beeper indicating the day's legislative session had been cancelled.

As they sat there looking around at each other blankly and wondering what was happening, a police officer hurried down the hall towards the staircase leading upstairs to the House floor.

"Hey, Radar," shouted Thompson to the officer who was so familiar he called him by his nickname. "What's going on?"

Looking over his shoulder as he stormed the stairs two steps at a time, he shouted back, "Someone's stolen the Mace!"

Acknowledgments

As with my first book, *The Maximum Contribution*, I could not have made it through the endeavor without the help and support of many people.

I have a circle of friends who act as my editors and beta readers who helped me with this book more than they could ever possibly imagine. Jeff and Penny Landen (who make enough changes to deserve a byline), Robin and Wade DeHate, Debbie Strietelmeier, State Senator Damon Thayer, Dennis Hetzel, Jim Brewer, Greg Greene, Lytle Thomas and Aref Bsisu all gave a read (or an idea) to this book before I sent it to my publisher. As usual, Vicki Prichard gave it more than a read and kept encouraging me throughout the writing of the entire manuscript.

Senator Jim Bunning taught me a lot about how to properly: a) watch a baseball game (apparently, it's all about the pitcher), b) be a good public official, and c) live life as a good husband and father. As this book goes to press, he is making a decision on whether to seek a third term in the United States Senate. If he runs again, I have the campaign theme song:

We've been through some things together,
With trunks of memories still to come,
We found things to do in stormy weather,
Long May You Run.

As you can tell from my writing, I love placing real people and places in my fictional meanderings.

At Kentucky Lake, Lytle Thomas taught me and fellow Ludlow pal, Jim Lokesak, how to sail on his parents 43'sail boat. While the boat is real, I can assure Dr. Laurie and Ann that I never had sex with anyone on their galley table.

John Cooper is a great friend and a lobbyist that any public official can truly trust. I do, however, think that he colors his hair. Dr. Lawrence Neack, was so precise with his analysis of the use of DMSO to kill a Congressman that he actually scares me.

Thanks to Russ Jenish for letting me watch a ball game from his perch at Great American Ball Park. What's the cost of a season ticket up there?

Once again, Kevin Kelly helped with the cover design and Denny Landwehr took my glamour shot.

Rodney "Biz" Cain gave me a great line that I used in the book. Josh Quinn, of the Boone County, Kentucky's Sheriff's Department, assures me that there are still Elvis tapestries out there to be had. John Carey carried my bags in LA like a champ. Robin Arcuri—if they ever make this into a movie, you'll be in it.

I'm probably not supposed to thank book stores for fear of angering one chain or store over another, but there were a couple which showed particular interest in my first book, *The Maximum Contribution*. Borders at Crestview Hills (which my wife keeps in business with her personal purchases) and Borders at CVG plugged me to their readers whenever they could. The Trover Shop is the bookstore on Capitol Hill and they were great friends every time I called on them.

Special thanks to my publisher, Cathy Teets, and all the folks at Publisher Page, an imprint of Headline Books. Cathy not only publishes me, but seems to employ some of my biggest fans. Thanks for answering each and every email from me with the patience of Job.

Finally, as always, special thanks to my family—Linda (my best editor), Josh, Zach and MacKenzie. I spend a lot of hours in the basement chasing my muse. Thanks for understanding why, at times, you have a hermit for a father and husband. I continue to love you all more than you could possibly imagine. I couldn't do this without you.

About the Author

Rick Robinson has thirty years experience in politics and law, including a stint on Capitol Hill as Legislative Director/Chief Counsel to then-Congressman Jim Bunning (R-KY). He has been active in all levels of politics, from advising candidates on the national level to walking door-to-door in city council races. He ran for the United States Congress in 1998.

Rick's first book, *The Maximum Contribution*, was named Award Winning Finalist in the 2008 Next Generation Indie Books Awards in the genré of political fiction. It also won an Honorable Mention at the 2008 Hollywood Book Festival. His last book, *Sniper Bid*, was released on Election Day 2009 and opened on Amazon's Top 100 Best Seller list at #46 for political fiction. *Sniper Bid* has earned 5 national awards: Finalist USA Book News Best Books of 2009; Finalist Best Indie Novel Next Generation Indie Books Awards; Runner-up at the 2009 Nashville Book Festival; Honorable Mentions at the 2008 New England Book Festival and the 2009 Hollywood Book Festival. Throughout 2009 both books appeared on Amazon's Top 100 Best Seller List on the same day. Author Robinson was featured at Book Expo America in New York City May 2010.

A graduate of Eastern Kentucky University and Salmon P. Chase College of Law, Rick currently practices law in Ft. Mitchell, Kentucky with the law firm of Graydon Head & Ritchey LLP. Rick, and his wife Linda, live in Ft. Mitchell with their three children, Josh, Zach and MacKenzie.

Third in this series, *Manifest Destiny*, hit bookstores April 2010. In *Manifest Destiny*, Richard Thompson looks into the murderous eyes of Communist rebels living in Romania's Carpathian Mountains and comes face to face with his own ideals, values and morality.

Follow Rick Robinson on Facebook, MySpace and LinkedIn and visit www.authorrickrobinson.com

Top selling author, Rick Robinson follows up his award winning novels *The Maximum Contribution* and *Sniper Bid* with a thrilling tale of political intrigue which will rock his readers to their very core. Read *Manifest Destiny* and you will understand why Robinson is quickly becoming known as the only author who puts "real politics" in his political thrillers. His stories are as real as today's headlines.

"Taut and tense political drama wrapped in American history and tradition. A solid and compelling journey."
—J. A. "Jack" Kerley, author *The Hundredth Man* (Carson Ryder series)

I'm confident that this will be Rick Robinson's third consecutive, award winning, book. His writing skill and lifetime as "insider you need to see" shine through with a riveting novel that keeps us on the edge of our seats.
—Don McNay, syndicated Columnist and *Huffington Post* Contributor

"I maintain that the best storytellers hail from Kentucky and Rick Robinson is among them. A political insider in the Beltway and the Bluegrass, Robinson masters the vernacular of both. Anyone who knows anything about Kentucky politics—and Robinson does—knows it's often stranger than fiction. Once again, he has crafted a page-turning, can't-put-it-down-until-the-end, political thriller. *Manifest Destiny* is his best yet."
—Vicki Prichard, scriptwriter, Emmy award-winning documentary, *Where the River Bends*